DEATH: FOURTH HORSEMAN OF THE APOCALYPSE

Four Horsemen Series: Book 4

Angie Porter

When the Lamb opened the fourth seal, I heard the voice of the fourth living creature say, "Come!" I looked, and there before me was a pale horse! Its rider was named Death, and Hades was following close behind him. They were given power over a fourth of the earth to kill by sword, famine and plague, and by the wild beasts of the earth.

REVELATION 6:7,8 NIV (NEW INTERNATIONAL VERSION)

Chapter One

Death

Kaboom!

Awareness shifted into focus as I awoke underwater on a rocky slab. Blue-stained scalloped ice covered the walls and ceiling, shining like crystals, translucency allowing light to penetrate my secret sleeping place. I grinned; my seal broke, so I could finally shapeshift like my horsemen brothers! But only in emergencies.

My reapers still ran the show, but consciousness further sharpened, alerting me to eight dark souls nearby. On the other side of my cave skylight, silhouettes crawling over the blue ice confirmed; all females.

One of the shadowy female figures swung a curved weapon, *tink, tink, tink,* chipping away at the ice wall. Were they trying to reach me?

Although I could breathe underwater, that ended my plan to wait for my brothers and Bram. War better not have balked about me wanting his son soul-chained to me—like Bram was to War. Only Bram. Then when I didn't kill him immediately after the soul chain formed, I could never carry away his soul. The best end-of-the-world protection the Angel of Death could offer the boy.

Divine knowledge flooded me. So...God did give Famine, like War and Pestilence the Conqueror, a woman. That didn't bode well for me as the last thing I wanted was a wife. Another wife. It directly related to my favor asked of War...find me before any female attempts to thwart my purpose. Yet above, eight women chipped at the ice around me.

Tink! Plink! Chip, chip, chip.

My typically excellent global pinpointing system—to locate my brothers anywhere on the planet—seemed to reset when God sent me to sleep. However, I sensed I was deep underground. Surrounding lava tubes created a labyrinth, which crawled with five more female presences. The women aboveground chipped away at the ice, each silhouette in a different place above me.

Fine. I'd portal into a nearby city and await them there. I cast a glamour, an illusion strong enough for anyone knowing my authentic appearance not to recognize me as a blue-eyed blond.

Rumble! Crack!

The ground groaned and dropped, falling from beneath me.

Kaboom!

Surrounding ice and lava tubes crumbled into a chasm. A sinkhole? Instead of summoning my wings, I opened a magical manhole under me and dropped out in a nearby city.

Underground? My coordinates were no longer above ground! This was the first floor of a hotel when I last visited in the 1800s! Now I stood under a brick archway below ground? Metal beams secured small glass blocks inside a sidewalk above, allowing dirty yellow sunlight to highlight a tall wooden beam. Collapsed faded signage littered the concrete floor. Chipped wooden window frames, missing glass, remained in the closest brick wall. Five metal pipes ran overhead next to a line of wooden support columns.

Snap! Crack! Boom!

A seismic wave rumbled like a muffled explosion as a chasm opened under me again! Debris battered me; wood, dirt, bricks, metal, and concrete broke apart. *Bones* pummeled me like hail as I dropped! Ivory carcasses rattled, coalescing into skeletons; they crawled along the sinkhole lip.

This was Hades' doing! Not the sinkholes, the foretelling of my horseman seal breaking, but the bony skeletons rising from them! Power-hungry Hades had already cracked open a doorway! He was releasing non-heaven-bound souls from his temporary holding cell, a realm meant to house them until final judgment.

I dodged the bang of falling bricks and scattered rubble. The surface level above the caved-in underground collapsed, dropping a street-level building into the cavernous sinkhole. My swerve landed me in the path of a rusted metal beam rocketing straight toward me. Still at my weakest state after waking, the beam didn't bounce off me but cracked open my head. Then blood rivulets ran into my eyes.

Above, in a dust cloud heavy with sinkhole fallout, a woman screamed; not a death scream, not fear, but warriorlike. Then a narrow wooden plank swung over the rim at the underground level, slamming into the bones of a fully formed skeleton. The hit sent bone fragments flying as the creature broke apart.

Thud! Thunk! Boom!

More debris hailed from the sinkhole's unstable lip. Prone, knocked to the ground by the beam, my vision of the female figure swam. Through the hazy dust cloud, she looked almost like Zehra as she decimated more bones creeping over the crater's rim. How badly did the beam crack my skull? Was I delirious?

"Hold on," she shouted while smacking another skeleton to bits from the crumbling edge. "I'll help!"

The heavy beam didn't crush me, but I stayed there, head wound pouring separate blood rivers down my face. Pestilence would find me soon to heal me. My vision of the woman smeared, darkness crowding the edge of my consciousness. The Conqueror better hurry because Hades came out of the pit swinging, giving up the dead from the land and sea. I had to stop him. Together, we were tasked with wiping out a fourth of the remaining souls in this world. However, Hades and I were not friendly.

How long did I sleep? Sinkholes and women coming after me? Courtesy of the Fallen, no doubt. I closed my eyes, desperately trying to recover underneath the beam, further buried by bones and dirt dropping from the expanding edge of the sinkhole. I could not afford to sleep to heal.

The female, smelling of honey and sweet pea flowers, descended from a rope at the underground level, slowly lowering over the edge into the sinkhole. Despite the layered coat of dust from the collapse, her ponytail was long and black. But, regardless of her similar scent and shape, it couldn't be Zehra! Not when I personally escorted her soul to heaven so long ago. Grrr. Then returned to learn Lilith had stolen and possessed Zehra's body before it was buried! Spelled to the age of when I met her.

This definitely was not the underground city where I met Zehra so long ago in 1 AD. No, not her. Younger, thinner. Long black hair, not straight but corkscrew *curls*. I let out a shaky sigh. Of course not. Yet....

While securing the rope around the beam, the woman flashed bright green eyes my way. The resemblance was uncanny as she repeated a mantra, "I've got you. Hold on. I've got you."

She heaved, her entire frame climbing the rope, leveraging her weight to lift the beam. It didn't raise, but it was kind. I gave her a little help, pivoting it off me with her pully.

She slid down the rope, kneeling beside me, green eyes searching. Now I noticed differences from Zehra's appearance. A darker green circled her irises, straight nose thinner, lips fuller, curls showing in her long black ponytail.

After pulling off her faded blue flannel shirt, she pressed it against my head, stemming my blood flow.

Was she bleeding? Cause. Hell. No. I was not opting for a life with a bonded mate, bound through blood, genuinely married in an angel's custom. Grabbing her hand, which gently pressed the shirt to my head, I spoke in the same language as she...the same language as Ashi and Serenity. Grrr! "I do not need your help. Don't. Touch. Me."

"Huh," she muttered. "From where I'm sitting, you look like you need some help."

"My brothers are on their way."

She swiped a hand through her dusty black hair as cries for help, moans, and screams sounded in the distance. "Thank God. I wasn't sure if all the underground pathways collapsed after that last sinkhole. And I'm wigging out about bones rising, stitching into skeletons to attack!" She blew out a slow exhale.

"Whew!"

The words no sooner left her lips than a skeleton with a cracked skull pulled together, immediately lunging at her beside me. Her eyes flashed frosted green as she ducked, lifting a plank as she rolled.

With a slight roar, she bashed the wood into the skeleton. "This! Is! The! Worst! Day! Ever!" A smash of wood punctuated each growly word until it was a pile of bones again. Wide angled eyes flickered back to bright green as her gaze landed on me.

Above us—not my brothers, not Bram, but two dark female souls approached the sinkhole lip. One woman, with short orangish hair, smelled like Nephilim. Another redhead smelled like Eljo. I growled. I was glamoured, so how were they tracking me? They didn't know my magical signature.

Bram needed to hurry before one of them directly caused me to bleed. Although being soul-chained to two horsemen would burden him when the fated task kicked in, he needed my protection in the form of a soul chain to keep him alive. Had the cursed fated role triggered in him yet? How many years did I sleep before my seal broke?

The Nephilim pulled a bow from her back, nocked an arrow, then fired.

The woman beside me screeched as she batted at the arrow flying toward us. When it embedded into the plank, she dropped it.

Hooking her elbows under my armpits, grumbling about how heavy I was, she yanked me behind a thick beam for cover as the Eljo fired a crossbow at us. After the metal projectile hit the wooden beam, the black-haired woman muttered, "What kind of crazy crap do you have going on? Are those assassins?"

"I suspect they are keepers."

"Enemies from a zoo closed for fourteen and a half years since the apocalypse began?"

Corrupted guardians, but she wouldn't understand that answer either. Yet her question answered how long I slept before my seal broke. Over five years, Bram was now thirteen.

If I portaled out, the woman who battled skeletons and attempted to save me would undoubtedly die. So I summoned neither my wings nor my scythe—I didn't want the woman beside me to know my identity. The two attackers were not enough to push me into my new emergency shapeshifting form. Instead, I merely lifted a hand toward the Nephilim and Eljo. I hit them with a blast of death magic. One dropped above the lip at street level; the other died before tumbling off the edge.

Although my magical stream was not visible to her, the woman beside me still whispered, "Who are you?"

Before answering, I caught the flash of mother of pearl, copper, and golden wings over the sinkhole. My brothers had finally arrived!

With her focus on my face, she had yet to spot them. I leaned toward her and whispered a command in Angelic. *Sleep!*

Then I caught her as she fell asleep standing, shedding my glamour disguise.

Pestilence immediately flew into the pit, lifting a hand glowing with golden light, healing me before thumping my back in a hug. "Good to see you, brother. Though Hades is already raising hell."

"Keepers," War grunted, pointing at the dead woman splattered on the ground. "Morningstar planned for one to find, stab, and bond you the instant you woke, and your invulnerability ended."

Famine thumped his greeting on my back before pointing at the sleeping woman in my arms. "Who is she?"

Shrugging, I realized I didn't ask her name. "Someone kind."

Then I searched War's teal eyes. "Where is Bram?"

He pointed straight up. "Big portions of the Seattle Underground collapsed, too dangerous. Bram is flying above us."

I gaped. The boy was not magical.

Famine nudged my shoulder. "He's riding Samson, a dragon. My Eljo wife Eden and I…have a dragon ranch. And two-year-old triplets. Ready to meet them?"

I nodded, summoning my wings, carrying the woman up,

then landing. I left her reclining under a brick archway; nearby, a stairway led underground.

Then, I remembered it; the second floor was now ground level. The town had built-up dirt to raise the city. When the plague ran underground in the 1900s, I sent my reapers to collect the dead. My last trip here was in the 1800s. This was the most bizarre, disorientating portal I'd created since Day One.

Taking flight, I stared at the devastated terrain. Sinkholes had eaten entire blocks, dotted with fires and black columns of smoke, more visible as I lifted higher. Otherwise, thick vines climbed buildings; trees sprouted through city roadways.

Did I have Famine to thank for my underwater bed? He controlled the weather and definitely had a hand in nature reclaiming the land. Maybe not, if the planet continued to increase temperatures; weather erratic since the Conqueror awoke. Now, the Four Horsemen and Hades were loosed in this world. Chaos would roll over the globe.

"Humans beware. I am Death. And I am awake!"

Pumping my wings, I reached my brothers and Bram riding a red dragon! Once I enacted the soul chain with Bram, I would recall my reapers and begin my divine reign over the world's end.

Chapter Two

Death

Nine dragons! I slept for only five years! The one I knew, Ashi's colossal dragon Stormbringer, stretched. His mate, a massive light gray dragon with a red heart on her nose, snuffed me with enormous nostrils. It ruffled my gorgeous, long black hair. Not that the Angel of Death was vain.

"Shangri-la," Famine supplied.

My head swam, utterly stupefied, as four more young, sizeable dragons from two litters rushed through the open cavern to snuff me. Before I slept, the creatures weren't real—only Ashi's and Lucifer's summoned ones. Nearby, three more newly hatched dragons screeched baby wyvern noises.

The Conqueror's towheaded twins were babies no longer but ten—older than Bram when God sent me to sleep. Now, the family babies were two-year-old's, two boys and one girl, all dark curly-headed like Famine. The triplets had their Eljo mom's hazel starburst eyes.

Eden, Famine's guardian wife, explained how the Fallen sent keepers after me. To bond and soul-chain me instantly after waking!

On overload in the dragons' den, triplets yelling over each other while running around me, I needed to sit.

However, Serenity shook long platinum hair, misting me with her Valkyrie soothe power. "Come to the beach. My hubby and I need to talk with you."

In the distance, a decrepit wooden ship, fresh from its sea grave, floated in the ocean. Coral-encrusted like its skeletal crew and cannons, it sailed closer through a break in the reef. After another glance down the mountain, iguana bones crawled over the beach…as well as an ivory-boned cat. I growled, "I need to find Hades."

But Ashi slid one arm around my elbow, Serenity the other, walking me down the mountainous dragon cavern to the white-sand beach.

Ahead, with one swift swipe of his black sword, War scattered a bone iguana into a sinkhole. Then he stepped in front of me and dismissed his sword. His meaty hands fisted on his hips. Light brown hair shook as he growled, "You worked out a plan to soul-chain Bram when he was eight? Without running it past Reni and me?"

Nodding, risking him going berserker, I smiled in the direction of the gangly boy. Now a teenager, but only age six when we made the deal. They didn't need to know if Bram didn't bother to tell them. Not sorry, as when Famine's seal would break was an unknown variable. It also signified when God put me to sleep until the breaking of mine. "It is the best protection the Angel of Death can provide him during the world's end. Or do you really think he plans to ride out the chaos war in hiding?"

When his adoptive parents exchanged a look, I knew they knew...no way Bram would hide, so I added, "Bram is like my own. And now he has a dragon! He's mortal. It's happening, brother."

Ashi sighed, digging her toes into wet sand before seawater lapped her prints away. "You realize that will double-curse him with two fated roles once he matures? I barely survived one! You were there, Death; you saw it! So your plan is cruel and kind at the same time. But I get it; you are ensuring you can't reap his soul."

"I am Death. I know best."

"Here we go," Eden said with a laugh as she joined us on the beach. "I heard you like to brag about that, being Death."

I glared at the redheaded Ashi, but she bounced a palm-sized illusional unicorn at me, the white puffy thing farting a rainbow right in my face. At that instant, I both wondered why and understood why I was so fond of Kobayashi Maru. I wished I never claimed rainbow-farting unicorns wouldn't work on the

Fallen, giving her the idea. However, my original estimation stayed accurate as she was kind and fierce.

No sooner did my smile form than it curled down at the edges. Ravens gathered, blocking the sun glinting off the nearby coral-coated ship carcass. The unkindness of ravens swirled into a growing ebony mass, funneling until the upstart Hades appeared on the deck in grand fashion.

"Whoa, whoa, whoa," Ashi called in a magically infused momma bear voice, hands raised, warning Hades to come no closer to the kids. The woman had chaos magic. Not wise to rile her. Her dragon thudded to land behind her, standing steady like a ginormous pit bull.

Worse than the usurper? A deep purple portal spun like an expanding pinwheel, announcing Hades' cohort. Morningstar. No! Hell no! The you-must-be-joking scene was exacerbated when Lilith stepped next to Lucifer, waving her long, highly polished red nails my way.

All Four Horsemen stood on the beach, facing off with three souls bound to burn in everlasting hellfire after the final judgment. They and the remaining Fallen would do anything to stop that. They long expected me to join them, to at least deserve it when cast into the pit with them.

I summoned my scythe, the thumping echo on the sand unnaturally loud as red runes, proclaiming how ticked I was, flashed up the handle. "Hades," I called, voice supernaturally enhanced to carry over the water. "You rule over the realm of humans' disembodied existence. No one told you to return unholy souls to their bony carcasses."

The Titan spawn laughed like a jackass, throwing back his short blue-black hair, sharp cheekbones, and silver eyes prominently displayed. "Death, we share the right to extinguish a fourth of the world's souls." Cocking his head toward Satan, Hades added, "We thought it was a nice touch while the Four Horsemen seed chaos into this realm."

Lilith grinned. "Are you worried the risen will end someone near and dear to you, Death?" One long red fingernail pointed toward our family's only fully human boy.

Panic setting in, my gaze bounced to Bram; he wasn't safely soul-chained to me yet.

The Conqueror nodded at me. *No worries. They can't land here; we blessed it.*

I summoned my wings, launching toward the ship's deck where I hovered.

Lucifer, surrounded by animated pirate bones, nodded at me. "Welcome back to the land of the woke, old buddy."

Glaring, I studied him, same short blond hair and sky-blue eyes, impeccably dressed in a black suit. How was he ever my buddy, even on Day One? He sent corrupted guardians—keepers —to find me. To enact both soul chain and blood exchange marriage bond simultaneously!

Then my glare swapped to Lilith. Black hair, green eyes, staying as close as she could to the body she possessed for a millennium before I ended it. Zehra's. Lilith had pursued me for ages.

Hovering, I finally stared at Hades. Flamboyant as always, wearing a lime green suit and an orange bowtie, using the coral-coated ship for his stage background. On the other hand, I wore jeans, a t-shirt, and tennis shoes—the opposite of trying to stand out.

I sighed. "Hades, stop releasing souls. Close the door to your realm. Or I will close it for you."

I grinned at a flicker of doubt in his silver eyes. I had always been stronger than Hades…and now I could shapeshift. Shift into what he didn't yet know. Despite how much I wanted to transform…to knock Hades' come-out-swinging attitude down several fathoms, this was not a break-only-in-case-of-emergency situation.

"Braggart," Hades growled.

I cupped my ear. "Call me that one time more." When he didn't, I sighed. Guess he wouldn't provide a reason to transform.

To my disbelief, Bram took to the sky with Samson, flying in our direction. Teenager and red firetruck-sized dragon heading toward Hades, the King of Hell, and Lilith!

Perhaps I failed to hide my alarm as Hades honed in on my one vulnerability. Four black stripes appeared in the air, the flow of ravens thick as streams; the unkindness raced like spears toward Bram.

That was as good as any reason to shapeshift!

Tapping into my new power, it roared through me, shifting incorporeal. My body. My wings. What basically amounted to god-mode power flowed through me. With it, I reached into another realm from here. "There," I said with a sneer toward Hades. "I shut it for you."

Thousands of my reapers gathered in the air around us, obliterating his ravens. I essentially recalled them all, temporarily out of work. Because in this form, no matter what, murder victims or trying to commit suicide....

"No. One. Can. Die."

My new power pulsed as I faded, my physical self nearly see-through, but the magic was magnificently potent and addictive. Better than any of the millions of glamour illusions I cast. Because when transformed, I felt nothing. Not fear for Bram. Not the sun or wind on my wings, hair, or skin. Not all-powerful like God, but elite archangel strong. That heady thrum of conceit was why it was emergencies only. Plus, the whole no-one-can-die magic.

Lilith whistled. "A rock star incognito is still a rock star!"

Would she never stop pursuing me? I gave her no hint of interest for millennia!

But I nodded at Hades. "Go. Don't open it again."

Hades bristled. "We are loosed together to take a fourth. Expect to see me soon."

I grunted. "Not if I see you first." With a nod toward Lilith, I added, "And I'm observant like that."

Flames flashed like uncertainty within Morningstar's pupils.

I pulsed magic again, sinking the coral-coated ship and crew. Sadly, the trio of evil wouldn't drown as I manifested the meanest undertow to pull them down, down, down through a sinkhole to a watery grave.

Turning to Bram soaring toward me, I dismissed my reapers as he shouted, "Let's do this, Uncle D!" He mime-stabbed his chest. "Soul chain. Ready to bleed?"

That's all it would take. Directly causing a wound to welt a drop of my blood. The stabby-stabby motion at the chest was something we never discussed. It wouldn't kill me, but....

"I cannot while shapeshifted. Yet neither can you die. It's first on my list as soon as I shift corporeal again."

"Do it then." It was adorable, dark curls down to his shoulders, his boy voice cracking, red dragon hovering. "You're nearly see-through. Weirdo."

"It's my first shift. I cannot say how long it will take to gradually shift back. Until then, I will eliminate bony minions roaming from sinkholes and send them back to the holding cell in Hades. You can make me bleed for a soul chain when my form solidifies. I'll be back the minute before it happens."

When I mimed gently pricking my finger, he laughed. "Wimp!" He circled his dragon in the air as the previously sweet, loving boy, now a teenager, chanted, "Uncle D is a wuss!" Then he added, "Joking. See ya later."

I tapped into Team Horsemen group comms. *The next time I shift, there is no guarantee I will still be able to fly.* They didn't object when I flew over the deep expanse of ocean solo. My duty awaited me.

Almost transparent, utterly detached from this world, I took in the devastation. The ivory pockets of skeletal armies below. And the humans in misery, seeking death but unable to find it. Scents reached me while transformed, but I'd never been this disconnected from the world. Nothing touched me. Strangely unable to feel the wind or dwindling sun as I flew. Did I miss it?

With no shortage of skeletons to fight, the lack of feeling sent me back to where I last felt something. In the underground, with the woman who reminded me of Zehra. If her area was not clear of reanimated bones, it was as good as any place to end Hades' minions.

The kind woman who tended my head wound wasn't kind enough to be where I left her sleeping. Instead, a large smear of dried blood greeted me as if a bleeding body had crawled down the stairwell. That much blood indicated a near-mortal blow; if it occurred before I shifted, my reapers had come for the person's soul, which might have escaped Hades. If it happened after I shapeshifted, the person could suffer endlessly, lose every drop of blood, and still not die. A downed beam and blood path started where I'd left her sleeping…and, therefore, vulnerable.

Yet now, in the darkest hours of the night, I sensed a female presence below; she smelled like sweet peas and honey. The nameless one was near.

Chapter Three

Death

I followed the path of dried blood, past a downed beam in the stairwell, then dismissed my wings and squeezed through the only opening in the crumpled brick wall. Weaving around collapsed columns, the actions stirred up dirt and pulverized brick dust to drizzle upon me. By the time I passed a rusted metal gate, then a rusty broken sink hanging sideways on a wooden wall, all types of debris had stuck to me. Odd not to feel the grime. Finally, the blood path stopped under a sidewalk skylight. Dirty, yellow moonlight spilled through glass blocks onto a dead man, hands folded across his chest in a funeral pose.

Further out, in the darkness broken by a single candle, I spotted the top of the nameless woman's black curly hair, visible above the rim of an old-timey metal bathtub. With her eyes closed, a frayed quilt covering her, she whisper-sang a dirge as I moved closer. Did she sleep there? Her song cut off as a clang echoed from the nearby sinkhole where I first saw her.

She sighed heavily, climbing from the tub to pick up a nearby plank. Then she neared the sinkhole rim. "Why won't you stay dead?"

An ivory bone hand appeared before a skeleton climbed from the pit. She swung the board into the bones, scattering them back into the sinkhole as I approached from behind.

She whirled, green eyes wide in an olive-tinted oval face. Her long black hair swinging, she pivoted the plank in my direction. With her hair no longer bound by a ponytail, her curls resembled long springs. She did not recognize me, not glamoured into a blond like when I first met her.

Though nothing could harm me in this form, I lifted my palms to show I was no threat. Despite standing nearly seven feet tall, I looked human, wearing jeans and a t-shirt. The common look was my longstanding habit, ascertaining I didn't stand out. Thankfully, I appeared solid due to the dirt and brick dust.

She pointed the plank at the dead man, saying, "It didn't end well for the last male who jumped me." The blood on her shirt and jeans testified to that. "What do you want?"

Facing me, she didn't see the risen redheaded Eljo crawling over the lip behind her. I dodged her swing, rushing toward her to knock the dark creature back.

She lowered the plank upon realizing I was fighting the undead. Then she joined me, whacking skeletons that climbed over the rim, returning them to the pit.

With a sudden spurt of power aimed into the sinkhole, I forced the unholy risen souls out of their reanimated bones. As Death, I could sense the death cause. They'd returned to the scene. Some had died of the bubonic plague. Others involuntarily committed suicide by falling from the regraded ground level into the underground, formerly the first floor. As one, I crammed the damned souls back into their pocket dimension, Hades' holding cell until final judgment.

When the coalescing bones collapsed in the dirt below, she dropped the plank, leaning forward, bracing her arms on her legs, panting from the fight.

I held a hand toward her. "Come above ground. This underground is unstable."

She straightened, lifting her chin. "I live here. Name's Zadie. Who are you?"

"A friend."

"Nope. Not even an acquaintance. Your name?"

"I go by many names." Yet, I loathed to give her any of them and divulge my identity. Since she was back to looking at me like a threat, I offered, "Some call me—"

She shrieked, wheeling her arms as the sinkhole rim crumbled, about to topple into the pit backward as the hole expanded.

I reached for her outstretched hand. One yank later, her other palm landed on my chest.

My skin tingled under her fingers before releasing her hand and stepping back from her palm. Her grip brushed off the grimy coating, but my fingers and palm appeared solid. Her handprint over my chest was also filth-free and no longer semi-translucent. Indeed, sensation returned where she touched me, my feeling of touch.

The surprise galvanized my retreat as if she scalded me, yet I nodded at her. "Come with me."

Her green gaze landed on the plank before bouncing back to me. "Nah. I'm not in the habit of leaving with super tall strangers who just saved my life." She picked up the wood, walking closer to the candle. "Come into the light."

"Are you in the habit of leaving with strangers whose lives you tried to save?"

Zadie waited near the candle, drinking from a canteen before holding it toward me. "Only if they need medical attention."

"What would it take for you to leave here?"

When I didn't walk into the candlelight, she lowered the canteen. Then her green eyes narrowed like I definitely was a threat. "It would take a front-row seat to watch the aurora borealis light show."

I grunted. "These skeletons will rise no more, but it's unsafe underground."

"How do you know they won't reanimate?"

"Their souls returned to the lower level of Hades."

"Hades…?" Her wide eyes widened.

"Where souls not bound for heaven are held until final judgment."

I pointed toward the bloody dead man. "How long ago did he die? If he attacked you, that attests to his evil character, so he may or may not have escaped when Hades opened the door between the worlds."

Smoothing long springy curls from her face, she whispered, "The dead are returning? Did the Angel of Death quit his job?"

I cocked my head, determining she definitely did not know to whom she conversed. "No, the final horseman's seal broke today. He shapeshifted, then closed the door to Hades, but that recalled his reapers. So now humans seeking death will not find it; death will elude them."

Zadie grunted, rolling green eyes like she decided I was crazy. "Bye, doom whisperer."

Suddenly the clouds parted, silver moonlight streaming into the sinkhole, quickly followed by a swarming unkindness of ravens.

Zadie shook her head, disbelief the strongest of her surface thoughts. "A conspiracy of ravens over a sinkhole. On the worst day ever." Then her mouth dropped open because the ravens formed a funnel under which Hades appeared.

Lime suit exchanged for purple, Hades ignored her entirely, immediately launching into a diatribe. "Shutting that door was completely unnecessary. We share power over ending a fourth. That's why on the coming full moon, a blood moon, I'll let loose the wild animals on mankind."

"No!" Zadie exclaimed. "This is not real. That man did not appear under the ravens."

Unfortunately, she drew Hades' attention. "I am real. I'm Hades." He flashed her a wicked smile, standing under a beam of moonlight, the upstart always trying to shine. "And you are?"

A blink later, Hades stepped out of a travel portal directly in front of her.

She jumped back, slapping a hand over her chest, uttering a surprised squeak. Her mouth gaped when Hades stood between us.

"She is no one. Human," I clarified. Then I turned from her "hmph" to leave, knowing Hades would follow. Hopefully, before he threw a temper tantrum. If he killed Zadie, she wouldn't die. No one could while I was transformed. My only solid parts were where she touched me when she nearly fell. But a mortal wound would be fatal immediately after my shapeshift ended. That she did not deserve.

Indeed, Hades couldn't stand it that I walked away from him without my okay to kill by wild beasts of the earth. The shared power to end a fourth meant he needed my agreement. However, I was in no hurry to reap a fourth and bring on the chaos war.

"Fine," Hades huffed. "I'll ride along behind you."

The air picked up an electric vibe, a dimensional doorway about to open. Thus far, since waking, my timeline folder labeled Are. You. Kidding. Me? Was the fullest. I sighed deeply as Lilith stepped out of a dark purple portal wearing a bright red dress, wagging long red fingernails.

"How did you sleep?" Lilith laughed. "Did you dream about me?"

At my scoff, she twirled a finger to indicate our forlorn surroundings. "Why are you in a collapsed underground?"

Lilith pointed toward Zadie, still standing in candlelight. Perhaps frozen in place? Her surface thoughts popped, each a big bubble of disbelief.

Lilith huffed. "Her? Reliving the underground with your wife? Wasn't Derinkuyu eight stories down?"

I swerved around her, hoping both would follow, but Lilith didn't. Instead, she neared Zadie, asking, "Is she the latest model? Curls are new, though still black hair and green eyes...."

Perhaps the sense of touch returned an equal measure of emotions, which developed after my brothers woke. Because a tiny sliver of fear raced up my spine. That was Lilith's thing. Trying to possess the precise Zehra-like body. Anything to hold my attention. She would happily try it; of that, I had no doubt. Lilith would kill Zadie, then possess her body once I transformed, and people died instantly of mortal wounds.

I growled for bringing this on Zadie by returning to check on her, repayment for her initial kindness. Since possession was Lilith's favorite obsession for millennia, and Lilith mentioned a new model of Zehra, Zadie would die if I took no action.

Pivoting, I swerved around Hades and Lilith before stopping beside Zadie. "Time to leave." I nodded toward the crumbling sinkhole, then the dark souls following me. "It's not safe here."

"I *live* here! I'm not leaving."

I sighed, then slid one arm around Zadie's waist, ignoring her squeak as I guaranteed, "You are."

Pulling her against me, I jumped off the crumbling sinkhole rim and instantly summoned my wings. Her scream from the jump didn't end, changing frequencies when we went from falling to flying.

Based upon how strongly she fought my hold on her, she found no comfort in being removed from danger. My side solidified in contact with hers; her connecting kicks turned those pummeled parts solid. Huh. Human touch or just her touch helped me shift closer to corporeal? Each bit of physical sensation she unlocked also returned an equal measure of access to my emotions.

Eventually, her bright green eyes raked over my wings. When those eyes finally met mine, I announced, "I am Death."

She gaped as I poured on the speed, her honey and sweet pea scent heady, her body soft against me as my wings pumped.

Her gaze bounced from the wreckage and sinkholes below to my wings, entranced by the red rune markings flowing over the silver. She inhaled deeply. Humans were too easily overwhelmed by an angel's smell. Women couldn't resist angels, but I wasn't sure how long before she would be overcome. So I flew faster.

At last, I slowed, murmuring, "Isn't this the price for you to leave?"

She looked past my wings to the bright green smear of a dancing aurora. Not a front-row seat below, but hovering above the light show.

"Oh, wow!" Zadie watched the swirling lights stream over the starry expanse as another line of blue and pink fired beside the green. "Don't drop me!"

As if I would when I didn't while she was fighting me. I chuckled. "Does it make up for the worst day ever?"

But her shock and awe gave way with awareness, her thoughts sharpening into focus as she whispered, "You are the Angel of Death?"

"I thought we covered that. Humans, sadly, are rather dull-witted."

"As in the Grim Reaper?"

"I have reapers. They are on the first vacation of their existence. Would you like me to show you where?"

"Are you asking if I want to die? No! I do not."

"No. Asking if you wish to visit my pocket realm. I merely wanted your name. But you are not safe where you live in a collapsed underground. Also, Lilith has seen you now. You should know that she will kill you to possess your body. Or Hades will kill you for giggles. I do not know where else to safely stash you."

"I need to sit." She pointed at the snowy ground. After landing, Zadie plopped in the snow despite her short sleeves, jeans, and tennis shoes. She'd sacrificed her flannel shirt to my bleeding head wound.

When she immediately shivered, I summoned my horse for the first time since waking. Before God sent me to sleep, my steed's beautiful black coat fell off him like ash. I braced before seeing him, not black now, but so very pale. Yet I gave him a nod, picked up the woman, and placed her on the saddle. "Sit there; it's warmer for you."

"This is the sickest-looking horse I have ever seen! Not sick cool; he looks ill. In fact—"

"He was black."

Zadie scoffed. "He's not now. He's beyond pale, either yellow or light green cream. Is that a vitamin deficiency? I'll round up some carrots."

I huffed a laugh, then swung one hand to indicate all the snow. "No nearby carrots. Not that Horse would eat them."

"You named your horse, Horse? Yet you called humans dimwitted?"

Still, she shivered, so I vaulted on behind her. "Horse doesn't need to eat. Neither do I."

"Well, I do. What will I do for food in your realm?"

I leaned forward, peering down at her oval face. Then, when

she shivered again, I settled my left hand holding the reins onto her waist, pulling her back against me to share body heat. Now, my entire front and inner thighs were corporeal. "You are no longer afraid?"

"That depends."

"On what?"

"There is a story regarding the Angel of Death, passed down from generation to generation like family mythology. It's an actual book!"

It was my turn to shiver.

"Once upon a time, a woman moved to Cappadocia, where hundreds worked to dig subterranean dwellings. She cared for the sick, moving deeper underground as each floor was dug. One night, eight floors down, a man grabbed her from the shadows; he raped her. Within a couple months, the people wanted to stone her to death, an unwed woman carrying a child. But the Angel of Death made her an offer. To bestow upon her his name. Not a true marriage or ceremony—"

"But Zehra," I interrupted, "and her daughter had the protection of my name. She was my wife of a sort." Relief followed, saying it aloud. "Zehra was kind. Allowing her to be stoned to death was out of the question; the woman once anointed the Lord's feet and wiped the oil away with her long hair!"

Zadie swiveled, throwing a leg to sit sidesaddle, first staring at the colorful dancing aurora, then at me.

Her thoughts pounded loudly now. *I should go, running and screaming into the snow, freezing to death under the aurora's glow.* She must like her mental dirges; she had been whisper-singing one when I came upon her.

Her deep exhale huffed a billowing puff of cold as she nodded. *See if it's true.* "My family has the weirdest tradition. If you are who you say, you know my middle name. The middle name of *all* the girls in the family?"

Her question soaked in deeply, touching me that Zehra's line had honored it. The same middle name she asked me to choose after her daughter was born. She'd vowed the middle name and story would pass down; I didn't know why I was surprised. Deeply honored.

My brothers did not know of Zehra, though the Conqueror and War thought Lilith taught me to lie—because I told Ashi my wife died. Still, I'd dodged those questions about lying or a wife. Either by ignoring them. Or exiting fast, claiming I was busy. As Death...I was.

If Zadie came from Zehra's bloodline, it suggested Zadie carried a gift that I bestowed upon Zehra after she took my name. All in her line could potentially possess it. I couldn't teach Zehra magic without falling, so I gifted her with a power while she was pregnant to help keep her safe when I off doing Death's duty. Which was almost always. All she really needed was a husband to claim her.

Zadie's sweet scent carried no magic. Still, now I had to know if she was born a memitim with the power to kill people no longer protected by guardian angels. Like the man who raped Zehra...and the man who attacked Zadie?

Yet Zadie held my gaze. "Do you know my middle name?"

Chapter Four

Zadie

"**G**race," Death supplied, gracing me with a breathtakingly beautiful smile. The man—*angel*—was already gorgeous, with long black hair, a perfectly square jaw, and stunning green eyes. I was on my way to drowning in his eyes when he added, "I ended him."

Sitting sideways beside him, I asked, "Who?"

"The man who defiled Zehra." He paused before his baritone dropped a notch in bass and volume. "Did the man defile you before you ended him?"

I looked away, watching the lights dance. That didn't lessen his scent of teakwood and leather with the tiniest hint of smoky amber. "Waking to him groping me wasn't pleasant, but for the record...I didn't kill him. A metal beam fell at the top of the stairs, then another cracked his skull underground as he chased me. It surprised me because a guy was full-on whacked with a beam this morning; it didn't kill him."

"I apologize."

His green eyes appeared so solemn, but why? "For?"

"Commanding you to sleep and leaving you vulnerable where people could reach you."

"I've never seen you before tonight."

The air shimmered for a split second before Death no longer had black hair and green eyes. Now he was the blue-eyed blond from the sinkhole this morning!

To my gasp, he grinned. "Recognize me now? That was kind, rappelling into the expanding sinkhole to help. Unnecessary and reckless, but kind. That kindness is why I looked for you tonight; I wanted to know your name."

I didn't feel very kind. It was ridiculous; I would've helped anyone, but the fact he tricked me? I almost wanted to punch him.

"Go ahead."

After gaping like a fish, I finally managed, "You read my mind?"

Apparently, he took it as rhetorical. But at least he didn't accuse me of being dimwitted again. When he grinned as soon as I thought it, I added, "Stop it. Stay out of my head! It's one of the few things the government never managed to wiretap… thoughts. Or, that's what my mom said. She worked for the Mossad before the world ended nearly fifteen years ago."

Staring at the smearing aurora dancing above us, I sighed. "Thank you; I always wanted to see this but never thought I'd get an opportunity to appreciate it."

"Did your mother die?"

I shrugged. "In a post-apocalyptic world, Israel might as well be in a different universe. It's not like I can fly there and check. And she might not have been there when the world ended. She wasn't allowed to discuss where the agency sent her. Usually, she went on a mission when I wasn't there."

I shivered, teeth chattering despite the ridiculous heat radiating off his big body beside me. After stealing another glance at him, I decided he was still sexy as a blond, but I liked it better when his hair was black and his eyes green. Then I growled when he changed his appearance, clearly still reading my mind.

"You're cold." He pulled me in closer, rubbing his hands up and down the goosebumps on my arms. "I'm taking you to my realm before you grow ill. I'm sorry I ruined your warm shirt."

Death lifted one hand in front of us. A symbol appeared vertically in the air, then spun faster and faster until opening like a window to another location. "A portal," he supplied, riding through upon his hearty yet eerily-colored pale horse.

We rode from a snowscape under an aurora into violet shades of twilight. No possible way that this was the same planet! A massive moon stretched across half the horizon. Shallow water reflected an entire universe's worth of jeweled stars. In the center, one sizeable black rock jutted like a throne.

I gawked, utterly awed. Then, pointing at the glittering stars, I managed, "What universe is this? I don't recognize those constellations."

"Those," Death grinned, "are my reapers. Brighter than normal, but they don't know what to do for vacation, having never had one. It will be over soon. You have helped."

Death magically removed our shoes before he vaulted off the back of his super pale stallion. Then he held out large hands, hesitating for a beat too long, a vulnerable instant as he asked, "What do you think of my realm?"

"Amazing, of course, but…?" Any number of things entered my mind. Like…did reapers or their horseman boss actually need to breathe oxygen? Cause, if not, then…I needed a space helmet!

"You don't need a space helmet," he chuckled.

"Stop reading my mind!"

After lifting me off his very tall horse and setting my feet in water up to my ankles, he added, "You poor dimwitted human."

Death moved to basically the only seating place out of the water. The black rock, where the enormous moon backlit him perfectly. Ludicrous mode of perfection.

"Competing with Hades' ravens? It's really no competition." I followed to the rock, but the perfect seating height for him meant I practically needed an elevator.

"You don't need an elevator." Then he grabbed my hand and hoisted me up like it was nothing.

"Seriously, stop it with the mind-reading! And for your information, I've not been in a working elevator since I was five."

Death raked long hair from his face. And with the whole twilight sky full of extra-bright stars, which were *reapers*, with him centered in that ginormous moon? Two choices. Drool, of course, was the obvious choice. The other option took great restraint, but I looked away from him to the water reflecting glittering reapers.

"Hmm," he uttered. "Why live underground? What about

your father?"

"Also a spy, but for an NSA-CIA squad. I was young, so... Dad explained it like he was an elf. He hid devices that listened in foreign countries. So Santa could keep track of who was naughty or nice. Working for different governments, my parents concealed their marriage from their spy buddies. Guess it would have been frowned upon? I was visiting him when the world ended. Unfortunately, Dad died the day the world did. Work called him in, internet, electricity, everything crashing, but he never returned."

"How old were you?"

"Five."

He gawked at me. "Who raised you?"

"First, I stayed in his apartment. I ate all that food and used up batteries for flashlights. Then after looters showed up, I hit the streets."

"At five?"

I nodded. "Kind folks at soup kitchens let me sleep inside while it lasted. And they taught me to read and started my word-for-the-day quirk. With today's events, my daily word is how I feel...discombobulated." I winked. "People are the good thing about the streets; many teach you numerous things."

"How long have you lived underground?"

"I moved out of the rain into Underground Seattle at age eight. Found a hidden section not fixed up and secured for tours back when that was a thing, so it was pretty safe. Hidden from traffickers. Then I learned to make and sell candles providing light and pleasant scents. Cause the end of the world may have ended manufactured pollution, but nowadays, some people stink worse than places. Meaning I dabbled in soaps, too."

I pointed at the perfection around us, asking, "Other than raking your perfect hair from your perfect face, what do you do here? Cause, essentially, this is a rocky throne on a beautiful shallow-water world. The lighting, framed perfectly by the insanely huge moon, everything about it...is the Angel of Death vain?"

He scoffed, which also managed to sound conceited, before saying, "I am not conceited."

"Mindreading know-it-alls are the most hated people."

He huffed a laugh. "Your parents were spies."

"Yeah, not mind-readers. Besides, we wouldn't have seen eye-to-eye on privacy issues. I didn't really have those at five. Do you live here?"

"I come here sometimes. Rarely. My reapers need a place to rest between retrieving souls. I brought Zehra once. Brought Ashi for an interrogation."

"Who's Ashi?"

A slight grin tugged at his full lips. "Nephilim woman with chaos magic. Kobayashi Maru is the wife of my brother, Pestilence the Conqueror. I appeared to Ashi in three different glamours before hijacking her to discover what she did to Pestilence the Conqueror. My brother was riding the land, smiling. Laughing!"

"There's not much to do here. No wonder your reapers don't know how to vacation better than their boss."

After a slight wave of Death's hand, an aurora danced over the water. Pinks, blues, and greens skimmed the surface. "Better?"

"Yeah," I uttered reverently while watching his magical light show, reflection dancing in the mirrored water with the jeweled reapers. "Hella cool." It was a fantastic spot to think, but what else was there to do? Did he make out with Zehra here?

Death suddenly looked surly. "It was never like that with Zehra. I brought her here shortly before she died. She wanted to see it."

In agitated Grim Reaper mode, Death completed the look with a massive scythe that appeared out of the air. He rested it over one broad shoulder, the sharp-looking curved blade glinting like chrome. Red markings flashed up the midnight handle, much like his magnificent silver wings had done. Then he jumped down from the rock, thumping the base in the otherworldly glimmering water.

Thump. Thump. Thump. No way the sound should echo like

that in shallow water. Supernatural. Ripples extended outward over the glassy surface for every knock, matching the red racing symbols on the handle. His green eyes were now as unearthly as this place, a glowing yellow-green as pale as his horse.

"I am Death."

"You sound like you're—"

"Do not say bragging."

"What kind of mind-ninja skills do I need to stop your thought police invasion? I don't care for that any more than Orwell did."

"Who?" When I didn't reply, Death nodded at me. "I'll leave you here. I need to visit my family, need to see Bram."

"Who's Bram?"

Death smiled, devastatingly beautiful, stealing my breath. "He's as close as I'll get to having a son."

"Ah. Important then. Drop me off at the entrance to the underground."

"Pfft. I cannot do that. It is unsafe."

"Thank you for the aurora. I'll never forget it. But I can't stay here."

"I am the Angel of Death. I know best. I'm a realist. You are homeless now, thanks to that sinkhole."

"I at least need my stuff. Before someone finds and nabs it. Or it falls into the pit! My picture of my parents," I whispered. "You whisked me away, but there's not so much as a place to sleep here…nothing to eat unless I'm supposed to fish. Can't say I see any."

"Lilith," rumbled from his chest. "I saved your life. You can *never* disregard her now. She's relentless; trust me in this!"

I opened my mouth to protest, but he grabbed a curl, pulled it down, then released it to *boing* back in place. Death shot me a sad smile, green eyes reflecting that same sadness. "Though your hair is long curls, you resemble your ancestor. You will never be safe from Lilith now that she's seen you. Then there's Hades to consider. No. You cannot live there, but I will return for your things. Where are they?"

"No! You can't read my mind, banish me to this reaper realm, and then rifle through my belongings. I don't have much, but it's mine. If I choose to show you something, that is one thing. You digging through it is something else entirely. Besides…you wouldn't understand what to grab if I told you. Have you ever made candles? Or soap?"

Even his smirk appeared superior. "I have no need for candles. I see in the dark. My daily divine regeneration means I have no need for soap."

"You've never bathed simply because it feels fantastic?"

He swiped his scythe through the water, then raked back his hair. "It's primitive."

"And what about my yak?"

He blinked, black brows spiking. "You have a yak? I didn't see it underground."

I laughed. "That's cause Chuckles doesn't live there with me. Nah. I hide her, where she grazes, so no one—you know—snuffs her for nom-noms." At his blank look, I mimed shoveling food into my mouth. "Yak butter is required to make my candles and soap."

Green eyes twinkled, edges of his full lips threatening to curl into a grin. "Your yak is named Chuckles?"

"She's a barrel of laughs. Like a dog. Except taller. Wider. Hairier. Milkable too."

"So not like a dog at all."

"Chuckles and your vitamin deficient horse can be carrot-eating buddies."

Death's scythe disappeared as fast as it appeared. "I will ask Famine if he has room on his dragon ranch for your yak."

"*Dragon* ranch?"

He nodded once.

That's all it took for me to jump off the rock into the ankle-deep water—which only submerged his toes. His eyes widened when I hooked onto his elbow. "Yes, to the dragon ranch. First, I need my stuff. Then, I'll see a dragon!"

"You met the Angel of Death today. Hades. Lilith! But meeting a dragon is what spurs you into action?"

"Pfft. No woman would ever say no to meeting a dragon in person." But then I stopped, scenarios starting in my head, no sooner finishing the first than—

"No," Death chuckled. "The dragons will not regard you as a food source."

"Is that true for Chuckles?"

"I don't know where yaks fall in line with what dragons—yes plural—like to eat. I didn't see any on the island." His full lips tipped up like he fought a smile. "Unless they were nom-noms."

"Knowing Chuckles isn't a dragon chew toy is vital. Also, is the island tropical? Yaks like the cold, winter."

"Let's gather your things. Then I need to see Bram; I'm nearly corporeal. Afterward, we'll ask Famine or his wife, Eden. I hope you like kids. They have two-year-old triplets."

"Post-apocalyptic babies are gifts; all those kids are tough. They never had the things that most people miss about the world ending. I remember stuff, but not really. At five, I wasn't lethally hooked on the internet or a smartphone."

Death was right about needing a new place to live. Yeah, most assuredly, I wanted to see dragons...but Chuckles and I would not be moving in with his family. Meeting him was like coming face-to-face with family mythology. In it, he played the hero.

So far, I'd learn the fourth horseman was entirely vain, the way he continued to rake his long black locks away from his gorgeous, perfectly squared face. Chiseled muscles on his arms showed from his plain black t-shirt, which stretched over broad shoulders and a defined chest. But watching him open a portal, a doorway leading to my underground housing in shambles, I figured if anyone looked like him...they had a right to be vain.

Arm-in-arm, we stepped through.

Chapter Five

We no sooner stepped out than I pulled my arm from hers and summoned my scythe, swiping to disconnect the head from the dead man's body. Although Zadie shrieked, the reanimating corpse's fingers still twitched under sidewalk skylight sunshine. Thumping my scythe once, I crammed his unholy soul back into Hades, where the realm exit was still locked. The escaped dark souls could only roam so long before returning to their bodies. Transforming from my shift would not end the escapees from before I shut and locked the door. However, shifting would end the lives of every person mortally wounded but unable to die.

I didn't unsummon my scythe when I pivoted her way. One quick side-step later, she could no longer stare at the severed head. A master at dodging Lilith over millennia, the fact she found me last time down here niggled at me. "Gather your things."

Zadie's housing mainly consisted of a sinkhole now. The one remaining wall beside the old metal tub was not brick but old stone, green from wetness and age.

"Turn around, so I can change."

"Flesh does not interest me. It's about as interesting as studying the stone wall." But I humored her by looking down at the wreckage in the deep pit.

Her soap-making supplies were buried in the sinkhole, but she wore clean jeans and a t-shirt. She stuffed her threadbare quilt and her parent's wedding photo in a pillowcase with her surviving candle-making supplies. The woman certainly didn't have much. Except for her sense of humor. A yak named Chuckles?

She interrupted my musings. The darker circle around her

irises grew more pronounced in solemn green eyes. "So you are sort of like my great-to-the-Nth grandfather?"

"No!"

"Uncle?"

"The child wasn't Nephilim! It wasn't mine. I merely provided protection. And a family name."

Zadie tossed her arms. "So why help me?"

"Lilith." I sighed. "Zehra." Both true. "You were kind."

"I'm not her. Zehra."

This time, I did grin. The woman was ridiculous. I leaned forward, pulled down on a soft, black strand of her hair, then released it to spring back into a long corkscrew curl. "Obviously. Should I know something about your brainpower? It is discombobulated, isn't it?"

Despite using her word for today, she frowned. "You're a real heartbreaker."

"Of course. I am Death." Intentionally, I ignored her smear—plenty of practice with Ashi—to point out that obvious fact.

I didn't mention wanting to know if she possessed the magical power potentially bestowed upon females in Zehra's line. Zadie didn't mention that in her mythology tale about me.

I lifted a hand to open a portal. "To Bram. Then Chuckles." The name alone had me fighting a grin.

"Wait!"

Her surface thoughts pounded loudly, so I smiled at her. "No. You won't die instantly in the company of the Four Horsemen."

"Okay. Why is your scythe out when going to see your in-your-heart son?"

I frowned. "Bram used to play with it when he was young." Then I held up one hand. "Don't mention that to Serenity or Ashi."

Now, she gaped at me as the gateway window cleared, showing the white beach at Famine's Arcadia—a dragon ranch.

When she didn't step through, I placed a hand on her back, escorting her across.

Zadie gawked and pointed. "Is that a ghost ship—er—um—is it

un-sunk? Seaweed-coated skeletal crew and broken mast?"

A different ship, a Spanish galleon, floated nearby in deep blue water. Before the ravens' unkindness showed, I told Zadie, "Hades cannot set foot upon blessed land. You are safe here."

Then I turned away from the upstart, heading up the mountainside toward the dragons' den where Bram waited.

Perhaps I should have given Zadie more warning? Immediately after she crossed the den threshold, six dragons thudded forward to snuff her. Her long curls stuck out in different wild angles when they were done. But the wide goofy smile plastered on her face indicated happiness.

While Eden introduced each dragon by name, I sauntered toward the grinning teenager. He lifted one dark eyebrow while mime-stabbing his chest again.

Yet I turned toward Zadie's squeal as Eden handed her one of the newly hatched babies. The red-striped black wyrmling latched onto her arm, climbing to her shoulder, nuzzling curly locks in total disarray.

"Do. You. See. This?" She squealed again.

Stormbringer huffed a smoke ring her way, his stamp of approval.

"Do they eat yak?" She asked Eden.

"Not yet," Famine replied. "Why yaks specifically?"

"Do they eat dogs? Cause Chuckles is just like a dog. Except—"

"No," I laughed. "We established your yak is not like a dog in any way. That's before you get to milkable."

Famine grinned. "You have a yak named Chuckles?" Then he shook dark curls. "So, who is this woman you said was kind?"

"Zadie," she spoke up and held her hand to shake his. Baby dragon perched on her shoulder, walking down a line as Ashi and Serenity took over the introductions.

I turned back to Bram, nodding, "Ready? I can shift now. Do you still want this, Bram?"

"Of course." It was adorable. His voice cracked. He stood, lean and long, at least a foot taller than before I slept. Bram wrapped one arm around my back, thumping me on a numb spot that wasn't solid; oddly, it didn't solidify. So only Zadie's touch?

After angling my head away from the others, Bram followed my climb on the mountaintop path. Practically a Garden of Eden, but this was Famine's place. I stopped above the den to survey Arcadia.

With a mental broadcast into my realm, I warned my reapers to be ready. All mortally wounded would die instantly, a busy time for soul gathering. Then with both hands held away from my body, I summoned my wings, thumped my scythe with a resounding *boom*, and shifted to corporeal.

An immense sigh escaped, keeping a running death toll as thousands perished. Yet thousands of reapers were only too happy the reprieve was over. Nevertheless, I was in no hurry to reap my fourth.

Bram stepped in front of me, about chest-high now. As I braced for the boy to stab me, he laughed hugely. Then, shaking shoulder-length brown curls, Bram pointed at my finger, holding up a needle. Just like that, he poked the tip into my thumb.

Instantly, a drop of my blood welled. Bram's soul latched onto mine. He lifted a hand to his sternum, then I touched mine. The soul chain. There was no decision about killing him or not for causing it. That was the point. Though, I would not wish the fated role on him. Hence, the curse to try to kill me repeatedly when he matured—just as it would kick in on War. *If* the world didn't end before he reached maturity. But now, by not killing him, Bram was safe. I would never be able to reap the mortal boy's soul.

The most intensely bizarre sensation of liquid sunshine flowed along his chain, the accompanying newly acquired sense. But Bram grinned, tapping a finger over his sternum. "I feel that, Uncle D. Aw, you love me."

Love was the feeling flowing between us? Huh. His love for me and mine for the boy who was now closer than a son.

A shared soul chain. The very reason War adopted Bram after a metal shaving in the two-year-old's blanket pierced a drop of blood—while the toddler hugged War's neck.

War developed emotions through that chain. Soon, I would. All my brothers agreed; brace! Emotions were confusing and overwhelming. Developing empathy was not for the faint of heart.

Thinking of the berserker acted nearly like a summons; War ambled to the mountaintop. He was *peeved*. Never a good thing. Two beads hung in his beard and two in the braids in his light brown hair. As if the berserker look wasn't enough, red glowed in a rim around War's teal eyes. "You soul-chained my son."

Bram scoffed. "More like I soul-chained him."

"Our son," I added with a wink. "He cannot be reaped now. No matter what."

War blew out a deep breath, shifting away from his berserker; the red in his eyes dissolved as fast as his beard and hair braids. He nodded at me once before sending me his thoughts. *That's a relief. Lucky you; unlike his temper tantrums at two, you get to share puberty. Two was a lot easier.*

Before asking what that meant, I felt a little *zing* of excitement through that chain as Zadie and Serenity joined us.

My brow crinkled. While wondering what *that* was about, I tracked Bram's eyes to Zadie, picking up his thought bubble of *wow!*

War smirked. *See?*

Pestilence joined us. Even after all these years, seeing the Conqueror without his crown seemed wrong. He grinned at me, long golden hair nodding at Zadie as he opened up Team Horsemen men-only comms. *That was fast. And War worried you'd never allow a mate.*

Horrified, I quickly cleared up the misunderstanding. *No. She was kind. Homeless now.*

Famine joined us. *She has a yak named Chuckles.*

Pestilence locked his hands behind his back, then rocked from heel to toe. *Kindness has always meant everything to you, brother. Don't be too quick to discount that you could have met the one immediately like I did Ashi.*

I scoffed, but the kindness remark struck true the same as it would if he shot an arrow my way. *I don't want a mate. Zadie did not shoot me like Ashi did you. She tried to help me. She was—*

Kind, War supplied with a dimpled grin.

Zadie swung one arm toward me. "Great-great-great Grandpappy didn't tell me there were nine dragons!"

"Grandpappy?" Ashi repeated as the twins ran behind her, playing hide-n-seek with the triplets.

Before we wandered too far down the path of discovery, I sidetracked Ashi with the truth. "I am sorry you lost your granny when I wasn't here to escort her soul. She's in a better place; I guarantee it. Only unholy souls were set loose when Hades cracked the door. So you won't see her in that way, like Eden's cat. But all animals can rise; a heads-up before seeing Cerberus again."

A span of emotions flittered across the redhead's cobalt eyes, sadness, gratitude, repulsion, and shock. "Thank you? Wow." She turned toward her bonded. "Lance, did you hear what Annihilator Anubis said? My mastiff hellhound! I don't know how to feel about that. Of course, it's better than the nightmare of Granny as Skeletor. But still?"

Eden added, "It's strange, but Delight is still my cat. I'm happy to have the extra time with her."

If my mission was to throw Ashi off track of Zadie's crazy comment, I more than succeeded as Eden's skeletal cat joined us to rub in and out of our legs.

Sadly, however, Famine was not so easily sidetracked. He shoulder-bumped me. *Grandpappy?*

Are you sticking up for a Nephilim? And to think I was worried you might not like her.

"About that," War said. *I used my peace power, just not in the first minute of introducing him to our wives. Famine killed Ashi instantly —well, impaled her on a spike after roasting her with his fiery wings failed.*

I roared, "You what?" Every head snapped my way. Now the triplets eyed me warily.

War grunted. *Pestilence said her relic navel ring saved her from the first mortal blow.*

Famine raked a hand down his face. *Not my finest moment. It birthed a Fury; that's a whole other story.*

The Conqueror grunted. *Stormbringer devoured Famine immediately after that. Thankfully, I ensured Ashi was as immortal as I am. Best not to dwell on it. She slept and woke. Nothing festering; we forgave him. The roughest patch in horsemen history.*

"I knew it," I muttered. "After all—"

"I am Death!" hollered Ashi, Serenity, and Eden.

"That's two," Eden added.

Scowling, I clarified, "I did not say it."

Zadie snorted. "You were about to. The Angel of Death is so very vain." She shrugged. "What else do you call it when a huge rock, like a throne, is the only seat in shallow water? When the person on the throne is backlit perfectly centered in an enormous moon that takes up half the horizon?"

Ashi cocked her head. "I've been there once when he hijacked me. The water was awash with a universe of light, mirroring starry reflections."

Zadie cocked her head. "Reapers. Not stars." Her green eyes landed on me. "It wasn't a super-secret lair, was it? You called it a realm."

Ashi gawked at me as my brothers shot me with smirks. Clearly, they wouldn't let it drop. Therefore, I turned to Zadie. "Ready to collect Chuckles?"

"Sure. Bye." Zadie waved in a big arch to include the dragons, then picked up her pillowcase, holding everything she owned.

I needed her to picture the yak's location to hone in on those coordinates. Still, the longer we stayed, the more my family would pry. So without those coordinates, I opened a travel portal to quickly escape, escorting—closer to dragging—Zadie through.

Chapter Six

Zadie

With a muscular arm hooked around my waist, Death swept me out of the portal, ignoring my scream as we stepped out into the sky. His hold tightened instantly as magnificently enormous silver wings appeared and pumped, lifting us higher above a sandy landscape. Red rune markings—perhaps words in an ancient language—glimmered and shimmered along the length of those wings.

Heart pounding, I swapped the pillowcase to my right hand and latched onto one broad shoulder with my left. "Don't drop me!"

His scoff managed to drip conceit.

"Where are we?" It came out in a breathless whisper, surveying destruction, sinkholes in the sand. I knew the answer when one contained a crumbled pyramid.

Yet he replied, "Egypt. Temporary travel portal. Picture your yak; I'll take us there."

"Why Egypt?" Flying felt freeing once I trusted he wouldn't drop me. We soared in a bright blue sky streaked with white puffy clouds. Too bad the land was in ruins with sinkholes.

Large forest green eyes studied me, bright like lit by a divine inner fire. It was as if Death searched for the answer to a vitally important question. Except he didn't ask one. He held his silence so long that I thought he didn't intend to answer.

Finally, in a quiet deep voice, Death stated, "I suppose thousands of deaths in the same instant reminded me of here. Where, long ago, I mass-reaped firstborn sons from every home without lamb's blood smeared over doorways. But I was here many times. Pestilence wiped out hundreds of thousands with his plagues. Famine, too."

Bemused, my brain spun, trying to process Death as a killing machine. Was he trying to frighten me? I wasn't scared of him as in creepy Grim Reaper; he was part of a family hero myth—and middle name—passed down for millennia.

I thought it was an ancestry fairytale, vowing I wouldn't name a daughter Grace. But my mom, whose middle name was also Grace, said she claimed the same thing. That I'd understand when I was older. Well, I was older. Still, I could not wrap my head around the weirdness of so many Graces in our family line.

Golden sunshine stained the tan sandy waves and sinkholes below. Exhilarating, but Death was a horseman, so why wasn't he riding?

Death sighed. "We fly because shapeshifting could eventually lead to no more wings when I transform into corporeal."

I gasped, staring at those gorgeous silver wings that I wanted to—but didn't dare—touch, to learn if they felt as much like feathers as they looked. "Then don't shapeshift. Problem solved."

His wings entranced me, holding my attention instead of sightseeing wrecked Egypt below. His scent was exotic, teakwood and ambered leather, stronger now as he flew. Why shift if he could lose those wings?

I didn't know what to make of his slight smile—it didn't chase the sadness from his green eyes—so I changed the subject from potentially losing his wings to a happy one. His son. Or almost son. "Bram will be a heartbreaker in a few years."

It worked; that smile chased away his melancholy as he answered, "Yes."

"Why do you wear jeans, a t-shirt, and tennis shoes?"

"To blend."

I laughed. "You are not successful in blending. Nice try, but you stand out."

"Of course. I am Death."

"Pfft. Your scythe, if not height and beauty, kind of gives it away. And, you know, you have wings."

He lifted two fingers to my temple. "Picture where you hide

your yak."

As the image immediately formed in my mind, a portal window materialized in the air. On the other side, Chuckles grazed as Death flew through and landed.

Her black and white fur was moppy from rain and sinkhole debris. Fluffy tail up, Chuckles lolled her tongue as she ran circles around us.

Waiting for her to calm down and stop grunting, I smiled. "See. Just like a dog!"

"If that dog weighed five hundred pounds and was milkable."

Then I squealed, finally spotting what Chuckles was showing me. I pointed. "Look! It's Yippee!"

Death looked at the little gray ferret riding along my yak's back. "You have a ferret named Yippee?"

"Nah. He's friends with Chuckles. Best buddies. You know, like yippee! A buddy for Chuckles."

"I fear for the children you will someday have and name." Long black hair swayed, head shaking as he muttered, "Chuckles. Yippee." As the ferret ran to hook onto Chuckles' small horns, he added, "Grandpappy."

"Ah." He disliked that label.

"It's not so much disliking the ridiculous name," the mind-reading angel replied like I commented aloud. "It's that I told you; we are not related."

Oh, I'd embarrassed Death in front of his real family. Not like his fake family with Zehra. That mistake was likely one he never shared with them. Fine. I'd find a new place to live, been doing admirably on my own for a *long* time.

Just that fast, I cut Death loose. "The stink factor is high with this one," I stated, pointing at the wet ferret, then the wet yak. "Or both of them. Bathtime!"

Back arched, the little ferret danced on Chuckles' shaggy black fur, running along her back, jumping sideways, excited like always about bathtime. However, Chuckles' big brown eyes gave me her best yak stink-eye stare. I arched one brow, pointing at her white furry underbelly, so dirty as to appear tan. "Don't give me that look, smelly."

Death blinked, face aglow with what looked like incredulity.

I marched to the nearby semi-collapsed barn. A large rainwater trough waited directly outside. After lifting a piece of wood in the only solid corner of the barn, I retrieved a metal pail storing soap, a yak comb, and a ponytail. I'd sleep here tonight, exhausted as I was. Probably before bathing them, but after he left.

When Death finally approached me at the trough, his scythe was back in his right hand, the curved blade glinting in the sunshine. It thumped with his every step, each thud causing red symbols to race up the ebony handle.

He had the lightest complexion of his three brothers, but everything about him was dark when he scowled. Darker than the other three horsemen. His stance was arrogant. "I don't have time for yak and ferret bathtime. I am Death. I'm busy. My seal just broke."

Nodding, I semi-tamed my long curls into a ponytail. "I know. Thank you for the aurora, petting dragons, a quick view of destroyed Egypt, and a visit to your realm."

Then I held up two fingers in a peace sign. "Bye, Death. Don't work too hard. As in…don't be in too big of a hurry to finally end the world."

He thumped his scythe again, starting to look hot under the collar of a tight-fitting black t-shirt. "Did your dull-wittedness already forget about Lilith?"

I shrugged, not rising to the bait but stating, "If she wants to help with bathtime, I won't say no."

Thud-thud! His otherworldly scythe reverberated unnaturally loud for thumping on grass. His head cocked, black eyebrows drew down to a V. A dark beauty stalked my way. "Lilith will kill you to possess your body."

That was frown-worthy. "Lilith is looking for you, not me. If you aren't nearby, how will she find me?"

He sighed like I was truly the most dimwitted human he'd encountered. When the mind-reading thought-cop didn't interject, I knew it was true.

"Lilith is relentless. I'm not explaining magic to you. Suffice it to say, she'd hone in on you before you finished bathing your yak."

The yellow-green glow around his bright green irises flashed brighter. Death held his scythe in front of him, a massive magical gateway opening to the third horseman's dragon ranch. He glared at Chuckles, still carrying Yippee, before commanding, "Go."

Chuckles charged onto the white sandy beach, where a skeletal cat frolicked. At my hesitation, Death placed his left hand on the small of my back and propelled me through.

The portal spun closed in a smoky swirl as dark as his baritone. "The plan was to collect your yak. Consider it successful. A plus one, in fact."

Unlike in daytime Washington, the sun had clocked out, swapping shifts with a strawberry moon. "I can't stay here. With your family."

"You're homeless. Famine and Eden grew you a cottage. The land is blessed. You're safe here. I know best. I am Death."

"What if they ask about the grandpappy remark? What do you want me to say?"

"Angels cannot lie. My brothers, at least Pestilence and War, think I can." Then he tapped one large hand over his chest. "They think Lilith taught me. Because I told Ashi my wife died. Serenity, too, has tried to get the story. But my brothers are ill-informed. Intentionally? Some on my part. I get them back by pushing their buttons, portal in at the same instant as ringing to announce I'm on my way."

He shrugged, raking long black hair from his face. "I ring while stepping out near them immediately. It's not my fault they mate constantly."

"Gosh." I rested my palm on my forehead. Mind blown. "The Angel of Death's overshare has my mind spinning. Lots to unpack."

"I was forthright with Zehra. We talked. I decided over Egypt to be straightforward with you. We will talk."

I pointed up toward the dragons, then the main house. "I don't want to embarrass you again."

One eyebrow hiked on Death's perfectly squared face. "Zadie Grace, you did not embarrass me. I wanted it clear to *you* that we are not related. Family book or not. I'm certainly not ashamed of Zehra. My brothers all slept at the time. I'll tell them."

"I'm not her," I whispered. "Not Zehra."

His eyes narrowed. "The Conqueror can heal. Does he need to look into your memory?" Death reached for a curl hanging from my ponytail, pulling it to spring back in corkscrew place. "We covered that."

"Do you go around touching pregnant women's bellies? Cause the same type of guy pulls on curls to make them *boing*."

And the dark beauty seemed to grow darker.

I shrugged. What else was it if not seeing me like Zehra? Like some sort of familial obligation that he thought he owed her? How the heck did I end up with *Death* as an escort? I needed sleep; I hadn't in the underground because the skeletons continued rising.

Death stopped, pivoting my way before we reached the den. "Then sleep. If you can wrap your mind around any of it, then know. Lilith. Will. Kill. You. To possess your body."

"Call off your psycho ex! That is not cool!"

Thud. Thud. Thud. Red symbols flashed faster on his scythe. His baritone dropped a notch. "Lilith is not my anything. Ever. That was uncalled for. Very low. I thought you were kind."

Death dared to shoot me a glare like I should feel guilty. But I didn't know the magical chick at all!

He snorted. "You don't want to know Lilith. Know why?"

Why, mind-reading jerk? "Body snatching?"

One dark brow lifted. "If it is a willing possession. Otherwise? It is stealing. Your. Newly. Dead. Body. To possess you."

Nah, I wasn't living the rest of my life in hiding. "What is her hang-up with Zehra?"

"Angels don't have emotions."

"Pants on fire!" I scoffed. "I saw you with Bram. I thought angels couldn't lie?"

Death sighed. "No feelings or empathy before my brothers woke, chose inquisitive mates, then added Bram and other children to the family. But I cared for Zehra as much as I could at the time. I was fond of her; she was kind. She made me laugh. Or, more like she laughed at me. Zehra was a decade older than you when we met. When I made a deal with her to ensure she was spared from stoning."

He stared out over the ocean toward the colossal yet skeletal ship but didn't seem to see it. Nor the starlit sea waves crashing on rocks, frothy foam glinting like pearls.

Several minutes later, he blinked, then continued. "Eventually, long after her child married, and she was a grandmother twice-over, I took her to my realm as she had repeatedly asked to see it. Then after we returned to watch a sunset, I flew her soul to the pearly gates."

I didn't dare breathe; he needed someone to listen. And this was my family's story. It paid off after he sighed.

Ancient, sad green eyes stared at me, his voice low, rough. "Lilith possessed her dead body by the time I returned. Reversed her age to when I first met Zehra."

"Whoa! Is that why...you didn't," I drew a finger across my throat.

"For a millennium. I finally did. Lilith comes back in another body. I do not know why she pursues me."

Cause he was hot, dark, deep yet vain. Cause he stepped up to help a human. A supernatural entity, playing hero. Compelling.

He grunted. "Yes. I am Death."

"Stop it! Thought cop."

Famine joined us, laughing. "A little gray ferret is hanging on the yak's horns."

I nodded. "That's Yippee. They are best friends."

Dark brown curls shook as Famine laughed. "Yippee. Chuckles."

As Eden walked toward us, the triplets yelled and played from the mountaintop house.

Then Famine pointed to the left of the main house, toward the amazing living architecture that wasn't here when I met the dragons. "Getting the triplets down for the night can be quite the endeavor. I thought you might want a bit of privacy."

"Thank you. I'll stay tonight; I need to sleep. Then I'll be able to think clearly. Please don't let the dragons make nom-noms of Chuckles and Yippee."

Eden whispered, "Don't worry." She pointed toward a massive black stallion. "Rapscallion laid down the law. They are safe."

Then Eden hooked her arm through mine. She took my pillowcase of worldly goods and escorted me to a doorless little cottage. The building was created with flowering plants, trees, and woven vines, with fireflies flickering light in the otherwise dark room. It was *magical*.

"Thank you, Eden." I fell back on the leafy mattress, spotting the Angel of Death in the doorway before my eyes shut.

Chapter Seven

Death

The upcoming blood moon, Hades turning wild animals against mankind, unholy escapee souls reanimating bodies—all things worthy of discussing with Team Horsemen. But I knew the instant Zadie went out cold, that wasn't why Famine waited behind me. He was my closest brother; at one point, over the millions of human years that made up Day One, Famine, Lucifer, and I were the tightest of friends.

Famine frowned, crossing his arms over his chest. "Are you hiding her from Morningstar?"

"Lilith."

"Annihilator Anubis." Ashi joined us. "The heartbreaker. Took her to your super-secret lair...your realm? Who is Zadie, Grandpappy? Does she have something to do with the wife you once mentioned?"

I raked back my hair as we headed toward the main house; Serenity already misting me with magical Valkyrie soothe. The ladies on Team Horsemen were not about to let it go anymore than my brothers. Fine. I wanted to tell them. Basically, the Nephilim summed it up nicely. Therefore, I replied, "Yes."

We waited for Famine and Eden to tuck in the triplets, the twins inside reading them a story. Studying the massive skeletal ship nearby in deep water, I deliberated how unholy souls were tracking me. I'd been a master at dodging Lilith; how did she hone in on me and appear before I sensed her? God wouldn't do that to me...reset my expertise in avoiding her.

Once all the adults gathered outside the house, the Conqueror shrugged. "I don't get why you thought you couldn't tell us."

I shrugged. "It wasn't that. It's best not to dwell on Zehra. 1

AD was so very long ago. Her lifespan—a speck in time. You all slept."

Then I nodded. "And yes. I had God's blessing, His command to do this. And no, I had no emotions. Zehra was not a mate. I am Death, and I made an offer to the kindest woman I ever met. You don't anoint Christ's feet, wipe off the oil with your hair, and then be stoned for carrying a child of rape. God chose me to provide protection. Surnames weren't used, but the male's first name identified families; I was a husband in humans' eyes in that way."

When they held their silence, I added, "We talked." And we did—the closest thing to a best friend since leaving heaven. No emotions, no fleshly desire. As Death, I didn't generally sit with humans to chat before escorting souls. It was so dreadfully long ago.

Serenity faced me. Great, extra soothing mist coming my way. "You missed her."

Ashi nodded. "Yeah. Sad, ancient eyes. That was without developed emotions. You may be the reason God created new rules for horseman angels. He more than anyone knows how much you miss your companion."

"Hrmm," War grunted. "Could be. If so, thank you, brother."

"Yes. Thank you." Pestilence cocked one golden eyebrow, a ghost of a smile on his lips. "Whew! Lilith didn't teach you to lie. You had a wife."

Serenity sighed. "You once said the first time you felt rage was after you flew a kind woman's soul to heaven. That Lilith possessed her body. Was that Zehra?"

The memory always produced a slight growl. "Indeed."

Eden added, "You were her guardian."

The Conqueror hitched a thumb over his shoulder toward the cottage. "Why is Lilith after Zadie?"

I growled. "Zehra. Lilith has done this over the ages. You know the look, always the look Lilith wears. She's seen Zadie—asked about a new Zehra model. Zadie will never be safe from her now."

Ashi sighed. "Lilith is the biggest psycho I've met. And I've met Morningstar. So Zehra and Zadie are that similar?"

"No," I stated, looking at each of them. Then I recalled first seeing Zadie in a sinkhole dust cloud. The resemblance was uncanny before being closer to her. "And yes." Yet that was after a beam walloped my head. Zehra was nothing like Zadie… the woman with a she-yak named Chuckles and the yak's best friend, Yippee. "But no."

Famine blinked at me.

Ashi laughed. "That's the squirrelly-est thing I've heard the Angel of Death say! It tops his 'angels rule, Nephilim drool' claim after a whiskey-made healing rune."

The Conqueror snorted. "Does Zadie understand she's Lilith's target?"

I huffed. "I've told Zadie repeatedly. But humans are slow to catch on."

Serenity laughed. "Oh, she will like you if you talk like that."

"Angels," Ashi laughed. "So eternally clueless about winning hearts and minds."

I shrugged. "I do not need to win hearts and minds because I —"

"Am Death," Eden chimed in, making the women laugh.

I nodded. "Therefore, I'm inevitable. It's why I do not need to win hearts or minds."

"Way to go," Ashi muttered. "Drew Downer."

Then I announced, "On the blood moon, Hades will sic the animals on mankind, using both living and dead beasts. We share the duty. Turning wild beasts is the least deadly option. Compared to killing by sword, hunger, or sickness. I am in no hurry to reap my fourth. I will allow this, but nothing more. He will be done and one less problem."

Pestilence locked his hands behind his back, his pose enforcing his position as commander. "As the Four Horsemen ride to eliminate such beasts, it will stir chaos to blanket the planet."

War nodded, teal eyes solemn. "What the Fallen want more than anything. To harness it; their plan to kick off the war."

An ebony cloak glided through the air to a nearby swing at the mention of war. It billowed open, fluttering in the breeze, showing a crimson lining embroidered with midnight wings. The Fallen's prophecy cloak stalked Ashi after she accepted the gift to save Serenity. A redheaded Nephilim was prophesied to open the door to the bound Fallen. And they intended to free their leaders caged in solitary confinement, pitch-black space prisons.

Famine's gray eyes bounced from the cloak to me. His reflected dread and acceptance; he knew this was my God-given purpose. "Compared to plague, starvation, or skeletons wielding swords, it is the compassionate choice."

Famine had never before been a fan of humans! Or Nephilim. Nevertheless Eljo! Compassionate choice? Eden definitely opened his mind. And heart.

War crossed his arms over his chest. "Is there anything else we should know?" He cocked his head toward the cottage, long light brown hair swaying.

Serenity swiftly followed with a sweeter version. "That you might want to tell the people who love you?"

I nodded toward the cottage. "I gifted Zehra with a power while she was pregnant, to protect her while I was busy with Death's duty. It could potentially pass down the line. But I've seen no evidence that Zadie has or knows about it."

Ashi smiled. "As the recipient of quite a few gifted powers, that rocks! What is it?"

Really, it wasn't something I wanted to answer. Right now, the plan was to protect Zadie from Lilith. And Hades. A position she was in only because I returned for her name. That was what Zadie got from me in repayment of her kindness. That absolutely did not work for me.

If I told them, and she displayed a destroyer's power, my brothers would definitely want a memitim on Team Horsemen —the opposite of why she was with me; safety from Lilith. If Zadie inherited Zehra's power? A destroyer went after entities no longer protected by guardian angels. "It matters not. She manifested no indication of having it."

Yet, Zadie didn't hesitate to fight skeletons reanimated by unholy souls at the sinkhole. That was fight or die. I sighed. "I'll be back. I have to deal with Hades."

An odd *zing* shot from Bram's soul chain. Still new to me, I lifted one hand to my sternum.

War grinned, dimples flashing. "Bram. Dreaming. Welcome to puberty." He laughed hugely. "As Reni said to me, welcome to flesh…101. Probably appropriate for you."

I grimaced at his teasing.

War inclined his head toward our brothers. "This land is blessed. Everyone is safe. The families need sleep, but Lilith may show wherever you go." His dimples flashed. "I'm looking forward to it. The Four Horsemen. Sounds fun."

The Conqueror grinned at War. "Stealing the spotlight from the instigator."

Eden yawned, patting me on the back. "That's you. Have fun. Be wise."

Serenity smiled. "No worries. We'll be there when Zadie wakes."

They all kissed their mates.

Ashi shot me a sad smile before the Four Horsemen rode out of a travel portal. Like Pestilence, I believed her power would increase the more chaos the horsemen created while riding together. But, she didn't want that power; it hovered topmost in her thoughts, shining in cobalt eyes.

We exited to the mountaintop where the ark parked after the Nephilim-annihilating flood. Immediately after watching the last of their children die, the Sons of God were bound. I sighed. That was before we learned of the thousands hiding in dimensional portals.

Mounted, seeing no nearby sinkholes, we took in the beauty of this world before the view was utterly destroyed by a funneling unkindness of ravens.

With his shiny bright blue suit and matching hat perched low over one eye, Hades smiled at me and pointed up at the nearly full moon. "Full moon tomorrow night. *Blood* moon."

First, he'd cracked open the door to cells holding unholy souls awaiting judgment. The death toll would continue to rise from that until all were chased back into Hades. Now he champed at the bit, ready to hurry the world's end. I wasn't. The sooner Hades was out of the equation, the better. "Wild beasts. *No* turning pets or reanimated versions against owners. But wild beasts can rise. That's it."

Brat, egotistical Titan child that Hades was, he threw a tantrum. First, he kicked at the ground, rocks rumbling and rolling as he opened a new cave. Then, after a long exhale, he growled. "That will take forever to reap a fourth."

"Still, it will be reaping. Slowly but surely. Congratulations. Your work is done after the blood moon. Enjoy being out of your cage."

"What am I supposed to do after that? Besides, follow along after you?" His tone implied Hades found that option as distasteful as I.

"Perhaps entertain Lilith?"

"Only if I saw the blacksmith first," Hades muttered. "And to crack open the door to Tartarus, you must stir up copious chaos."

I laughed. "You think the Titans will get out? Missing your family?"

"No," Hades huffed. "Saying that before I agree to entertain Lilith, I'd need the blacksmith imprisoned there to forge a demon dagger."

The Conqueror nodded toward us. "Let's go." Then as one, the horsemen galloped away from Hades.

Before God sent me to sleep, my stallion resembled Famine's black steed. Now my horse was eerily pale; the yellow-green lightness of his coat seemed to cut into the darkness. Could carrots help? Then I shook Zadie's suggestion out of my head.

We rode from one sinkhole to another on our last night before the blood moon spell would trigger a newer apocalyptic hell version than sinkholes. Animals would turn on mankind. For now, we fought through ivory-boned patches in the open, sending unholy souls reanimating bones back where they belonged.

Hours later, a strange *zip zap zing* series shot through Bram's chain. Although I managed not to touch my sternum this time, I turned to War when the subsequent three unnamed emotions pinged me hard.

Shrugging, War's dimpled grin plastered across his face. "He's crushing on Zadie. That's what Reni called it when I described the bizarre sensations. Zadie is attractive and the only unattached female he's been around lately."

The following three fast feelings zinged the hardest yet; War nodded at me. *Sexual attraction. You'll feel an echo of what he does. Brace, while his feelings pump through you. It will tint how you see Zadie. He's human, so maybe tint everything?*

Chapter Eight

"**S**leeping?" A young child's loud whisper penetrated my consciousness.

An even louder whisper to my right declared, "Mommy said no wake."

That was quickly followed by a shushing, made almost at a yell level, from the foot of the twin bed.

Scenting salt, water droplets hit my face as I opened my eyes to see the triplets, the only girl tossing green seaweed over the bed at her brothers.

"I'm telling." One boy declared before he held out his hand. Red seaweed appeared in his palm before he threw it at his sister!

I jerked upright, rubbing at my eyes, then the droplets on my face as yellow seaweed formed on the other boy's hand. He tossed the sloppy wet mess at his brother.

Eden ran in. "I'm sorry, Zadie, that the little varmints woke you with magically-enhanced temper tantrums. They'll be three soon."

When she said varmints, the little girl gasped and slapped her hand over her mouth like her mom cursed. Then three sets of long dark curls swung as the toddlers looked down at their toes.

Eden pointed at the boy to my right. "Hunter." Her finger swiveled to the boy at the foot of the bed. "Forrest." Then she nodded at the only girl. "Ryder. What do you say to Zadie?"

"Sorry," they said in unison.

"That's okay."

Last night, I noticed the cottage had no door but overlooked details in the dark before crashing hard. The walls were a leaf weave the color of a tiki hut; magenta and coral flowers bloomed from four of six trees serving as support frames. Red and yellow apples hung from the remaining trees. The high ceiling flickered with magical fireflies.

Eden threw open two sets of wide woven blinds. Tropical sunshine streamed inside as she told the tiny magical trio, "Go help Daddy."

Ashi stood in the doorway.

Usually, I woke solo inside an old-timey metal tub in the sidewalk skylight's dim light. Sometimes, I'd wake nearly freezing in winter after the coals buried beneath the tub turned cold. But I could shift from sleeping to thinking fast with the best of them; I had been a child raised by the apocalypse. So I asked the two women standing there, "Do you have any carrots?"

Eden laughed. "Yes. Famine grew bunches. Death said your yak needs them."

"His poor pale horse, too," I muttered, trying to smooth my wild hair. "Thank you."

Ashi held up a cup of steaming coffee.

"Gosh," I accepted the mug. "Caffeine? Super rare. I haven't had coffee since my dad let me take a sip of his at the airport. I was five."

Serenity entered with a plate of fruit, another rarity, placing a tray beside me. Her light violet eyes glowed a darker purple, the air above her now lightly tinted green as a mist dappled me.

"What is that?"

"Magical soothe. A Valkyrie power. Sorry for the ambush right after your eyes opened."

Ashi grunted. "She's doing better than me; I have zero brainpower first thing after waking. Drink up before stepping outside. Either Eden's skeletal cat or Death dropped a dead rabbit outside your door. Just wow! Spoiled meat sounds closer to a post-apocalyptic mob's death threat." She sighed. "He means well. He's the most clueless of all the brothers."

Serenity snorted. "The vainest."

I shrugged. Death was the hero in my family story. "If you look like that, you probably deserve to be."

That seemed to galvanize a grinning Ashi. "Death's disdain

for human intelligence may make you doubt what he says, but Lilith is no joke. And he is an angel." She sighed and nodded. "He cannot lie."

Eden supplied, "Lilith is a mighty demon; possession is her favorite obsession. You're safe here on Arcadia."

Ashi patted my back. "It's a lot. I know. I didn't use to believe in any of it. But you're not alone."

Nodding, I walked outside. It wasn't hard to breathe here before, but suddenly, I couldn't get enough air. Furthermore, a creepy brown rabbit carcass waited outside the doorway.

Serenity rested a hand on my shoulder, misting me in a near overdose of calm. "Death meant well."

Rare caffeine kicked in; I burst into action, retrieving the yak comb, soap, and ponytail from my pillowcase. "Can we talk while I bathe Chuckles and Yippee?"

I held up the comb. "It's warm here, so that will trick Chuckles into shedding. I plan to knit the vain Grim Reaper a yak sweater in appreciation for putting me on Lilith's radar. I think you may agree that wearing it is the least he can do?"

Ashi laughed, stepping out with us and waving an arm at the twins I met yesterday. "Bring carrots. Let's help Zadie bathe her yak and ferret."

"Oh," I turned to her as Zed, Bram, and Zoe headed our way. "Yippee is Chuckles' best bud. Not mine."

Bram quickstepped, catching up, striding beside me down the mountain to a shady trough. He was super cute, like from a boy band poster. If the world didn't end, the boy would be a heartbreaker. Despite his tan, his cheeks burned red before ducking his curls, hiding his blush.

The herded triplets flipped water droplets on each other at the trough as Eden sighed. "There's no worry over a soul chain. That's all Bram."

The boy nodded, but as I hand-collected shedding yak fur, no one explained that terrifying jargon. While I puzzled over a soul chain, the kids formed an assembly line from the trough to where Chuckles grazed, passing my pail down the line to drench her.

Serenity stated, "Suppose Death bleeds. And so do you? Then only let him touch you, exchange blood with you, if you want to be married to him. The angelic custom is called bonded. Not that it would happen, but it's good info to have to make an informed choice. If given one...."

"Yeah. Important." Also, super creepy. Was that why blue-eyed blond Death was skittish about me holding my shirt against his profusely bleeding head wound, insisting not to touch him?

Brain spinning, my gaze bounced from the Valkyrie Serenity, misting me with a miraculous soothing calm, to the dragons' den, then my magically grown cottage. Furthermore, offshore, I spotted a floating skeletal ship with an equally bony crew.

Flabbergasted, each exploded like mini-brain bombs—before the skeletal cat rubbed against my legs. My curls blowing from my ponytail might as well be blown-mind confetti shooting out the top of my head. It often happened since meeting Death, not a fairytale angel but a living, breathing myth.

Shaking my head, I looked at Ashi. "How do I stop Lilith? She can't ruin my life."

Ashi blew out a long exhale. "I can zap her out of that body; holy magic I acquired through my bond with Lance. But Lilith will come back fast in another nearly identical body. She can't inhabit an unwilling host, but she can kill her, then possess her. Usually, there's no shortage of women willing to trade their souls for comfort and magic in the devil's dimension. But, lucky you, Lilith has eyes for only your body. She wants Death. Thus, your problem."

Tossing my arms, I decided upon a full nuclear option. "Can't Lilith be killed?"

The tall redhead nodded. "Yes. With a demon blade. But you must kill her host to trap her in a dying body. Lilith can possess the dead. But if a living body she possesses is stabbed with the blade, if she can't remove it to escape before the willingly possessed body dies? That is the only way Lilith can stay dead."

Soaping Yippee, I asked, "Where do we get a demon blade?"

Serenity shrugged. "Books suggest a blacksmith in Tartarus, also called Abaddon. It's a big no. Ashi searched for one for years. We've looked into it."

While we finished the bathing process for my massive yak and the tiny ferret in record time, Bram talked about flying on Samson. Then he asked if I wanted to ride his dragon during the eclipse.

Before I could answer, the air swirled like a giant smoky pinwheel—*whoosh!* Death stepped out. One midnight brow up and one down. His long black hair lifted in the breeze, head cocked, staring at Bram. Death looked...? Confused!

War followed him through, except deep dimples showed in his smile. He nodded at Death, then Bram, laughing, "Told ya."

Death looked at me, then back to Bram, then me again. Finally, he grinned as forest green eyes traveled down my body. "Yeah."

Weird layered on weird, but that was okay. I lifted the bag of collected yak's fur, planning to kill the angel with kindness by creating the tackiest sweater ever knitted. If I couldn't treat him like some long-lost relative, which he seemed like with all the family mythology, I'd hit him kindly but directly in his weak spot. His vanity. Until he helped me clear up the mess with Lilith.

If I was trapped here, for now, I needed to know if Death saw Zehra or still wanted to when he looked at me. Especially like *that*...standing next to Bram, staring at me, and tapping one finger over his sternum.

Yet Death sighed, muttering, "Poor dull-witted human." He pointed at me as Pestilence exited a travel portal. "She may need help with her brain. Specifically with her memory, recalling conversations."

"Stop snatching my thoughts."

Long golden hair swayed as the blond cocked his head, clear, bright aquamarine eyes studying me.

Could all angels read my mind?

Death steered me away from the group, then stopped in some semblance of privacy outside the cottage, where the carcass waited.

"Thanks for the rabbit, but the meat is no good if it isn't field-dressed quickly. Please don't do that again; I'd rather not spot a carcass first thing out the door. Did you leave food for Zehra like that?"

Death nodded. "Until she started waiting for me to show up and leave it. Then we began our talks while she cooked for herself and later for her child."

I shook my head at him. "I'm not her."

"How many times must we cover that, Zadie Grace? Moreover, how long before you stop thinking of me in a related grandpappy way? I don't know precisely why it annoys me. Oh, but it does. Do you enjoy taunting the Angel of Death?"

"When did I go from not Zehra to Zadie?"

"Before you told me your name." His scythe appeared in his hand! He used it like a shield when uncomfortable...that vain angel did. Honestly, how could I be scared of the guy written as a hero in family lore? Which ended up not being a fairytale!

With a swipe of his glinting scythe, the dead bunny disappeared. Just poof! Hero or villain, Death was here to end the world.

"Hey," I settled a hand on his forearm. "I won't hide from Lilith during the end times' conclusion. There's no need to dance around it, so I'll flat-out ask...can you acquire a demon blade?"

Long black hair shifted as his head shook. Then, staring down at me, green eyes holding mine, he uttered, "Destroyed. The Fallen long ago collected all that existed."

"How about from the blacksmith?"

He barked out a laugh. "The Olympian's blacksmith imprisoned by the Titans in Tartarus? There's a reason Ashi hasn't gone after it. It's the bottom layer."

"Of?"

"Hell. Nephilim can't enter it. Heaven either."

Darker and darker...yet my fairytale-related angel still sounded like mythology. The lowest level of hell? Closer to nightmare now than legend passed down. "If you know where the blacksmith is, why haven't the horsemen fetched a blade for Ashi?"

He scoffed, a veneer of conceit. "You know not what you ask. And I'm still not explaining magic to you."

"Think about it."

"You really have no idea. It's nothing to consider."

I approached his pale horse, holding a carrot bunch. "Nom-noms," I murmured lowly to him. "You need vitamins."

The yellowish-green cream horse pointed yellow eyes directly at Death like the steed silently asked if he must.

Death laughed. "Can you humor a human? Chomp on your first ever carrot?"

The stallion stomped, snorted, and nodded. Then, the horse chewed on the first carrot in his life.

With a sigh, Death added, "Horse likes bacon."

I gasped. "No wonder he looks so ill. That's not good for him!"

After focusing on the almost pale light the stallion emitted, I smiled. "You should name him Ghost. Then you can be a Ghost rider."

Death groaned. "That was bad. Even for a discombobulated human."

"Hmph." I pulled out my ponytail, massaging my scalp as long corkscrew curls whipped in the tropical wind. With a sigh, I swept an arm down the mountainside toward the beach, announcing. "This was a lovely pitstop. But Chuckles needs a cooler climate."

Black eyebrows lowered over forest green eyes. "Pitstop?"

"Before obtaining a demon blade. The blacksmith. I'm not hiding for the rest of my time on this planet. From a demon! Who wants to snatch my body, living or dead?"

His large palm lifted to my cheek. "I am sorry, Zadie. I meant to repay your kindness, desired to put a name to the nameless one...not center you in Lilith's bullseye."

Then he swept an arm toward the far-left beach below.

"Is that snow?" I laughed.

"Famine created a pocket of cold for a dusting of snow on

Arcadia. For Chuckles."

Snow on a tropical island! Back in the fairytale department. "Thank you!"

Death thumped his scythe once, the thud otherworldly. "If you cannot be comfortable here, Pestilence lived in many blessed locations. Still, Zadie Grace, you cannot stay there alone. Demons are wily."

"Calling me dull-witted again?"

"If a toddler screamed for help, or an infant cried? You would go. You, who rappelled into an unstable sinkhole to move a beam, fighting assassins and the risen. Lilith is wilier than most."

He sighed, shaking his head. "No. Besides, after the blood moon, the beasts will attack mankind. If you don't live where I know you are safe while I carry out my duty? You must ride with me."

Just like that. The fairytale flipped right back into the legends and super-intense nightmare category. Lifting the bag of yak's fur, I shrugged. "Guess I'm knitting then. Maybe we can talk about the blacksmith when I next see you?"

Chapter Nine

Death

"Eschewing," I announced from outside the cottage. "Your word for today." It fit. She spent the day avoiding me, which was *completely* fine; instead, she stayed busy spinning and stretching yak fur. Yet, smoke-like shadows slowly crawled over the blood moon's orange-red surface; when it reached totality, it would invoke more than howling coyotes. In under an hour, wild beasts, living and dead, would attack mankind. I needed to go.

Zadie sighed, winding her new ball of yak yarn. "It's not habitual avoidance. Yet. Unless you eschew telling me about the blacksmith?"

After I raked back my hair, a habit, she joined me outside, adding, "Are you signaling for me to cut those long locks and steal your deathly superpowers?"

I grinned. "I'm not Samson. Besides, it would regrow due to my daily regeneration."

She pulled out her ponytail, unleashing fabulous long curls, then massaged her scalp. She studied the lightning flashes revealing high billowing clouds over the mainland. Then her gaze flicked to the lunar eclipse. "For a busy guy, you sure hung around."

"Reapers." She was why I stayed; Zadie seemed to settle in by all accounts. "Sleep. Don't leave this island."

"Don't make animals turn on humans!"

"Your pets, the dragons, and the bony cat won't attack you. You're safe here. This is Hades' last play. I am not in a hurry to end a fourth of humans. It is, in fact, the...." I thought over what Famine labeled it. "Compassionate choice. Compared to a plague."

She shuddered. "Speaking of compassion, how do you propose we get a demon blade?"

"It is not worthy of considering, Zadie."

She flipped her unruly curls from her face and widened her stance. The darker forest outline around her narrowing green eyes deepened a shade. "May I be candid with you?"

I smirked. "I'll know if you're not."

"I don't know how to deal with you. You were mythology." She twirled a finger in the air. "Then you grew wings! All this magic? Hades and Lilith? You were a family lore hero. Enough that I carry Grace as a middle name. Yet we clearly aren't family. I'm not magical; I don't fit in, so why am I here?"

I sighed. "Lilith. How many times must I explain?"

The breeze blew long curls to lash across her oval face as she asked, "Is there an answer to ending Lilith that doesn't include a demon blade?"

"Eternal hellfire after final judgment."

"So you literally expect me to hide from her, to not leave this place until the world is so long gone that it is final judgment?"

I sighed with relief. "Finally."

Oddly, Zadie didn't appear relieved when she squared her shoulders and glared at me. Instead, she spun away, walking toward the den.

After summoning my scythe, I thudded it once. Then, as the boom thumped supernaturally, I reached into her mind. *Where are you going?*

Except Zadie not only stopped walking but slapped her hands over her temples, yelling, "Ah! Mind voodoo! Never do that again!" She huffed out a breath, then muttered. "No to the Angel of Death whispering inside my head."

Bram stepped out of the dragons' den, hiking one eyebrow. A *zing* shot through his chain when his large brown eyes landed on Zadie.

The next *zap* echoed through me after I turned toward her. It was distinctly uncomfortable to view her in that light. Angels didn't care about flesh.

A big dopey smile on his face, Bram asked, "Did you change your mind?"

Perplexed, I asked, "About what?"

Bram snorted. "Not you. Zadie? About watching the blood moon from the back of a dragon?"

Zadie nodded.

I hooked onto her elbow. Then, pointing above us with my scythe, I inquired, "What is that?"

She shook me off before shrugging. "Air? The sky? Night? In-progress eclipse?"

Since she still seemed not to comprehend, I pointed my scythe toward the ground. "What's this?"

She shrugged again. "Land? I don't know, scythe slinger."

"The ground is blessed, hallowed." Pointing up again, I added, "Not the sky. Not the water. So anxious to give Lilith a shot at you?" Hitching my thumb toward Bram, I then hitched one brow. "You put him at risk."

Bram grinned. "You made sure I won't die, Uncle D." He tapped his sternum.

I growled. Maybe it was in their water? This time, I pointed my scythe at Zadie. "But she will. It is Lilith, Bram."

I squared my shoulders as her thought bubbles popped; she doubted the veracity of the threat. I clasped her elbow again. "You want to learn how fast Lilith can find you? Is that what it will take for you to live here with Chuckles and Yippee? I will kill Lilith. You will see how fast she returns."

Dismissing my scythe, I summoned my horse and mounted. Taking advantage of Zadie's stun, I swung her onto the saddle. Then I declared, "We do this tonight under the blood moon. Do whatever you need to do for your tiny human brain to deal with seeing magic. Once you experience it, you will be happy to return to your yak. Where it is *safe.* It will tell you everything you need to know about Lilith."

I opened a travel portal to Easter Island—an isolated location where the wildlife would not threaten her life after Hades spelled the animals. Yet I didn't urge Horse through. Instead, I clarified it for her. "Don't leave my side if you dismount. Nod that you understand."

After she nodded, we rode through only for her to ask, "Those gigantic eerie figures dotting the hillside?"

"Moai," I provided as a shadow cast darkening red shades on half of the moon. Hades would not release the beasts until the blood moon was fully eclipsed.

Fifteen minutes later, full event minutes away, Zadie glanced toward restless wild brown horses raising a ruckus, running beside the moai. "Why Easter Island?"

"She's coming."

A deep purple swirl appeared vertically before opening like a window. Lilith stepped out and wagged red nails my way.

Immediately, I hopped off and summoned the sword given along with my duty. Then, I lopped off Lilith's head as her eyes narrowed on Zadie.

Zadie screamed precisely when the total eclipse cast the moon fully behind a dark red shadow.

Lilith's dark essence flowed away from the possessed woman's body.

Wherever Hades was showboating, he blasted out a shared power given to us. The wild horses immediately charged. But a burst of divine energy pushed a barrier shield outward, so the horses ran the other way.

I jumped on behind Zadie.

The five animals no sooner cleared the moai before a deep purple swirl announced an incoming Lilith. Black hair shorter than usual, but green eyes, someone from her reserve.

Lilith hissed. "That seemed personal, Thanatos."

Zadie opened her mouth but emitted no more than a squeak. Thought bubbles exploded with disbelief that Lilith was back immediately. And had the same look as the dead, headless woman on the ground!

Lilith sneered at Zadie. "What are you waiting on? For me to say, I'll get you, my pretty? That's obvious. You mean something to him. As did Zehra."

I nailed Lilith with a harpoon of death magic to the face this time. As she keeled over and her dark essence escaped, I glanced at Zadie in front of me. "Do you need to see it again?"

"No. Why is Lilith after you?"

"Lilith once told me that we'd spend eternity together in the lake of hellfire." Although Zadie gaped, I added, "She's coming again."

I opened a travel portal, quickly exiting onto holy land outside the lodge at Mission Mankind.

I vaulted off the back, then lifted her from the saddle. "Easter Island because it was solitary for Lilith with few animals to possibly attack. That's why we're here. I told them I'd make a sweep for wildlife potentially attacking humans near here."

Her lips opened, but the howling wolf in the distance cut off her words, green eyes widening.

I nodded. "Stay inside the fence." Then I nodded at the lodge. "Or sleep on the couch in the Conqueror and Ashi's home until I'm done."

Of course, she chose to do neither; instead, following me outside the fence. Suppressing a growl, I pivoted toward her.

Yet she clapped her hands and squealed. "Look! It's a bunny!" She moved closer as it did toward her, then bent to a knee. "How cute!"

"Zadie—"

"Eek!" Too late, the rabbit launched at her, teeth hanging from her shirt.

She jumped to her feet and made a shooing motion to the rabbit attached to her clothes. Then, hopping in place, she scolded, "Bad bunny!"

Zadie no sooner shook it free before all its friends headed her way. "Eek!" She hollered and ran deeper into the forest toward a deer that stood still in the ending eclipse. Nearly reaching it, she glanced back at the fleeing rabbit herd. But she turned forward just in time for the deer to headbutt her. A screaming mountain cat, sounding like a woman being murdered, scared away the doe.

"That was...." Unable to stop my grin, I strode her way, then offered her a hand, hoisting her from the ground. "Are you alright?" And I'd thought maybe Ashi overestimated the threat from the nearby woods.

"Yes." Immediately, Zadie picked up a dead tree limb. Then, after a couple practice swings, she rested it on her shoulder.

Another howl set off a flurry of others, signaling the end of the supernaturally enhanced eclipse.

"Want to return inside the fence?"

She swung that club again. "Nope. The bunny tricked me with adorableness."

"Lilith will be more than a little peeved. Stay on blessed land." When she didn't make a move, I escorted her inside the fence, then shut the gate. "Stay."

Not three strides later, she opened the gate and ran to block my path. "Oh, you *so* did not order me to stay like a pet?"

She flipped around at a sound like a woman screaming, finding a mountain cat instead. The tan beast bunched, readying to pounce, but a charging pack of wolves stopped, scaring it off. Except these wolves were long-gone, skeletal beasts howling. Suddenly, the wolves hunched, cowering; they ran as a deep purple swirl signaled an incoming Lilith.

Growling, I scooped Zadie into my arms and blasted away on summoned wings. "I am Death. I know best. Stay on blessed land."

Brushing aside long curls blowing in her face, I issued a command in my language. *Sleep!*

Apparently, I still had room for one more entry in my timeline folder labeled Are. You. Kidding. Me? Bram dreaming. *Zing! Zip! Zap!*

I blamed my deep inhale of her honey and sweet pea scent on the attraction zapping through me as I cradled her soft body closer. So small compared to me, so humanly fragile. It all started with a rabbit. She was likely picking out pet names as she kneeled by it. But Zadie could have died.

Another series of tingles zapped me as I stared at her, seeing her as Bram did. Would she try to leave the island? If that were the case, it would be safer for her if I knew where she was at all times. In my realm. Or riding with me.

After finally returning her to the cottage, I spotted Bram waiting outside—not dreaming, not sleeping. How? I'd felt his dreams, his carnal fascination with her.

Large brown eyes solemn, Bram tapped his sternum. "I feel that. I'm backing off. Zadie is beautiful. I'm not blind, but I'm only thirteen. I wanted to let you know."

"Look," I held up one hand. "I know you are attracted to—"

"*You* dig Zadie." Bram shot me a smile, tapping his sternum again. "That's all you. I backed off as soon as I felt it." He nodded. "Good night, Uncle D."

Chapter Ten

Stumbling from bed to throw open the woven shutters, I blinked at Death outside as he smiled my way.

"Good morning, Zadie."

Great! While I had bedhead, he was devastatingly hot—in a legendary family hero sort of way. Last I recalled, we were flying. I didn't remember anything past a musical-sounding word he uttered. But I slept amazingly well.

Ready to jump to it, I clapped my hands once. "Hi! Okay, so Lilith! Doesn't stay dead. Evil, magical, maintains a distinct look. Long black hair, green eyes. She was fast like that hunting you or me?"

"You." Death stepped next to me after I exited the cottage.

Pivoting his way, I tossed out my first suggestion. "You had blond hair and blue eyes when I first saw you in a sinkhole, so can you change my appearance with an illusion?"

"Why would I want to change your appearance? That's not how she's finding you. I'm not teaching you magic."

"Is there no way to stay off her radar?" At his blank look, I revised, "her tracking system?"

"Besides blessed land? Protective rune markings could shield you and make you much harder to find. Not impossible for Lilith, but challenging."

I tossed my arms. "Well, why didn't you say so when I asked about the blacksmith? Let's do this. Is it a symbol on a rock to wear like a necklace or what?"

He smirked, green eyes glinting like a challenge. "Tattooed runes." Then he flicked one finger up and down my body. "On your skin."

While I wasn't against tattoos per se, I wasn't a fan of their permanence. And that was of a fabulous design that, at a later date, I might not consider so fab. Not rune markings.

"Henna." How did I forget the conceited angel read my mind almost nonstop? He must have. "Yet that would need *reapplying* every week to ten days."

"Sold!" I pumped my arms over my head in victory.

His mouth dropped open; apparently, Death assumed I'd say no to the dare in his eyes.

I lifted one brow, grinning. "Are you offering to paint henna rune markings on my skin?"

Surprise, surprise, Death summoned his scythe, his shield when uncomfortable. "I wasn't—"

"But you could. And you don't care about flesh; you said that. Angels can't lie. So let's get the henna."

"It's more than one tattoo!"

I nodded, not seeing the problem. After all, he saw me as interesting as the coconut trees lining the way to the snowy patch of cold for Chuckles. So painting henna runes on the back of my hand was seriously not a big deal. "Will you please procure it? I have a yak to comb and milk."

I grabbed the pail and comb, then left him sputtering. On the beach, I waved for Chuckles to join me in the noncold section. Yet my yak grunted three times, circling me.

"What is your problem?" Then I saw the issue. The cute sweet ferret was feral; he turned against mankind! Yippee charged my way.

"Death," I bellowed.

Although he pointed his scythe toward the ferret, it didn't occur to me that he might kill the little guy under Hades' spell. Because that would be the act of a villain, not a hero. Family mythology assured he was the latter. And sure enough, Death magically swapped feral with tame.

After letting out a relieved sigh, I presented a straight face. "You should talk to Pestilence."

Joining me on white sand, overlooking a skeletal ship and crew, he inquired, "Why?"

I fought my grin. "So he can look into your big angel brain memory problem. I told you Yippee was Chuckles' best bud! Not my pet."

"Now, your pet's pet will stay at peace while on blessed land."

"Thank you. Do you still not have the henna? Tell me where to acquire it, then you can milk Chuckles while I fetch it?"

Long black hair swayed as his head shook. "I'm not milking Chuckles. Ever."

With a little shooing motion, I dismissed him. "Off with you then. Henna duty."

Thud. Thud. Thud. When I didn't glance toward the vain scythe thumper, Death muttered. "I'll return. Do not set foot off this island until you are covered in tattoos. And then, only at my side."

I wasn't one hundred percent convinced it would go like that, but I milked and combed Chuckles. The island's heat still played in my favor, hand collecting another bag of fur to spin into yarn…for Death's sweater.

Ashi, Serenity, and Eden joined me on the beach with a picnic we quickly devoured.

Eden studied me. "Do you miss anybody?"

I shrugged. "Not really. I can sell candles anywhere. The longer the apocalypse goes on, the fewer people see a point in being nice. Friends shift away like blowing grains of sand."

After rolling the fur, stretching it to eventually make yarn, I asked, "Can any of you draw rune markings to hide me from Lilith?"

Three shaking heads later, Ashi added, "That's a good idea, though."

Eden's skeletal cat stretched out beside us. Creepy, but not rabid like the rabbits.

I stared directly into Ashi's cobalt eyes, whispering, "Would you kill Lilith if you had a demon blade?"

Serenity sighed. "She wouldn't. She doesn't kill humans. And that's what it would take."

Eden nodded. "Lilith stabbed, unable to escape the blade while possessing a willing living human body."

"If the human asked you to? The one she possessed before possession?" I shrugged at the trio. "If she gets me, and we have a demon blade, I'm asking now for you to end me and, therefore, her. It will be a mercy if she possesses me. As a bonus…ending Lilith will stop her grand plan about an eternity in hellfire with Death."

"No way," Ashi stated. "*If* we had one, it wouldn't work on your dead body. Unless you agree for her to possess you. And I know you're too smart for that. But, unfortunately, that doesn't stop her from dreaming and scheming for some hellscape ending with Death."

Serenity turned my way, minty green mist in the air. "I was an orphan, so I asked Death about your family. He is sure about your father's passing, but not your mother's."

My heart rate kicked up like I was a kid running from traffickers.

In the background, up the mountain, the triplets sang, "Barmint! Barmint!"

Eden groaned, rolling to her feet. She pointed toward the house. "As far as they are concerned, they're chanting a curse word. If they could say V." She rushed that way.

Bram flew over on his firetruck-sized red dragon. He waved before performing a diving, aerial spin. Zed and Zoe repeated the spin while mounted on truck-sized Hail—blue-speckled gray—and Raine—bright blue.

"A dragon parade! That more than makes up for bad bunnies." I pointed at the massive bone ship. "And that."

While everyone watched the show, I ambled toward Death's pale stallion, waving a carrot. Then I stopped, letting the massive steed come to me. "Good boy," I murmured as he chomped on the carrot.

Turning, I caught Death leaning against a tree, intense green eyes locked on me.

I sighed. "Why do you always look like you're awaiting an answer to a question you don't ask?"

"I have the henna." He pivoted toward the cottage before striding inside.

I stopped beside the cottage. "How about out here in the breeze?"

Death pushed open the shutters on the second window, grumbling, "No."

When he returned outside, I held the back of one hand, fingers down, pointed toward his chest.

Black eyebrows drew down as he gave the dimwitted human award again. I could tell. He didn't interject, so....

Shaking his head, he asked, "What are you doing?"

"Do that one first, okay?"

"You need four tattoos. None of those are on your hand. Come inside."

After joining him, Death pointed at the bed. "Your back first. Stretch out."

Instead, I tugged my t-shirt off one shoulder.

"Your back, Zadie. Not the back of your shoulder. Do you want the runes or not?"

Before pulling off my t-shirt, I announced, "Turn around."

Ice in green eyes, Death warned, "My timeline folder labeled Are. You. Kidding. Me? Is full."

"Well, when you put it that way," I grumbled, pulling off my shirt and stretching out, my back exposed.

With a huff, Death plopped beside me. "Your whole back." Then he whispered a musical note. Except the whisper held magical power, brushing down my shoulders and back.

My bra vanished! "Eek!" Stomach down, I huffed. "You better be able to bring that back from magic land. They don't grow on trees."

"Hold still." He swept my curls away from my back.

I nearly bolted straight off the mattress when tickle-soft wetness touched my nape. Immediately, I shivered.

"Hold still."

"You're applying it with a feather? Find a paintbrush!"

This time he laughed. "The spell dictates a feather. My

feather."

His silver feather painted whisper-soft from nape to one shoulder, dipping into a deep V, connecting to the other shoulder. My whole back. He wasn't joking.

Actually, it felt amazing. First, the touch was so light as to almost not feel it over the wetness of the henna. Then the brush mark patterns felt random, fast, and small, feathering out to fill the rune. This felt better than my remembrance of Mom washing my hair.

Death grunted. "Do you wish to find her?"

I opened my eyes, cocking my neck to study him. "You'd help me do that?"

He shrugged. "I can fight reanimated unholy souls and wild beasts anywhere. We can look."

With a brush of his fingers, Death kept my shoulder down. "Hold still." His fingers pressed harder when he blew onto the giant tattoo covering my back.

Still, I shivered. He said four of these?

"Yes."

"Please stop reading my mind." Then, at his grunted non-answer, I clarified, "Before you mansplain my dull-wittedness, just tell me. Where are the other three?"

He tapped one finger on my hip, sliding it down my outer thigh. He nodded before I asked the question. "Both sides." Then he tapped one finger over his stomach, plucking his black t-shirt.

"Listen, dirty old man—"

"You are ridiculous."

If he wasn't affected by carnal things like flesh, it shouldn't matter if I were naked; but it mattered to me. "I *will* need my bra back for that one."

His snort dripped conceit. "Of course. Dimwitted one."

Another whisper of power vibrated my skin as my jeans went the way of my bra. Poof! Faded blue undies on display. "Ah!"

Death sighed, but then with a wave of his hand, a magical aurora danced beside the woven wall. "Better? Hold still."

The feather whispered across my hip before swirling to my

thigh. He bent, sitting beside the mattress, drawing with henna. Teakwood, leather, a drop of smoky amber, his musk scent as exotic as his eyes were ancient. Leaning in closer, he rested one hand on my hip, concentrating, his palm smoothing in the path before the wet feather painted. "Watch the aurora." He sounded a tad breathless in his concentration.

"Talk," I suggested.

"What is your word for today?"

"Simulacrum. All representations I've seen completely concocted you wrong. Cloaked or skeletal or both. Are your illusions why no one knew for sure? Face hidden? The family story had no illustrations."

The feather tickled over my thigh as he replied, "Illusions, so many, yes. However, it sums up how people regard death and therefore me."

I watched his magical aurora, tinted magenta and teal, shot through with green, dancing like a line of flames. "Tell me about Lilith's eternal lake of hellfire plan. Cause, clearly, she is intent upon that hellscape. That is why she pursues you."

"No simulacrum has nailed Lilith either."

"That's not an—"

"You make it sound like she'd need a reason. I am Death."

He followed the vanity by lightly blowing over the wet henna from hip to thigh, then back up. It effectively stunned me into silence before he stood and moved to the other side of the bed. Then he started in with the feather on that hip.

I turned my head before he waved the aurora into my view. Although I watched it dance, I could not ignore the wet feather tickling henna on my skin.

He continued painting before speaking in a low voice. "Death and Hades end up there."

It took me a couple seconds to recall what we were talking about before he blew on my leg and switched to the other. Oh yes, he'd used my word for today. Lilith. "Wait, what? You are a horseman, yes, but you are an angel! So you end up in eternal damnation?"

His hand clamped over my hip, keeping me from moving. "Yes. Also no. But death does."

"That is no ending a hero deserves!"

For once, conceit did not stain his short laugh. Instead, his fingers shifted, a different hold after I almost bolted upright with my declaration.

Finally, he lowered the bowl of henna and the feather. "Zadie, remember my simulacrum. Death isn't a hero." Then he blew upon my henna-wet thigh, the path slowly skimming up to my hip, then back down. "Death is a villain."

I shivered. "I don't believe that. I think your green eyes are so sad because you feel all deaths."

He nodded, "I feel them." Then he breathed out another musical whisper over my skin. This time, my jeans and bra returned from magical exile; however, my jeans were unzipped and wide open. Finally, Death added, "Put on your shirt, but expose your belly."

Suddenly, I was not keen on him whispering his henna-dampened feather over my skin. Cause in a family hero sort of way, he was hot. Yet untouchable. Also, in that great-great-great grandpappy role, off-limits. He could not be a villain. That would yank him off the hero pedestal. And that guy at ground level… was painting me with a feather.

But he chuckled, likely eavesdropping on my thoughts. "I told you there didn't have to be a reason. Many humans try to seduce me. I am Death. And I am a villain."

More than his conceit reemerged, his posture changed as if utterly convinced I'd accept this new villain label and object to the last tattoo. As if claiming to be a villain automatically rewrote his hero history in my family storybook. In fact, he was a little too cocksure of it as one black eyebrow hitched.

He nodded. "I understand you may object to a villain painting the last rune. And you don't need the rune if you agree to stay here, where there's everything you possibly need. So it's not a hardship."

Chapter Eleven

Death

Right when I was sure she would steer away from me painting runes, a path that led to her leaving safety, Zadie laughed. "Spoken like a nonvillain's suggested plan to keep a homeless woman safe." She plopped onto her back and hiked her shirt. "Whew! Hero-like."

I swear if grandpappy crossed her mind one more time....

Still, she waited, entire abdomen exposed for the last rune. Her pants were returned unbuttoned and unzipped. I wanted her to back down from finishing it. I felt the softness of her skin, the curve of her hip, the silkiness down her thigh. I noticed her scent, the way she shivered when I blew on the tattoos.

I wanted to blame the zinging zap of it on Bram. His attraction for her, not mine. But it wasn't him; his soul chain woke new emotional cravings. I was developing feelings. That it would happen was a given, yet not while he was experiencing puberty. As an angel, I should not be affected by anyone's flesh. Oh, but I noticed hers now. It rattled me.

After settling beside her, I placed one hand on her abdomen. Her heartbeat accelerated. I shouldn't care, but it was confirmation. Like it or not, she was not unaffected by my touch. Sometimes she seemed so unimpressed by me that a less confident angel might take offense or doubt himself over the grandpappy thoughts.

I traced one finger ahead of the feather, brushing a path from hipbone to hipbone. "Close your eyes. I'm not teaching you magic. The how-to."

Long dark lashes replaced inquisitive green eyes, yet she jerked and wiggled. "It tickles. Multitask; talk, too?"

The sooner I finished, the better. Anything if she would stop writhing so I could complete the intricate designs, a large tattoo where the inverted triangle on her back was V thin.

When she wriggled for the umpteenth time, I growled. "Fine. Pestilence the Conqueror consumed the internet and all private government networks. Your mother was on assignment, not in Israel, but in Africa. She flew there the same day you flew to reach your father. If you hold still so I can finish this, we will search while your shield runes are fresh."

She stilled considerably, eyes closed, until I blew on the rune to help dry it. Then she jerked straight up off the mattress and fanned it herself with her t-shirt. "Thanks for the runes," she said breathlessly. "And everything, really."

After she pulled long corkscrew curls into a ponytail, Zadie clapped her hands once, declaring, "Let's go!" She marched toward Horse.

If we found her mother, they could stay together on blessed land wherever they wanted me to sanctify it. For a spy would not be naïve, would not fall for Lilith's wily tricks to lure them off the consecrated ground.

Then I could go about my horseman mission without feeling like I needed to keep an eye on her to ensure she stayed planted where it was safe. If she stayed with her mother, I'd only see Zadie every week to ten days to reapply the runes, to keep her hidden from Lilith. After all, I'd seen no evidence that Zadie inherited my gifted power. And she didn't mention it in her family myth of Zehra and me.

Although I opened a portal, she pointed at my stallion. "He wants to come, too. You're a horseman; don't you ride?"

"A portal is faster. And I don't want the wild beasts to charge him. Losing his color was hard on him."

Zadie quickly scanned the beach, grabbed a club-sized piece of driftwood, then nodded. We walked from one coast to another on a different continent. This one under an ebony sky as she asked, "So not bunnies, but what—"

Bones rattled as a cadaverous lion skeleton hopped onto the rock behind her. She slammed the wooden club into the leg bones, scattering them. I pointed my scythe toward the ivory-boned male behind the lion, then ripped out his unholy soul and locked it in Hades.

Zadie spun, giving a little roar, before swinging at the next roaming skeleton in this pack. She battled, dropping the risen dead to scatter bones.

I returned the three escapees to Hades before they could rise again. "Good job," I credited her. A human.

She nodded, breathing heavily as the curtain of indigo lifted to lavender.

I pointed at a large thatched roof, silhouette barely visible. The spy agency's villa sat perched upon a hill, overlooking everything. "We'll check it. I sense a life force."

She squeezed and released my hand. "Thank you. Either way, if it's her or not."

We followed the path as the sky shifted into striking hot pinks and oranges. Although I sensed a swell of life energies, we couldn't see the top of the steep hill. The ground rumbled as we neared the villa. I frowned, wrapping a hand around her waist, moving Zadie behind me.

Ahead, a rhinoceros trumpeted. Seconds later, the detected human life force quickly dwindled.

We rounded the path; a colossal elephant carcass bellowed, charging through the open-air villa. Stampede!

Zadie's club would do little against the beast hurtling headlong her way, spelled to attack mankind.

Pulling her out of the charge and behind me, I blasted a spell from my scythe, shoving them back with an air barrier wall. The stampeding herd pivoted, running to keep ahead of the power push.

Zadie ran through the destroyed room toward a wooden pillar where a black-haired, green-eyed woman was impaled. "Mom?"

"Zadie?" She asked from her slumped position, pinned against a pillar by a bony rhinoceros' horn. The creature's bones were scattered around her. "Beautiful. Grown."

Zadie dropped to her knees beside her mother, holding her

hand. "Mom!"

After a shuddering breath, red bubbles frothing from her mouth, her mother uttered, "Will pass to you. Find our book."

Her eyes closed, her soul ready to go with me. Her mother exhaled her last breath before desperate bargaining with me occurred to Zadie. For that, I was thankful. War had done it, a bargain not to take Serenity's soul, instead to suspend her in a coma until he made her immortal.

Zadie burst into tears. I didn't want to leave her here, but her mother, a descendant of Zehra, deserved a personal escort to the pearly gate. Zadie was freshly runed.

Her mother's spirit waited beside me, having shed her mortal coil. Moreover, I smelled her power before she passed. Memitim, a destroying angel. Little wonder now why her life's work pursued the worst of the worst. Those so bad as to be abandoned by their guardian angels.

Reaching to cup Zadie's wet face, I vowed, "You cannot come along on this journey, but I'm taking her to a better place. She says she loves you. I warned death is a villain."

I summoned my wings, escorting her mother's soul from the shadowy valley of death. Then up, up, warping in a light tunnel into another realm. Here, the pearly gates glistened with an unearthly light. *Home.*

Returning in what were mere minutes for Zadie, I found her right where I left her. She didn't rail against life's unfairness when most would. As Death, I'd heard that many times. But being on her own since she was five, she knew that lesson well.

I wrapped the body in a sheet after removing the horn impaling her. "She's not here anymore. This is a shell. We must ensure Lilith doesn't find your mother's body."

After telepathically reaching out to Famine, my brother came to quickly melt the ground into a grave. Then, under the deep orange and red rays of a lurid African sunrise, Zadie stood beside him as I lowered her mother's body to the reddish-orange ground. In a matter of minutes, she was buried. Safe from Lilith's possession.

Famine offered to bring Eden or travel home with Zadie, but she declined. Instead, she shifted through the wrecked rubble. The open-air house experienced a rabid safari stampede.

I followed her, bending to retrieve a small wallet-sized photograph. A man with curly dark hair and deep blue eyes, his arm around a woman with long straight black hair and green eyes. Her parents. Captured in the hug between them was a curly-headed little girl. Her family's photo. Zadie sniffled when I handed it to her.

"Thank you," she said in a rusty, quiet voice. Then, after clearing her throat, she tried again. "I didn't see the book. She wanted me to have it. Or, you know, pass it down to me."

Since it was my gift, no one could better help her with the power than I. But the book would uncomplicate it. Zadie *Grace* accepted it, if not as fact, as family mythology. It wasn't the book her mother passed to her; it was memitim power the book must explain. Only one in the lineage could possess the ability at one time. Perhaps her parents thought she was too young to know all the details at five or younger? After all, her father had explained planting spy devices by involving Santa.

Wrapping one hand around her back, I steered her outside. "Do you remember your address in Israel?" Then, at the spark of hope in her eyes, I amended, "Just picture it. We'll see if it is still standing. That region had major earthquakes when War's seal broke years ago."

Before touching her temple, I wiped away her tear tracks. "Your mother was very ill, but now she has no more worries, no sadness, nothing hurts. She is in heaven. Please don't be sad, for it is a happy occasion for her. Your father was there, waiting to fold her in his arms."

Her green eyes lifted to mine. "It doesn't feel real," she whispered. "I lost Mom a long time ago."

"For you, I wish it didn't happen like it did. Yet we can find the book she wanted you to have."

Once I honed in on her pictured coordinates, I amended, "Let me go first to make sure. The last time I went with an old memory of a place, those coordinates ended up underground, not on the first floor."

Yet, that was how I ended up in the same place as Zadie, a descendant of Zehra—who I also met underground. What were the chances of that happening? Oh no. Were my brothers right? Did God intend for me to find Zadie? And now she'd inherit my gifted power? Oh, no. No. Mate. For. Me.

It was irrational—since I found Zadie both times—but still, it irked me. At her. Suddenly, the setup was clear to me, maneuvering Zadie toward becoming my bonded mate. I barely survived losing Zehra as a companion with no emotions. To lose a mate, there was no cure for that. And I did not. Want. One! That would leave her suffering, losing a mate, when the eternal hellfire verdict was issued for death.

I stepped out into a sunlit hillside facing the Old City, a hill covered in nearly identical off-white homes packed closely together. Many on the hillside had split apart. Turning, I noticed the lack of the Western Wall, which crumbled years ago from earthquakes when War's seal broke. I sighed and turned away from the destruction now tinted with green vines, a jungle vibe from Famine's reign of accelerated growth. Finally, I escorted Zadie through to Jerusalem.

She blinked, shaking her head toward the rows of identical buildings on the hillside. Instead of saying she couldn't remember which one, she pointed at the third row on a hill. "I got into so much trouble for that. It is, in fact, the reason I had to go visit Dad."

Some unidentifiable stick figure with a big belly and horns had been painted on the patio wall. The orange paint was still so bright that, fifteen years back, it must have been neon against the white wall. So large that it resembled a caveman's mural.

We walked that way, but she didn't volunteer more, so I finally asked. "What is it supposed to be?"

Zadie tossed her arms. "Well, a yak. Of course."

I huffed out a laugh, then nodded. "Of course." The poor dull-witted human had no artistic ability at all. Or, I suppose she was five at the time.

Despite the earthquake so long ago, I sensed many life energies nearby, living in iffy, crumbling buildings. "Stay behind me."

She took it literally, almost like a challenge to be my shadow. The woman was ridiculous. So silly! In the end, we found broken windows, the place a wreck. Someone had lived here in the past.

Seemingly undisturbed by the destruction, she grinned at me. "Where is the heart of a home?"

I didn't have a clue, but I didn't intend to let her know. "And?"

Zadie walked into the kitchen, climbed the counter, and pushed the top tile. *Click.* A panel in the ceiling popped open. Then she pulled down a tied protective oil wrap. She hugged it to her chest. "The leather-bound book."

This would make accepting the power much more manageable. But it didn't mean Zadie needed to delve into it right here. And it didn't mean either of us would step into a trap...for a mate. "Let's go."

No sooner did we step outside next to the orange caveman painting, allegedly of a yak, than an unkindness of ravens swarmed. Hades appeared under the funnel, showboating in lime green again. Great.

Yet he did not launch into a diatribe, still pacified by the power he wielded to turn wild beasts, living and dead, against man. Instead, Hades grinned at me. "So I'm bored."

I snorted. "I told you, entertain Lilith."

Hades snorted. "I told you, only if I saw the blacksmith first."

Zadie stepped next to me, staring at Hades. "What blacksmith?"

Did the woman have no survival instincts? I knew she'd been on her own for a long time. She should be wise enough not to attract Hades' attention. *Again.*

While gliding forward to close the distance, Hades glanced at Zadie, then me. "You are keeping a pet?"

Zadie lifted one hand. "Now, I object to that." But she persisted. "Is it the blacksmith who forges demon blades?"

Now she fully captured Hades' focus as he shot her a sly smile. "The very same," he purred. "Mount Olympus' blacksmith. My father Cronus chained him in Tartarus. Dear old dad was a savage. Good thing we ended him."

"Enough," I growled.

Did Zadie listen at all or back down? Nope. Instead, she presented another entry for Are. You. Kidding. Me? Stepping around me, she focused on Hades. "Can you get one? Do you have a way to reach the blacksmith?"

Hades cocked a shiny black brow my way. "With enough chaos to crack open the door, yes. Titan blood allows me to come and go from the bottom level of hell." He laughed. "Unlike holy angels."

"I suppose a human would sizzle and die trying to reach the blacksmith?"

Although I stepped around her this time, blocking her from his stare, Hades shot me a slight smirk. "I could shield your human pet. Sounds like she wants to go."

Chapter Twelve

Zadie

"To trap or trade her?" Death scoffed immediately, moving away from the crumbling buildings and my yak painting.

I snapped my jaw shut after he answered faster than I could. Then I opened my mouth to try again before realizing Death wasn't done ranting.

"Because she is not smart enough to realize she didn't ask for a way back? Nevertheless, demand she return as alive as she left. Or payment?" Death snorted. "No." His scythe appeared in his hand, followed by an unearthly thump.

"Huh," Hades uttered, shaking short, shiny raven spikes. "You *do* have a pet. What is she named?"

"Now you're just being rude," I told Hades.

In return, Hades indicated the oil-wrapped package in my arms. "What are you clinging to, little human?"

Thud. Thud. Thud. Red rune symbols flashed up the length of Death's scythe. Ah, irritated Grim Reaper mode. I recognized the pale yellow-green supernatural glow surrounding his pinpoint pupils.

"Go," Death told Hades. "Be bored elsewhere."

"Where are you going?" Hades nodded once. "I'm supposed to follow along behind you."

Thump. "Consider it mission successful for the day, then be on your way."

Death's arm fastened like a band around my waist as silver wings exploded from his back, launching into the sky! His scythe vanished before my shriek of surprise ended. He folded that arm over mine on the book. Then he growled near my ear.

"How dare you act mad?" I glared at the destruction below,

earthquakes and sinkholes, nothing like my memories from here, then glanced at his face. "Do I look like a yak to you?" When he didn't dignify that with a response, I clarified, "I'm not a pet. Yours or anyone's!"

He lifted one hand, a portal window swirling open to show Arcadia, before blasting through and closing the spinning pinwheel with a *whoosh*.

Death released me like I scalded him. Ice remained in his eerily pale, glowing eyes. "Do *not*," he growled, "play with the mini-devil Hades."

"But he could take me."

"Did you ask for a return trip? About payment to the blacksmith, or what payment Hades would demand in return? You don't know what you're playing at."

"Then tell me what to ask for."

He turned away, scrutinizing me over his shoulder. "Your mother is in a better place. I leave you with your book for now."

Death sighed, swapping his study to the nearby white and pink coral-coated skeletal ship. "I feel like riding with my brothers and wreaking destruction. Clearing wild beasts turned on mankind. Ending unholy escapee souls reanimating bones. And building up chaos, which you do not even know you need to crack open Tartarus."

He spun back toward me. "In my absence, absolutely, do not leave this blessed ground." Then Death was gone in a gray swirl.

I sat on a banana tree hammock, then untied the protective wrap from the black leather book. I'd forgotten how big it was. This copy was two hundred years old, repeatedly translated as it was re-recorded from the original in 1 AD. The first page...*As recorded by Zehra, wife of Thanatos.*

That was what Lilith had called him as well. According to the book, Death was the only horseman given a name instead of their divine duty label. Yet Zehra's written account was the only recording of Thanatos in the fairytale; the name Death gave as Zehra's husband when he stopped them from stoning her. All other family fairytale references used Death or the Angel of

Death.

I knew the story, but it was contained in the front of the thick book. Folding my fingers over a third of the pages, I opened the tome to the heading *Charon*.

Shivering, closing, and reopening it, carefully flipping past the fairytale start, I scanned ahead for the next chapter. Then I scooted the open book off my lap onto the hammock, page titled: *If you are named Grace….*

You will now name your daughter Grace in gratitude for the gift of power given to you by the Angel of Death.

I snapped it shut, wrapping the cover and tying it. Mythology. I wasn't in the mood. Not because my name was Grace, like my mother's, and I personally knew the oh-so-vain Angel of Death. The same angel painted henna rune markings on me—with his silver feather—while proclaiming to be a villain, not a hero.

Leaving the book on my bed, I returned outside to stretch and roll yak fur into yarn. For. His. Sweater.

Ashi joined me in the shade, overlooking Chuckles in the cold section, the warm side, and then the skeletal ship. Finally, she sighed. "It's a lot. I know."

"If you were not Nephilim, and you could break into the bottom level of hell, how would you go about it?"

"Pfft! If I were that crazy, I'd put on the creepy, stalking cape of evil, the Fallen's prophecy cloak, and start on a path to unlock the lesser Fallen bound in Sheol. Then hell would literally be loosed on earth. Tartarus would crack open while the Fallen free their evil elite leaders imprisoned in space. Like my father. Actual hell on earth in the form of an angel war. And all their magic-wielding demon pets. Should I mention that the cloak will kill you, a non-Nephilim? Like it's soul-bound to me, despite never wearing it and destroying it thousands of times."

I dropped the yak fur. "That all sounds, you know, horrible. But what if there's another way in? Without what sounds like the end of the world."

"Such as?"

"Hades."

"Say what?" But it came from Serenity as she plopped down beside us.

Ashi shook her long red hair. "She wants to go to the blacksmith. For a demon blade."

Eden, too, joined us, asking, "For the sole purpose of protecting Death? Or ending Lilith?"

I shrugged. "Why choose?"

Serenity brushed back her breeze-tossed platinum hair. "I'm fond of Death, not fond of Lilith, not Nephilim. I'm human, also a Valkyrie, but War made me immortal. And I have a dragon. So I could go with you."

Eden shrugged. "I'm Eljo. But I'm not cut off from it either. Also, I'm a dragon owner who is as immortal as Famine. Dying is to sleep, then awaken." She turned to Ashi and grinned. "You can be our commander. Strategist."

Instead of brushing it off, Ashi looked at each of us. "We need to gather our friends, our allies. For Death is here. The Four Horsemen are riding. I intend to make allies protective runes, but I've put off handing them out, not accepting that the end is nigh. Yet the chaos that feeds my magic is growing steadily now."

She stood so tall, brushing sand from her shorts. "I wouldn't mind backup for talking to Liam, a pilot. Then, to Jericho." She glanced at Serenity. "His boat and his allies, bring them up to speed with Lana, Kai, and Maverick. Humans need to be ready; an angel war is coming."

Turning to Eden, she added, "Your uncle could help with the magical contract wording, ensure no loopholes with Hades to bite us in the hiney."

Ashi pointed toward the ship floating far above its watery grave. "Have you looked at the fustercluck lately? Skeletons and wild beasts—better yet—skeletal wild beasts attacking!"

"And bunnies," I muttered.

She nodded. "If we do not connect with these allies soon, further Mission Mankind plans for the survival of humans? It will be too late for them to spread the plan about magical protective domes. Angels fight with magic and weapons, superior to humans in every way. So it's not…go big or go home. It's," Ashi shrugged. "Go big or no home."

Eden nodded. "I'll stay with all kids but reach out to my uncle while the Four Horsemen are riding. Where will you go first? Who will be mad, Pestilence over Liam or War over Jericho?" She laughed at me. "I already know Death will be rootin' tootin' angry. He told Famine he shielded you with runes, so get while the getting is good. If you hurry, they'll never know you were gone."

This time, I wound up my yak fur supplies, dropping the bag beside the bed, where the book devoted to Death and a chapter for Grace waited. It could wait. The women were ready to move.

Before I left the room, Eden entered and hugged me. "I'm sorry about your mom. I'm here if you need me."

Serenity and Ashi hugged me as well.

Tears near the surface, I pulled back. "Thanks."

Yet Serenity faced me, settling one hand on my shoulder. "You are worthy, Zadie." Then, after lifting her hand, a light violet handprint, the same color as her eyes, shimmered.

Handprint tingling, I felt like I'd been blessed, but I nodded, not questioning the magic or the soothing green mist. I needed to grow accustomed to magical power, not feel mind-blown confetti constantly streaming out the back of my ponytail. For I would wheel and deal with Hades.

I wasn't the pet. Nope. I was the damn hero. I would save the angel horseman from an eternal hellscape with Lilith.

Death wasn't a villain meant for everlasting damnation; he was a hero. The book I didn't continue reading assured it in a detailed story I knew by heart. Strange as it might be, I didn't feel like I lost Mom today. That happened nearly fifteen years ago. Instead, I gained a book that meant everything to my family, including the why-are-they-all-named-Grace phenomena. Mom said I'd understand when I was older, but….

I wanted the demon blade before seeing the book. But the reminder of Zehra, of knowing Lilith inhabited her for a millennium, tortured Death that long...now I *needed* it! An actual craving for the weapon. Okay, that was a bit alarming. But this was the world's end, so why not save time by shooting straight for the nuclear option?

Apparently, Ashi agreed. "Liam and I were...friends with benefits. He's a good guy. The best pilot I know. I'm ready to go first; been dreading it. The rest will be a breeze for me."

Serenity puffed up a minty green mist in the air, nodding, "Let's go."

Ashi held up one hand. Golden light swirled before a circular gateway opened. "London." It showed dusk, a narrow, dirty street at the corner of a brick building. She stepped out, then waved us through.

Red hair swaying, Ashi cocked her head at the door. Liam's Pub, according to a hand-painted sign.

Inside, I gawked. The establishment's brightly lit lanterns illuminated posters hanging on all the walls. All of Ashi, black leather, tiara, lightning shooting from her hand. The following launching fireballs. Another upon a dragon, dropping a parachute of supplies labeled Mission Mankind.

Gosh. Was Ashi a celebrity? And she didn't look any older than in the posters.

She shrugged. "I used to drink here, back in the day. With Liam...before the world ended and he bought the place."

A dark curly-headed man—appearing over a decade older than Ashi, called, "Kobayashi! Wow. You look exactly the same as when I last saw you up close and personal. Well, minus fire or lightning crawling over you this time. I couldn't tell if you changed when you flew here and dropped supplies. As if it could be anyone other than you making deliveries by a dragon?"

"Liam," she smiled and nodded. "Suppose I found plenty of fuel and an old plane that still runs? Sort of a clunker. It would take someone completely braver than he is wise or exceedingly competent to fly it. Nevertheless, to network and drop rune markings in key areas to provide protection domes. Preferably before Fallen angels break out and annihilate any survivors as the world finally kicks it. Earth is our world. Not theirs."

He huffed out a breath, taking a seat on a barstool. Whiskey-colored eyes lifted to Ashi.

She continued. "By plenty of fuel, I meant I magically whammy-jammied it."

Then a slow smile spread across his handsome face. "You came to the right pilot."

Ashi smiled at him. "I never doubted it." Then she slid him some complex drawings on sticky notes, sealed in baggies. "That's why I made you protective runes. Keep one on you. I'll explain before you start the plane. Welcome to Mission Mankind, Liam."

I left them to drill into details, moving along the walls, examining a dozen posters. I'd seen one when I finally fled Dad's apartment, running from looters. Back then, the drawing wasn't laced with magical powers; instead, showing only her face on a black and white Wanted bounty. Then I found shelter in a soup kitchen and never saw it again.

Yet this powerful woman could not gain entry into pearly or fiery gates. That was on me. On Hades. I expected a realm, not a wonderful one like Death's. Also, extreme heat.

I returned to Ashi. "What if I can acquire more than one demon blade? The first engraved with Lilith's name, but others for people to use against the Fallen?"

Then I shook my head. "What kind of payment plan do you suppose the blacksmith offers? If hell and Tartarus are fiery, my candles—no matter how lovely they smell—probably won't be a fair trade."

The magical minty soothing mist still landed on anyone nearby Serenity. "We'll see if Eden's uncle can write that into the contract," she said. People were so calm that no one objected or tried to move out of the vapor. "But now that Ashi is dropping Liam at the plane, we'll find Jericho."

I bumped her shoulder and grinned. "So Jericho was before War?"

Serenity laughed, an incredibly delightful jingly bell sound.

"He was my friend and self-defense trainer. A pirate. My pretend-husband for a shared disguise."

My mouth hung open; did I actually deserve the dull-witted human award? Because I didn't know how to respond.

"Trafficking is...." Serenity blew out a breath. "Out of control, around every corner, in every shadow. Immediate evil swept through as soon as the world ended like it flipped a switch on some folks. My vacation plane landed right before everything smart stopped working. Jericho saved me. Then we shared a mission to free others. If I knew Jericho, he'll still have an extensive underground network and be able to move quickly."

Ashi led us out onto the narrow street, around the corner, and out of view. She nodded at Liam. "Exactly like stepping through a doorway." She lifted one hand, rune symbol spinning golden then opening to an airfield.

Beside the plane, she lifted her hand again, creating a magical golden swirl to some island beach, a hut hidden among trees. "I'll come after Liam starts the plane."

I followed Serenity onto a golden sandy beach stained apricot by the sun. She smiled, waving to indicate the tiny island. "We're partway between Australia and Tasmania."

A big burly guy stepped out of the hut, gawking. "Reni!" The petite woman accepted the big brute's hug.

Serenity smiled. "I can't believe you're here." She cocked her head toward the sea and large yacht.

"Yeah." Jericho raked a hand over his darkly stubbled face. "I needed a break to sleep; otherwise, I stay on alert. Too many ships returned from watery graves, piloted by skeletons."

With a wave of her hand, Serenity added, "This is Zadie. And Ashi," she concluded as the redhead joined us.

Jericho grinned, nodding at Ashi. "Thank you for Mission Mankind supply drops here."

As they laid the groundwork for networking, I wandered off, past the hut and trees to the tiny island's backside. I stopped on the water's edge, shielding my eyes against the bright blue glare. A skeletal ship sailed within view. Was Hades out there?

Was that how I'd contact him once we had the contract? Cause I needed to know about the payment plan option. The trade.

As if I sent out a message in a bottle, a conspiracy of ravens swarmed and funneled. Then Hades appeared beside me on the beach. Gosh, orange suit, lime bowtie. I almost needed shades.

The handsome devil grinned. "Let's talk payment, pet. And a pickup plan from somewhere like this. I cannot whisk you away if you are on blessed land. I can't step upon it."

"What payment would the blacksmith expect for one demon blade? Would he cut me a deal if I order in bulk?"

"You should first concern yourself with what payment I expect."

Thump. Thump. Thump. Death slowly stalked through the trees toward us. Otherworldly scythe thuds thumping for each step.

Chapter Thirteen

Eye twitching, scythe thudding, the runes racing up the handle announced my aggravation level. Too bad Zadie couldn't read Angelic.

Hades recognized it for what it was. Still, he couldn't resist. "He's come to leash you, pet." Instantly after the dig, he disappeared in a swarming unkindness.

Her full lips opened, but I cut her off. "I left you with the book." *Thud!* "Said don't leave blessed land. Showed you who Lilith was." *Thud-thud!* "Told you not to play with Hades." *Thud!*

"Oh, wow," Zadie muttered, kicking at the sand. "You mean like *stay*, right? Again, I ask, do I look like a yak to you?"

She lifted both index fingers to her forehead to create horns. Then she grunted, lolled her tongue, and ran in circles around me while I gawked, utterly speechless. Finally, she stopped. "See the difference? I'm not a pet."

The woman was ridiculous! And human. Fragile. Put directly in my path. Then I remembered why I was mad. All of the above. I did not like it, but I knew it for what it was. So, I opened a portal into her cottage, informing her, "Grab your book."

As soon as she had it in her arms, I whispered a command in Angelic. *Sleep!*

I swept her into my arms, book and all. I wondered why the Conqueror often did that in the first six months of meeting Ashi. I also recalled asking him if it wasn't exhausting doing anything other than that.

When I placed her to sleep, it was upon the black rock she called a throne and claimed she needed an elevator to reach. Asleep, she thankfully had no idea I brought her where nothing could get to her. And she could get to nothing that might endanger her. Then I summoned my cloak, part of my actual horseman gear and simulacrum, pillowing part under her head, spreading the rest over her. Before eight hours expired, I'd decide if I were keeping her here in my realm. But if she woke? She said there was nothing to do here. She could read her book.

With that decided, I sent my *ring* while walking into Pestilence's living room, knowing I would not interrupt something torrid this time. It started when he sensed Ashi in London. I was there when he met Liam years ago. It was not a lack of trust but curiosity about what sent her there. Yet when we arrived, the ladies were gone. Later, War felt Serenity's location on Jericho's hideaway island, where I found Zadie beside Hades.

Famine was the only horseman not agitated as we stood there staring at each other. Gray eyes bounced my way. "You tucked her away in your realm?"

I nodded, then flicked them each a glance. "What have your wives told Zadie about the blacksmith? There is something seriously wrong with her. Because the dull-witted one is entertaining the thought of accompanying Hades to obtain a demon dagger. Oh, not one…she asked about bulk."

With a flourish, Famine waved a scroll in front of us. After unrolling it, we scanned the basic magical contract drawn up by Ohya, Eden's uncle, a twenty-four-hour safe passage with Hades to and from Tartarus.

"Hrmm," War ruminated aloud. "Bare bones. She'd need much better terms than that."

I raked my hair away from my face. "Are you suggesting Zadie should go?"

Pestilence sighed. "Our mates want to give demon daggers to humans; better the odds once the Fallen are free. It would work on Grigori." Then he squared his shoulders. "Zadie is not, but our bonded wives are immortal. Still, I would not oppose each of them—our children too—possessing the blacksmith's blades."

The Conqueror turned to me, settling one hand on my shoulder. "Have you asked her to join Team Horseman yet?"

I perhaps overplayed my conceited scoff based on how their eyebrows hitched toward their hairlines. Nevertheless, I played to a strength we all shared. The truth. "It has never crossed my mind."

Famine nodded at me. "You should draw up the magical contract. The Angel of Death knows all the ins and outs, wheeling and death-dealing, contingencies with contingencies."

War grunted. "No. That's a team mission. She's not on our team. Not bonded to him. Most assuredly not immortal."

Yet I knew the same as what reflected in gray, teal, and aqua eyes. Demon blades would change the game. Human allies wielding them was an idea we never talked about when strategizing. Previously, we'd believed humans had no hope of surviving it. Of course, Ashi would not accept that.

Pestilence squeezed my shoulder, grinning. "Have you heard of taking one for the team?"

"Are you suggesting I bond Zadie?"

War nodded. "And make her immortal as soon as possible."

While I walked outside, Famine shrugged at me. "It's inevitable. You see that, right? You opened a portal to her first thing. She was kind. The second time, she landed in Lilith's sights. And she has a yak named Chuckles. A lighter side that you are desperately in need of, brother."

"Don't forget *Yippee*." The Conqueror laughed.

"The ferret isn't a pet. It's the yak's friend. Can't you tell the difference between what's a pet?" I'd leave them speechless since they claimed I needed a lighter side. I lifted my index fingers to my forehead to form horns, grunted, lolled my tongue, ran circles around them, and straight out a portal into my realm.

Their flummoxed expressions were beyond priceless. Of course, if they wanted to tell their wives, they would have to show them the move. The ladies on Team Horsemen would never believe I did it. They'd ask to see it again and again. I only did it once. Last laugh for me, then.

Slowly, I raked one hand down my face. Ugh. My brothers would *never* let me live that down. After raking back my hair, I gathered my cool around me like a cloak. I would not acknowledge that it happened.

I approached the sleeping woman curled on her side, wrapped in my cloak. As for bonding Zadie, my brothers believed it was inevitable. So how we did this next bit would be tricky, avoiding the mating bond. Not only for my benefit; but for hers. There was nothing worse than if a mate died. And part of me, death, was bound for eternal hellfire in Abaddon. After final judgment, I would not be the angel I was now, not be who bonded her.

We'd avoid it, not allow it to happen. To be kept from your mate caused madness and an uncurable broken heart. I didn't choose that for her if that was a consequence of my divinely splitting. And I did not want it for the part of myself that would be flung into the pit, forever separated from her.

The jeweled glitters reflecting in shallow water shifted to a dark blue glow as one of my reapers landed. I pivoted, then nodded at Rhea.

She didn't talk aloud, instead conserving energy by mind-speak. *You brought her twice. You rarely visit, then you bring her two times. You have never done this.*

With no emotions, she simply stated facts.

At my continued silence, Rhea sighed. *You ran through a portal into the realm with two fingers sticking up like horns. Sir, your tongue was…lolling.*

If only I could time travel to before I did that! With thousands of reapers twinkling above, it wasn't going away anytime soon. Never since Day One had I done anything so silly. I tried out the defense of not acknowledging it. Thankfully, it worked.

Or so I thought until Rhea pointed toward her many reaper sisters. *We were wondering what caused your irreverence for your realm. Was it the sleep you were required to undergo or the woman?*

I sighed, ready to give a partial explanation. These were my reapers, after all. *She has a pet yak called Chuckles.*

But I didn't get any further before Rhea repeated, *Chuckles?*

I demonstrated the difference between her pet and her pet's pet, Yippee.

She covered her mouth, then uncovered a smile. *Did the Angel of Death just say Yippee? Thank you. I'll spread the word. She is the cause of your strange behavior.*

Blue glow lessening, Rhea floated into the twilight sky until high above, her reflection glistening like a sapphire again. A plethora of reapers twinkled, spreading the word; punctuated light flickers due to them laughing.

Gazing at Zadie for the next several hours, sitting beside her, I drank in her beauty and scent while the unpretentious one was unaware. Finally, I admitted there was no way forward unless she joined Team Horseman. Then I would help her experience maximum control of the power I gifted her family. I could satisfy the blacksmith's terms and payment. For *bulk.*

Indeed, holy angels could not enter the lowest level of hell. In fact, the hellfire burn would eat into divine skin before bypassing the barrier into hell. But there would be no Hades' involvement. No deal. I would shift, no holy skin to melt away, nothing corporeal about me. Incorporeal, I would take Zadie to Tartarus and collect the blacksmith. It was a mission for which she was uniquely qualified; she just didn't know it yet.

Zadie stretched, slowly waking, before sitting bolt upright on the rock. She looked at the cloak, the book at her side, then up at me. "Why did you do that? Stop putting me to sleep!"

"Good morning. Here is the plan." Then I hesitated, remembering how Ashi reacted to the wording, *captive.* But I could keep Zadie safe in my realm, a captive until she accepted my gift and could wield destroyer angel power. Then we would venture to Tartarus.

One hand shot up in the air, waving around, while she said, "Oh!" Then, before I could ask why her arm was raised, she added, "Where is the restroom in your realm?"

Since neither I nor my reapers had any human bodily needs, it was the first time I'd been asked the question.

Freshly awake but sharp, Zadie pointed at the shallow water. "Cause I'm not peeing in the pool. Or in front of thousands of star-like reapers." She picked up the book, swinging her other arm toward the water. "Plus, I don't see Chuckles. I have a yak to comb and milk."

She'd been awake less than a minute and had already changed the plan. Very well, I would need to make changes to my realm to make it habitable for her. Until then, I opened a portal to her cottage. Zadie pitched the wrapped book on the bed like it seared her hands, pivoting in her hurry to the restroom.

Fifteen minutes later, I cornered Ashi in the dragons' den. She burst out laughing, lifting her index fingers to her forehead to form horns. After my scowl, she tossed a tiny illusional unicorn, which floated toward my face before farting a rainbow.

She opened her backpack. Yet her cobalt eyes shone with seriousness when she handed me a stack of sealed see-through bags. Each contained a written symbol on square paper notes. Rune markings. I did not so much as have to ask her if she would use her chaos for Zadie.

"Two dozen straight-on protection healing bubbles." When her eyes twinkled, I knew she was up to something. Indeed, she dipped into her pack again, pulling out a stack of skimpy female underwear. Seven colors. A symbol stitched in gold threads was embroidered on each lace waistband. "Bigger dome, bigger heals."

Ashi grinned. "Sealed baggie or not, sticky notes get soggy sometimes, so Zadie needs to wear those. I forgot to give them to her with the other stuff. I'll leave that for you to tell her. Soul-chain-wise, this is about at the level of Bram's puberty. Therefore, how about you guess which ones she wears daily, like polka dots or hearts? And, Death, henna body rune shielding was ingenious."

The woman was an instigator, not me like she usually claimed. Ashi walked away, the second female in a row who dismissed me.

I didn't have long to deliberate summoning my scythe to thump for comfort and importance before Zadie returned. She blinked at the baggies in one hand, the stack of female undergarments in the other.

Those I shoved toward her, gawking at her skimpily dressed body. A malfunction in my supernatural brain came up empty except for what Ashi said. So I mumbled, "You have to wear those. I have to guess which ones you're wearing."

Then one coffee eyebrow hiked. "Say what, perv?"

I raked my eyes down her figure again. Oh, this would not do at all. I blamed Ashi and Mission Mankind for clothing a homeless woman. Zadie wore denim shorts, short enough for the runes on her thighs to show. And upon her *tight* and tie-dyed midriff shirt, there were no words. Only symbols.

:):

I finally pulled my stare from her partially visible stomach and back, eyes stuck on henna tattoos and skin I recalled touching. My gaze met hers. "What is this?" I growled.

Her brow crinkled. "Which do you see? Half-full or half-empty?" Still awaiting an answer, she continued, "The glass?"

"What glass?" I summoned my scythe and thumped it once. She could not go around with that much skin exposed.

She pointed at the symbol on her shirt, cocking her head. "What do you see? Smiley face, proverbial glass half full, or frowny face, half-empty glass?"

What did I see? Too much skin, the symbols stretched over her tight shirt. What the...? I was staring at her breasts now! That definitely was from Bram's puberty, pumping through the soul chain.

She grunted when I didn't answer her, taking the stack of undies into the cottage.

Not one to lie about idle, Zadie called her yak into the warm section of the beach. Then, combing and milking done, she attacked the bag of shed fur, rolling and stretching it as if her life depended on turning it into yarn.

Finally, after her yarn was created and her energy was spent, I approached her as she fed carrots to Horse. I cocked my head to the side, indicating the cottage. "You wanted the book. Yet you keep too busy to read it. Why?"

Her thoughts swirled, coming up with and discarding

scenarios, so I said, "Talking only works if you are honest. I sense lies."

Zadie heaved a monumentally long sigh. "The next chapter after the fairytale is for Grace, who will now name her daughter Grace as some tribute to you and a gifted power."

I shook my head. "I never asked for that. What else does it say?"

She snorted. "I stopped right there. Not in the mood for mythology."

I walked to a Famine-created hammock, saying, "Bring it. Read it to me."

"No!"

"Okay, I'll read to you."

"No! It's personal!"

I huffed out a laugh. "It's about you *and* me." Ah, her surface thoughts popped like bubbles. "Because you *are* named Grace. And because you *know* me." His smile increased wattage. "I am Death."

"Can the blacksmith create mindreading-proof helmets? I never really considered myself a helmet kind of gal, but if that would keep you out of my mind?"

"I have a proposition for you."

Zadie shuddered, then winked. "Cue the creepy music as the Angel of Death propositions me."

"If you willingly join me on Team Horseman, we will go into the pit under Sheol, go to the blacksmith for demon daggers. I will tell you about your gift of power and how best to wield it. The sooner you do this and can control it, the sooner we leave for Tartarus. If you refuse, the gifted power will still come to you, passed down by your mother. But we will not delve into the bottom layer of hell without being on the same team."

Chapter Fourteen

Zadie

The vain angel horseman, the hero from family legend, wanted me to join him on a quest into the underworld's basement. The fact that he was a magic-wielding angel implied it would go well, despite him claiming Tartarus was nothing to consider. Of course, if he couldn't lie, that didn't make much sense. But if he would take me to the blacksmith…? "What does Team Horseman mean? Cause I won't help end the world."

Death patted the hammock beside him. "It means you are not a wildcard, no longer solo after calling all the shots for nearly fifteen years. Clearly, you are a survivor; I do not doubt that. But it means you will not continually disregard what the Angel of Death tells you."

I plopped beside him, then glanced at his devastatingly beautiful face, too divine to be human. "A prettier version of stay? I'm not a pet. I don't need a leash."

Warm fingers cupped my cheek while his teakwood and leather scent, with a hint of smoky amber, filled my lungs. "You need a teammate. But I am stronger than you. I wield magic, am supernatural, immortal, and know the magical world. So you will let me protect you."

His pale stallion approached, neighing, before Death added, "Horse, too, will protect you."

Not Death, not any of the horsemen acted like villains. Yes, they wreaked havoc right after their seal broke, but now they were riding to kill spelled wild beasts or end evil escapee souls. Them doing that, along with Death's agreement to collect demon blades, was to save human lives and prolong—not hasten —the very end. No horseman seemed evil; if so, I would never consider his offer because heroes didn't team up with villains. Not that I was a heroine like he was a family hero, but I certainly was not villainous. Good stuck with good; bad with bad. "What do you and your horse get out of it?"

"You. As a teammate."

I pulled back from his touch on my cheek, whispering, "Did you ask Zehra to join your team?"

Death growled. "No. We talked. Inviting others to join the team was an option that didn't exist before horseman seals broke. We were friends, not a team."

"Not to undersell my own worth, but...?" I shrugged. "I don't see any benefit to you by taking on a weak link."

"You make me smile. And growl. But smiling is rare. And you, Zadie Grace, are not weak." He grinned. "Dull-witted? Perhaps. You do not yet understand the power you have."

Then he tipped his head toward the cottage again, long dark locks swaying. "Join me on Team Horseman. Then let's look at your family book together." One ebony eyebrow cocked. "Change clothes while you are in there."

"No. I'm not changing who I am. I needed clothes after the sinkhole. And I like the clothes Ashi gave me. Do I have a voice, a vote, in this team?"

"Of course!" His conceited expression handed me the dimwit award again. "That's how teams work. And stop giving yourself the dimwitted award. You will know when I award it."

"Will you stop policing my thoughts? It's like the world's most annoying superpower."

His veil of arrogance dropped. Death shrugged, more than a touch of sadness in his ancient green eyes. "The dead do not speak with words. I started reading human minds when I collected my first soul, Abel's. I hear your thoughts popping without trying to pick up anything beyond the surface. Team Horseman will give you the ability to—if not to become a mind ninja—at least perform mind voodoo. You can speak into my head; perhaps hear my thoughts."

I laughed and clapped my hands once. "I could read *your*

mind? You should have led with that. Yes. I will join Team Horseman."

Immediately, a breathtakingly gorgeous smile lit Death's perfectly squared face. It chased the sad shadows from his forest green eyes. At the same time, a connectedness developed, a new sense birthed into existence under my tingling temples. A link to Death; another to his steed.

"Welcome to Team Horseman, Zadie." His voice then sounded inside my head, startling me. *Is it my turn to choose a word for today?*

"If you stop whispering inside my mind."

"Memitim."

I shot him a lopsided smile. "I read a lot, fed my brain nom-noms, but I've never heard that word. You'll have to define it if you expect me to use it."

Death nodded. "Get your book. It is in there, I assure you."

Eden and Famine headed our way, triplets running ahead to swarm us on the hammock.

Famine nodded at Death. "Congratulations!" He nodded at me, long dark curls lifting in the wind. "Welcome to Team Horsemen, Zadie."

Death bobbled the triplets and nodded. "We were about to—"

"Congratulations," Pestilence said as he stepped out of a spinning magical gateway, followed by Ashi.

Ashi immediately hugged me, saving me from the trio of toddlers smacking wet kisses all over my face. She pulled me to stand while whispering, "Welcome, sister."

War and Serenity followed; he offered, "Congratulations," as Serenity hugged me.

"Thank you." Overwhelmed by the warm welcome, I whispered, "Was there an announcement? How did you know?"

Serenity tapped right below my collarbone. "Do you feel warm flickers of light inside your chest? That is us, Team Horsemen."

I didn't know what she was talking about. I didn't feel anything in my chest; the new sense I acquired was under my temples.

"They are not bonded," War explained. "It takes both, Reni, to feel family like that."

Bonded was a term I recognized; they warned me about the creepy exchanging of blood with an angel, the how-to for horsemen to marry.

Bram, coming from the den above, joined us. "What's happening?" He tapped his sternum. "Was that a surge of happiness from *you*, Uncle D?"

But then his brown eyes bulged when he looked at me, up and down, eyes sticking to each partially visible henna tattoo. His cheeks flushed red.

"She joined Team Horseman," Death explained, but there was unnerving heat in his green eyes locked onto me.

Bram cocked his head. "Zadie is my aunt?"

War thumped his son on the back. "Yep."

Wow, an aunt. Ashi called me a sister. We did not and *would not* be exchanging blood to bond, but they acted like I was family now. There was apparently much more to joining the horsemen team than potentially reading Death's mind. Everyone, except Bram and me, was magical. The towering handsome men were *angels*. Dang it, mind-blown confetti streamed out the back of my ponytail again.

As the ladies escorted me away from the horsemen, I nearly shrieked from the surprise of Death's voice in my mind, hearing his voice in stereo under my temples. *Do not share our plan to enter the bottom level of hell. Not until you are trained.*

"Pfft." *I'm not a pet.* I had no idea how I projected that aloud to just him, but I did. The new sense under my temples apparently sent and received like talking and listening.

You're not solo, a wildcard. You are my teammate.

That sense of comradery with a teammate branded a hero by my family was why I didn't argue.

Pestilence nodded toward his brothers. "While the ladies eat, let's ride." Yet before the horsemen were out of earshot, he laughed. "It distracts me when Ashi dresses like that. You have the awakening of your territorial male to look forward to."

No, I silently disagreed. We looked forward to our secret mission to save the world. That goal was overkill high in the last days, ticking down to the world's termination. At least it was not hastening the very end. Demon blades could stop evil angels who detested humans but possessed them. The weapons could stop the Fallen from wiping us to extinction.

That mission circled back to the book. If it were to be believed as more than mythology, Death gifted a magical power to my family. And now, I needed to read that book as soon as possible. Hopefully, while the horsemen were still riding, killing wild beasts and reanimated bones.

Yet it wasn't until hours after the meal before I escaped for privacy. My yak reclined on the white sand, so I settled against Chuckles' furry back like a breathing couch, book in hand. Chuckles grunted, echoing my satisfaction about the beach lit by a bright buttery moon and smear of stars.

I carefully flipped forward to the chapter awaiting Grace.

As recorded by Zehra:

I repeatedly asked God to give Death a real wife. More than a friend, a companion, one to awaken his emotions. Believing it on faith is why I want the power to pass to Grace. So she is there when the time comes.

At the top of the next page, *Memitim.*

Female angels do not exist, yet all of Death's reapers are female. While reapers inspired art devoted to female angels, a destroyer is as terrifying as Death. His gift of power ensures our protection against nearly soulless people—like my attacker. The gifted ability rarely activates. Few souls are so saturated by evil as to be abandoned by their guardian angels.

I paused, thinking of Mom. She hunted the scum of the earth that tried to stay hidden.

The power of a memitim will trigger when you encounter a nearly soulless one. Then, you will supernaturally wield a portion of Death's magical power as a destroying angel, ensuring the wicked one's last breath.

That sounded...terrible. Assassin-y-ish. I looked up from the page as scary me-turning-into-a-killer scenarios started to form. Yet Death walked into view, shaking his head, grinning at me as I leaned against Chuckles.

I sighed and used his word for today. "Are memitim magical?"

Raking back long black hair while approaching me, Death said, "It is a power. Those have to be gifted. But yes, that power is magical. Being on the same team will magnify that magic."

The vain Angel of Death definitely did not intend to join me in reclining against my five-hundred-pound mound of furry, horned pet.

He grinned. "You always wanted a yak. Your caveman painting illustrated that. Why?"

I shrugged. "Some kids want a dog. I wanted a yak. Smart, fun, can't sit in my lap but makes a fine couch while keeping me company. And yaks provide milk, fur, and usable things—a base for soap and candles. More helpful than ever in a post-apocalyptic world."

One black eyebrow hitched. "I've noticed your obsession with gathering hand-picked shed fur and turning it into yarn. What do you do with it?"

I laughed. "Normally, sell it to someone who knows how to knit. Speaking of…I need some knitting needles."

Death didn't laugh off my request; instead, he nodded as he held out one hand to hoist me from the beach and my furry couch. "Do you want to share the book with me?"

I thought of my ancestor writing that she prayed for God to awaken Death's emotions, to give him a real wife. She clearly cared for him. He was the hero of her story, the hero of my entire family line. Zehra would have been stoned without him, and we wouldn't exist. "I don't yet know if it's like Zehra's diary. I suspect she didn't think you'd read it. It's been translated many times, but I bet you can read her language, her actual words. Do you want to do that to yourself?"

Although the angel's haughty expression didn't change, I immediately sensed the change before hearing his thought. *She still misunderstands.*

Great yakkedity yak! I read his mind! Hearing no more didn't dampen my excitement. "What do I misunderstand?"

"I was fond of Zehra. But. I. Had. No. Emotions. No empathy. All of that was beyond me, not in an angel's nature. I'm unsure what romantic scenario you believe it was, but it wasn't that. For her either."

I squeezed his hand. "Yeah, but you do have emotions now. Will her words comfort or pain you?" With that, I handed Death the book, willingly sharing it.

He didn't so much as open it, keeping hold of my hand until we reached the cottage. There, he placed the book on my bed. Then he pointed at the bag of yarn. "Will you try something for me before we hunt knitting needles?"

I nodded but quickly gasped as he stepped in, placing his palm on the henna tattoo exposed at my midriff. My stomach flipped under his fingers, humming, electrified. Yeah, that should not happen, not allowed, with the family hero. The problem was... that hero was flesh and blood touching me, not a character in mythology.

His other hand parked on my exposed back to stop me from backing away. "Close your eyes."

I did, but it made it worse to stand with my head pulled in close to his chest, intensifying his teakwood, leather, and smoky heat scent.

"Exhale. Let your other senses spread like a slow-moving fog, expand, and take in as much as possible. Reach out beyond these walls, toward the pounding waves."

The large palm tingled my abdomen, slightly vibrating my skin, then a blast of power pulsed into me. Suddenly, my senses pulled in one direction. Startled, I gazed into his eyes.

Death smiled. "Where is the skeletal ship and crew?"

Although unable to see past the wall, I still pointed toward the pull.

He nodded. "Unholy souls. Good job, Zadie. Let's find your knitting needles before you sleep."

Chapter Fifteen

"**Y**es, Death," Zadie sighed from the beach, big green eyes rolling while mentally handing me the dull-witted award. "I did say our team needed bear urine. Also, I explained that you need to calm one until it pees on the aluminum foil to collect it."

The first time I parroted her request into the evening sky, darkening to the color of plums, calming by listening to the sea crashing against rocks, not looking at her. Another day with too much of her skin showing. Her day started with her yak, but I heard knitting needles clacking from her cottage when my brothers and I finished riding. I was only now ready to train her. Still, the new glitch in my angel brain would not process her team request. "Why?"

Zadie turned from Chuckles, waving her free hand my way. "You smell."

I summoned my scythe, thumping it once.

She laughed at my scowl. "Not horribly, but potently holy. I'd imagine that's something souls in hell and its basement rarely smell. They can smell, right? Bear pee is a strong predator scent. Hopefully, strong enough to mask yours and mine. Wolf urine worked to keep predators from Chuckles and Yippee."

"Do you have on underwear?"

Her mental image flashed to me, brightly-colored curly strings shooting out the end of her curly ponytail. "Pardon?"

"With the embroidered rune on the lace?"

At her nod, I followed behind her, wondering which color while watching the sway of her hips.

Yes, Ashi was an instigator, but she was kind enough to make healing runes without me asking her to tap into her chaos magic. "Stash a bagged rune drawing in your pocket. I'll show you what it does later. What is today's word?"

"Bockety, considering you made me both unsteady and wobbly with the undie question." She laughed.

"Bockety? Is that what you call the curly streamers you picture pouring out of your ponytail?"

"Nah. That's mind-blown confetti. But strangely, you asking did make me a bit wobbly."

"Me asking about the state of your underwear makes you bockety?"

She shrugged, then nodded.

Zadie had no idea about the depths of opportunity that opened when she joined Team Horseman. The most significant included indulging in carnal pleasures; mating with her flesh without falling. If discussing underwear blew her mind, knowing about the new sex clause would make her bockety. Since the sexual pull did not apply to our union, I didn't intend to tell her. Or to mate her.

As soon as she tucked the sealed bag with a rune marking into her shorts, I clamped my arm around her waist, grateful for her shirt hanging long enough to cover her abdomen this time.

Then I strode out her cottage door, blasting into the air. After her shriek of surprise, I asked, "Are you afraid of heights? You tense up and have asked me not to drop you. As if that needed to be clarified as a goal."

"Not afraid, you gave me no heads-up. Humans don't have wings. It's not natural, suddenly sprouting wings and launching into the sky. That's like a superhero skill." As she said it, she relaxed, trusting me not to drop her.

Soaring above the ocean, I noticed she didn't watch the deep blue water but my wings lighting up the night sky. "Close your eyes, exhale, and let your senses ripple away from you. Then, search for an anomaly."

I didn't touch her stomach this time; instead shifted my hold on her until we were all but chest to chest. Her softness, her honey mixed with sweet pea scent, launched an assault on my senses. Instead of pulsing power, the magic radiating off my body vibrated her skin like stimuli for hers. With her eyes closed, lifted high face-to-face, I freely studied her perfect features. I flew until she pointed, then stopped to hover, asking her to open her eyes toward unholy souls inhabiting a risen ship below. Then I sank it.

Pleased after an hour of Zadie successfully pointing her power toward sensing evil anomalies in the dark, so she couldn't rely on her eyesight, I flew toward land with daylight. "Hunting unholy risen souls isn't how your gifted power triggers naturally. We are growing that ability; you're doing very well. Sensing and avoiding souls in hell is vital for my plan. After I shift, after transforming to enter the underworld, we cannot touch for me to pulse magical power into you. Or else my corporeal divine parts will melt."

Her large green eyes searched my face. "That sounds…? Yeah, we won't let that happen. Hopefully, my skin doesn't melt off as well. But what if I can't sense them on my own? How will we get around if you aren't flying us?"

"Sneak. We'll get to that. This is only your second day of trying to wield your power."

Immediately after landing, Zadie clapped her hands once and glanced around. "This beach doesn't really scream bear stomping grounds. And I don't have the aluminum foil! I don't want to hold the rune baggie while it pees."

The woman was ridiculous. "We're not here for bears. I want you to try it again; let your senses find what does not belong."

I didn't touch Zadie this time, not buzzing magical power into her. "Now, you'll get a taste of what triggers your power in the wild. I've been here many times to escort souls. The man in charge of this trafficking ring doesn't mind losing a female or two to his own depravity. He's nearly soulless, so steeped in oily evil that his guardian angel stopped protecting him. My gifted power will automatically activate when you sense the soul abandoned by his angel counterpart."

First, when her senses alerted her to the guardian-less male, her eyes glinted green frost. Her stance widened. Tiny smoky spiral wisps lifted from her outline until shadows swept in to cloak her aura. She jumped around, slapping at smoky strands on her shoulders, flowing around her, sheathing her in shadows. "Am I on fire? I'm smoking!"

Then suddenly, as the wind shifted to carry the male's scent, so too did Zadie. Like hundreds of candles blew out at once, grayish-white smoke replaced her human form. The smoky wisps morphed into dark tendrils cloaking her silhouette.

Sensing the man with no guardian angel, her gifted power took over. Moving in gliding hovers, zipping forward in a smeared streak of speed, she stopped for cover behind a rock, her shape reforming into shadows when she paused.

Stealthy and fast, Zadie made a beeline toward a little beach shack containing a nearly soulless man. Gray smoky shadows billowed behind her, taking the shape of wings. Darting forward in a blur, she followed him as he ran toward the water.

Zadie lifted one wispy, ethereal hand toward him. He swung his fist through her mist-like smoky face, not connecting; she was all but invulnerable until she killed him. Then, death magic blasted from her upraised palm, hitting him in the throat.

As he exhaled his last breath, a reaper appeared to take over. Rhea. She nodded at me, glanced at Zadie in shifted form, then shepherded the vile soul to Hades.

After a gasp, Zadie growled. "You turned me into an assassin? And a smoke monster!" The strands of smoke carried her image, but the reflection broke into stripes; wispy tendrils lashed like angry streamers whipping in the wind.

Before her form shifted from the shadows, I wrapped my arms around her and shot into the sky. "Breathe." I alone could touch her physical body while she wielded my gifted power. I could feel her as solid. No one else could. It was meant as protection, so why delight in that knowledge?

She didn't calm down and breathe, instead raged, "I had no choice! I didn't choose to go after him. It just happened."

"Concentrate on your shift. You'll need to do it again and

again. So you can phase in and out through portions of hell. Another vital skill for my Tartarus invasion plan."

"I murdered that man. With *magic. Yours.*"

"Breathe. Try to hold the destroying angel shift as long as possible. This happens to souls so vile that even their guardian angels gave up and deserted them. You were pulled to his malignant soul."

"Why would you do that to us, pass us that power? That was horrific! I had no choice. Look at me! I'm made out of smoke! I killed him!"

"You felt his darkness. It's a decree, nearly like a contract from his former guardian angel. Grim, perhaps, but I gifted it to Zehra because I, like my reapers, spent my time escorting souls. In my absence, if a vile soul like her attacker came near her again, she would be invulnerable until that soul was magically extinguished."

With the wicked soul passed on that triggered her memitim shift, the supernatural shadows around her body lightened. Finally, her form solidified.

After landing, I released her but added, "It is exceedingly rare for an angel to abandon his charge. I'm sure my gifted power never triggered for some in your line because they never encountered such a soul. Now you've felt it. You shapeshifted. It is that we will work on, as well as sensing unholy souls. I will not purposefully take you where I know it will trigger."

Zadie surprising me was nothing new; she narrowed her eyes on me. "Can I fly? That smoke looked like wings...."

"No. You would have to work up to a float."

After raking one hand down her lovely oval face, she growled, "You could have given the women in my family the power to fly. But you settled. For. Floating? Like a blimp power?"

"What is a blimp? Floating is telepathy."

When she frowned, I slid my hand around her waist, propelling her toward the nearby building. "I did not intend to turn your line into hunters flying around the globe, searching for evil. The gifted power was only if you encountered such a soul, ensuring you were invulnerable until you ended them. Nevertheless, it seems your mother was a globe-flyer to hunt. But she could not shift during the stampede because the memitim power did not trigger."

I gave her waist a little squeeze. "But *you* will learn to shift at will. And like when I transform, you, too, can interact with the world in your smoky shape. The same as if you are solid. You can toss a rock or carry a backpack. Yet no one but me can feel you as solid."

After reaching down to the dead man, I pulled a key from his pocket. Handing it to Zadie, I nodded toward the bigger building. "Now go. Free the captives you saved from that man. They are locked in the basement."

Bright green eyes blinked up at me before she ran into the building.

When Zadie reemerged, three bony women and two equally bony girls followed. The frightened females stopped hunching once they spotted their dead capturer, torturer—a flesh trader on the water's edge.

Thanks to earlier plans with War, a portal opened. But the newly freed females blinked at Serenity as her minty green mist landed on them. War waited in bright sunshine outside a massive forlorn Victorian mansion on the other side. The monstrosity, complete with turrets, was the orphanage where Serenity was raised.

After Serenity ushered the five through the magical gateway, she gave them a guided tour. My brother left food inside for them. A place to recover or to live.

Although Zadie stayed quiet, her thoughts through our Team Horseman link assured me that she was happy with the outcome, if not her power. Once the females were settled, she rejoined me outside in the sunshine, holding up a roll of aluminum foil. "About that bear pee."

War huffed out a laugh, but I warned, "Don't ask."

Although she had no idea of the significance of joining my team, her requests were not unimportant. She was my equal as a teammate. Therefore, I would grant her requirements the same as I hoped she would cede to anything I might ask.

I wrapped my arm around her waist and then blasted into the sky, flying toward an eroded landscape that humans called the Badlands.

Zadie watched the land, the sinkholes, and the devastation. Then, at last, she whispered as we flew. "Take my power. It's a gift from you; take it back."

"Are humans in the habit of giving a gift and then taking it back? A gift is a gift."

Reaching the Badlands, with the spell on wild beasts to attack mankind, grizzly bears roamed steep tan and gray slopes. We landed a short distance from a sinkhole; a deep ravine was on the other side. I gave her a nod. "Pull that rune from your pocket. I'll show you what it does."

She freed the rune from the baggie, then held it out to me.

Shaking my head, I said, "It is for you. Hold it in your palm. If you bleed and touch your blood to the rune, it will trigger a protective bubble filled with healing magic to surround you."

Her green eyes widened after I summoned my mission-given sword. "You don't plan to lop off my head?"

Huffing out a laugh, I reached for her other palm. Yet before I punctured her skin for a welt of blood, the rocky ground around us rumbled.

Zadie stumbled. The ground under us thundered; three grizzly bears charged our way. She squeaked with surprise, waving the aluminum foil at me. "Calm it so I can put the foil under it."

Yet the wild beasts were not running our way to attack us but to escape what charged after the bears.

The ground thudded before glimpsing ivory bones running our way. *Boom! Boom! Boom!*

A skeletal T-Rex, risen and enhanced by the spell Hades released, tilted back its head, emitting a nearly deafening roar.

"Nope!" Zadie hollered, dashing away from the bears *and* me. Yet the apex predator's footfalls shook the ground as it neared, which must be what tripped her. The foil shot out of her hand

and unrolled ahead of her on the rocky ground. Then she fell into the sinkhole on top of a bear.

She wasn't hurt, but the woman could find more trouble in thirty seconds than some find their entire lives!

When my spell exploded off my sword, the bear under her collapsed. The dinosaur toppled over, momentum flipping it end-over-end. Finally, it came to rest on the unstable sinkhole rim, its long bony tail hanging in the pit. Dead. Its bodily functions relaxed, releasing a waterfall-like pour down on Zadie.

She shrieked. "I am. Doused in. Dino. Urine! That is impossible! It was bones!"

"That is what happens at death." I grinned into her furious face. "It's an end-of-the-world spell. Nothing should surprise you."

"I've been attacked by T-Rex bones and a little bunny. And maybe, someday, I can *float.*"

Gingerly, she folded a massive foil pouch, urine collection captured. She sighed. "Apex predator. This is better than bear pee."

While I tried to process her doing that, Zadie reached for the end of her shirt. Green eyes flicked to me. "Give me your shirt, Death." Then she pulled her dripping, reeking shirt off, folding it in aluminum.

I stood there as if paralyzed. As an angel, I could walk through a crowd of naked women, and nothing would be interesting enough to stop for a second glance. But I wasn't glancing at Zadie; I was staring at her in a beige bra.

She cupped her hands over her mouth, calling, "Hello, family hero. Don't fall off your pedestal, Grandpappy; you'll break a hip. I need your shirt."

Growling, I jumped down to her. Then I pulled off my black t-shirt. But before handing it over, I leaned in to whisper. "Death is a villain." Finally, I dropped the black shirt over her head, swallowing her.

Zadie, too, seemed rattled. Yet she shook it off with a frown, muttering, "It smells."

"Worse than T-Rex waste?"

Her cheeks flushed, her heartbeat thudding loudly. Her eyes kept bouncing back to my chest. *Take that, grandpappy.*

Apparently, she struck back as she reached under my shirt, hanging long on her, then her sodden shorts plopped in a pile with her shirt.

She wrapped foil around and around them as a tendril of horror wound around me. Although it exposed no additional skin, shorts hanging shorter than my shirt, I wanted to strip it off her to see more of her skin.

Instead, I opened a portal, following her to Arcadia, outside her cottage.

She deposited the apex predator collection, then grabbed new clothes. Unfortunately, underwear was at the top of the pile; no way I failed to notice the color was dark blue with little red hearts.

Though not the plan, my mouth opened, and words fell out. "What color do you have on? Underwear?"

"Purple with gold stars." She turned to go, in a hurry, stinking up a storm.

Stepping in front of her, I grabbed her finger, quickly poking it with a needle. She yelped, then glared.

I nodded at her. "Touch your blood to the rune."

She jostled her items until smearing a droplet on the wet paper. Immediately, a golden oval bubble surrounded her. "Whoa," she muttered.

Before I left her, I grinned. "It serves as healing *and* protection. A wise woman would have triggered it around her before the T-Rex coated her in urine. Or shifted again."

With the golden bubble around her, Zadie hurried for the outdoor shower; her surface thought popped. *Sweater.*

Chapter Sixteen

Zadie

"**S**hark!"

One tall fin bearing down on me, and my dip in the ocean no longer seemed wise! Since three showers didn't stop me from winning the stinky award, scrubbing my skin with sand to remove the stink worked! Yet I retreated from the shark, back to the outdoor, waterfall-powered shower to rinse off the salt.

Late now, near midnight, the quiet gave me time to reflect on the gifted power simply overtaking me. My body turned into smoky wisps of shadows; no solid substance, no physical sensations. The price of that invulnerability? The magic zap. It shot from my palm into the man mere seconds after his fist swung harmlessly through me. I'd seen people die, but this time I saw a dark orb pop out of his mouth after his last exhale…and then I saw a reaper in action.

Death's *gift* made me a destroying angel? Ugh! But five females were rescued from a trafficker. Was this the greater good Mom talked about?

Tired, I finally crawled into bed only to stare at the fireflies lighting the ceiling; an incredible sight, until my mind stopped swirling. Except it didn't.

"Can't sleep?" Death stood shirtless in the shadows; one broad shoulder cocked against my doorway.

"Nope."

He moved with a confident, slow stride until stopping at the foot of the bed. "I can fix that." Then he uttered a whisper-quiet musical note. *Sleep!*

My world turned to silence.

The next thing I knew, a voice clanged louder than an alarm.

"Oh! No!" Eden's exclamation woke me. "What. Is. That. Smell?"

I jumped up and out the door in a long t-shirt to find her gagging, then clamping one hand over her nose. I'd forgotten about her supernatural sense of smell. So pointing toward the aluminum foil packages, I admitted, "T-Rex pee."

Joining us, scrunching her nose, Ashi blinked. "Where did you see a T-Rex?"

"The Badlands. We were there for bear pee and then—"

"Bear pee?" Serenity interrupted.

Nodding, I continued, "The grizzlies were running from the T-Rex bones. So when Death ended the dino, it whizzed all over me after it died."

"How can that happen from risen bones?" Ashi asked. "They have no bladder."

Serenity shrugged. "Wild bone-beasts kill and eat people—no stomach required; it's partly why the horsemen are so busy riding." She shuddered. "War didn't mention dinosaurs!"

Eden now used her elbow, covering her mouth and nose. "Why would you save it?"

"Predator. An apex. I'd imagine that could mask anyone's scent. I learned about marking territory from wolves; their wizz was a strong deterrent to protect Chuckles in the wild."

I carefully but quickly lifted the pouches. Then, I dashed where the beach had snow, partially burying them.

Yippee and Chuckles ran to greet me before pivoting and rushing away from the smell.

Death said to say nothing about our plan until I was trained. Having a dinosaur leak on me wasn't what I had in mind, but Death took me to the bears. He'd honored every one of my requests since I joined his team.

Bram provided entertainment again with flying stunts while I cared for Chuckles. This time, he ordered Samson to hit the nearby risen ship with dragonfire until it returned to a watery grave.

I joined the cheering women for sandwiches in a shade pavilion grown by the magical couple living here.

Bram joined us after he landed. A slight scowl marred his face as the airshow continued with Zed and Zoe performing aerobatics. Grabbing a sandwich, Bram sauntered from the shade to wet sand. Something seemed off. He should be celebrating after taking out that ship.

He left without a drink, so I carried a cup of water to where he stood, looking out over the ocean. Standing beside him in the blazing sun, I buried my toes in the sand before the wave erased my prints. Finally, I handed him the drink. "What's up?"

Shoulder-length dark curls shook. "I don't remember when I soul-chained my dad, but Uncle D's feelings are…?" Bram tapped his sternum. "I feel them both through their soul chains; I was the first to shed a drop of their blood after their seals were broken. It's how positive emotions, empathy, develop for holy angels."

I contemplated that. My team link with Death potentially allowed me to hear his thoughts while Bram absorbed Death's emotions in the soul chain.

After chugging his drink, Bram continued. "He's proud of you; I feel that and his confusion. His amusement. Sometimes flares of anger. Sometimes," his cheeks flushed a light red, "other stuff. All those flares of heat are likely the reason I thought…?"

"Thought what?"

Bram blew out a long breath. "That I saw a flame—a tiny flare of fire—on my tingling fingertips while Samson sank the ship."

Then he shrugged. "I'm not magical. So it had to be a play of light off Samson's dragonfire? But that doesn't explain why my fingertips tickled."

"Can the soul chain give you magic?"

"Nah. Just enough to enter dimensional portals. Although I was so young when it happened, I don't remember it."

"Can two soul chains give you magic?"

Bram shrugged again. "I'm the first and last person in this world to experience two soul chains."

"Want to find a quiet spot with fire retardant vegetation, away from prying eyes, to try?"

"You're serious," Bram said with a grin. "I wouldn't know how to start trying. I'd rather recreate it by Samson nuking another ship. Then see if it happens again." He pointed at the ocean. "I don't see any more ships."

"I can sense skeletal crews. Kind of. I need to be able to sense the unholy. Do you want to try it? I'll find it; you nuke it?"

His evident building excitement over the possibility of having magic suddenly deflated. Large brown eyes looked away. "Uncle D said Lilith would find you; if you leave sanctified land."

Bram did want to try. Closing my eyes, I touched my temple. However, I doubted it acted like a walkie-talkie button to activate speaking into Death's mind. I concentrated on that new sense under my temples and reached out to Death. *Your son needs you.*

Then I opened my eyes and smiled at Bram. "Now I have rune tattoos to make it harder for Lilith to find me." Today, I wore jeans over the sand-scrubbed henna tattoos.

I shrugged. "But I don't have any magical knowledge to wager how best to help...and my own magical mess to figure out. So tell Death, Bram, about the flame? Maybe he knows? You are the most important person to him."

Speak of the hero, a swirling portal opened before a pale stallion trotted through with the Angel of Death. Black jeans and sneakers, still wearing no shirt since he gave it to me. Stupidly chiseled physique on display. I waved bye, giving them privacy.

That gave me time to settle on the bed with my yak yarn and knitting needles, about to open the book. I'd watched women knit yak fiber into beautiful sweaters. Yarn made from yak down was warmer than wool but itch-free, softer than cashmere; each sweater was worth a lot of gold. The ladies had talked me through it and let me play around a bit for giving them a good deal. But yesterday, I started knitting and pulled it out twice because my creation looked like the yarn threw up. I'd work in a slower rhythm this time and be more careful about my stitches.

Satisfied with my progress, I flipped past *Grace* to the next chapter. *Lilith.*

Before I so much as started to read, I aggressively knitted his sweater.

Also called Eve. The most powerful force after Lucifer. That demon stalks Thanatos. She wears many faces and sheds many human bodies in her pursuit.

According to Lilith, like she split from Eve into her shade, Thanatos, too, will separate. Then he will be with her forever since God ordained the pit as Death's final destination.

I pray the last Grace will know how to stop Lilith and unlock Death's emotions. I pray for the man behind the angel to awaken and fight an ending in the pit. There is a way. God would not do that to his loyal angel horseman.

I stopped my ferocious knitting; it wasn't helping my lack of skill. But I knew how to stop Lilith.

With that, I left the cottage, marching to the backside of the den. Bamboo grew below cliffs overlooking the ocean. Death said we'd go to Tartarus as soon as I could control his gifted power. After another glance over my shoulder to ensure no one was watching the backside of the mountain, I tried to figure out how I shifted. Clenching muscles or striking poses failed, and since no grunting was involved...?

Moving on, I concentrated on *floating.* I repeated it like a mantra. *Float. Float. Float.* Then I jumped off the cliff. Thankfully, the ledge had another not too far under it. I found that out when I crashed down.

Death appeared in a flash, looking down at me. "Not floating. *That* was falling. Once you can shift, you can phase out before landing. It's how you'll avoid injury."

He appeared on the ledge above me in a blur, one large hand held out. After he hoisted me to stable ground, I stood as tall as his shoulder, staring at his bare chest. Basically, face-planted in chiseled muscle sculpted into ludicrous abs.

"Thanks. Did you give me your only shirt in the world?"

He scoffed, but I added, "Put one on."

Take that, grandpappy.

I heard his thought and laughed. "How do I shift? Without the whole murder-mayhem part?"

Death stepped in closer, nearly touching, breathing into my ear. "Thank you."

His baritone whispered a shiver into my ear, traveling up my spine. I jerked back, nearly falling backward off the cliff, arms wheeling ungracefully.

Grinning, the shirtless angel caught my hand and pulled me to him like at the sinkhole. His scent surrounded me; teakwood, leather, and the tiniest hint of smoky amber.

Whew! Abnormally breathless, slightly annoyed, I insisted, "No more ear voodoo. I almost fell."

"Ear voodoo? Is that what people call talking nowadays?"

"You shiver-whispered!" I slung it like an accusation.

"You liked it, so why leap back?" Then his chin lifted, a grin forming on his divinely sculpted square face. "Ah. Same reason. Because you liked it." He glowed with conceit...or maybe that was an actual aura, as in celestial angel?

Frowning, I informed him, "I intend to put in an order for that helmet from the blacksmith." Then I walked away. "Find a shirt."

But a large hand closed around my elbow, swinging me toward him. "Today's word is sublime."

Before I could comment on how boring that was, Death slid one hand up my spine, then threaded his fingers into my curls. "You are a sublime yokemate."

I shivered, inappropriately enjoying the family hero's soft caress. "Thank you? It makes me sound like an ox or something in the pet family."

"Bram...seems to be developing magic. Angels can't teach magic. You offered to find the unholy souls in risen ships, so ride with Bram on his dragon. War and I will fly alongside you."

"What if I can't sense them without you touching me? And *you* are teaching *me* magic."

One large hand smoothed over my long curls, stopping to rest on the small of my back, where he ran out of hair to stroke. "You will sense the unholy aberrations. And I'm teaching you how to wield your gifted magical power, not magic. Yet teaching magic is allowed since you joined Team Horseman."

"Then add Bram to the team so you can."

"That's not how it works. For each horseman, there is only one."

Before I could delve into that, Serenity flew by on Delilah, her female dragon the same firetruck size as Samson but lavender. She stopped to hover, appearing almost anxious, hollering, "Let's go!"

Death lifted me on behind Bram, already harnessed onto the saddle. Tall red spines provided handholds.

Right before we lifted off, Death's baritone whispered across my mind. *Don't depend on your eyesight. Use your power. You wear no harness, so I will catch you if you fall. Even if the blast of adrenaline from falling forces you to shift.*

Chapter Seventeen

Death

*F*lames!

A giant spike of adrenaline shot through Bram's chain into War and me as Samson streamed a river of dragonfire over the unholy crew and ship. Tiny flames danced over Bram's middle and index fingers. The teenager was indeed developing magic. It flickered out as Samson's dragonfire ended. Was it directly connected to his dragon, which ultimately was a creation of Ashi's chaos magic? Or a result of two soul chains? Or both?

Immediately after Bram's woot, Zadie sensed the next ship and pointed the way. Flames danced back and forth on three of Bram's fingertips when his dragon sank the next. The teenager held them up, showing us all.

Wild long curls whipped riotously around Zadie's face but didn't hide her bright smile. It reminded me of how shadowy bands of smoke spiraled away from her when she shifted.

Do I need to do this to turn it on? Zadie's thought popped into my mind before she lifted one hand to her temple.

Saturated with Bram's elation thrumming through the chain, I purred into her mind. *You don't.*

May I play tag with the next unholy crew before they sink? Would that work for me to shift?

Hmm. Good idea. If it weren't for the Conqueror's children, I wouldn't know what tag was. "Bram, please hold off before sinking the next, so Zadie can practice her power?"

Massive smile plastered on his face, Bram's voice cracked as he yelled, "Sure thing."

Serenity, who earlier admitted being torn about the possibility of magic emerging in her son, flew Delilah beside him. War joined her, dismissing his wings as they whispered.

I knew they spoke with their minds, so I wondered why War held her, whispering in her ear. He was comforting her! Using voice and touch, not needing his peace power. When his bonded wife brightened almost immediately, it was a lesson I took to heart.

After flying toward Zadie, I scooped her off Samson and into my arms. At least today, her flesh was covered by jeans and a t-shirt, no tattoos visible. It didn't alter her softness or smell, but at least I was not distracted by skin exposure and direct carnal contact. While I hovered far above the deck, I drew a crooked path in the air, overlaying the ship and crew below. "Phase out when you zigzag past them."

"Okay." Bright green eyes blinked up at me. "How?"

"You phased from stop to stop when you hunted the man. When it fired as intended. A gliding hover. So think of stalking them in the shadows. Think like a destroying angel."

She grimaced, so I stroked my thumb across her face as War did with Serenity. "You can't kill them with death magic. They are dead. Your power is magic that fires on its own, only in the presence of a person abandoned by their guardian angel. But you can shift from skeleton to skeleton like the tag you wanted to play. In this version, you shift invulnerable next to each instead of tagging them. It is a skill you need to navigate hell."

She nodded as we hovered close enough for the skeletal crew to wave coral-encrusted swords in the air. Although determination gleamed in her green eyes, no shadowy wisps of smoke emitted from her body. She couldn't kill them, yes, scatter bones, but if she didn't phase out beside them, they could injure and kill her. With the echo of that possibility reverberating in my head, the glitch in my angel brain fired, meaning my mouth opened. Words simply fell out. "Do you have on underwear?"

It broke the tension, but now she appeared annoyed. "Yes, Death. Consider that the answer anytime you might wonder. Save you from asking."

What color?

You said you'd guess. Not that I'd answer.

Now I really wanted to know, but her anger caused tiny tendrils of smoky shadows to grow like extensions of her springy locks.

As soon as her toes touched the deck, she puffed into a smoky form. Like hundreds of candles extinguished at once. Although she had no physical form, her reflection flickered in the smoky strands. She perfectly zagged past the first ivory-boned sailor. But her zig past the next was not phased out.

I summoned my scythe, pointing it that way. Yet, Zadie pivoted, charging toward me as her body reformed into tenebrous shadows. A half tock later, I sensed slimy darkness, the incoming of Lilith, a dark purple portal spinning open behind me.

The whir of dark smoke buzzed past me toward Lilith possessing a human body. Zadie fully sensed that the female's agreement for possession acted as the last straw for her guardian angel. Wielding true memitim power, Zadie's silhouette reformed behind and to the side of Lilith before holding up one palm. Smoky shadows billowed behind her into large wings as death magic hit Lilith's human shell right in the throat.

A reaper appeared, ready to escort the dark soul orb that escaped the female host.

The darkness of Lilith's essence swirled away. She did not prefer possessing the dead. She had only done so to torture me with Zehra.

But this time, Zadie appeared delighted about her gifted power. Better yet, she maintained her shift, counting on Lilith to reappear.

Lilith did not disappoint Zadie. A slightly stouter than usual female model—long black hair and green eyes—stepped out of the swirling purple portal.

Zadie spoke in a whispery growl. "Stay dead, Eve."

The short-lived female uttered, "Destroying angel? Too delicious!"

Lilith used that body as fodder, alive only long enough to land a taunt. A reaper appeared to ferry the unwilling female's soul to the holding cell in Hades. Lilith's darkly demonic essence twisted away from the body, disappearing in the wind.

Without waiting to learn if Lilith would return, I scooped Zadie from the ship while she was still in her shadowy state, but I felt her soft body under the smoky strands. Then I blasted past Bram.

Bram and Samson wasted no time before incinerating and sinking the aberrant ship and crew. But, this time, a more significant flame danced in the palm of his hand.

Although his chain pumped positive emotions, they weren't enough to diminish what I felt. I was unsure if I wanted to shake sense into Zadie or kiss her. Wait, what?

I held the smoky bundle, not reseating her with Bram, then leaned to her shadowy ear. "What if she used a dead body? You haven't mastered triggering your shapeshifting power; you would not automatically phase. Then Lilith would. Kill. You. Zadie!"

Still looking like she was made of smoke with shadows sweeping around her, Zadie smugly replied, "But she didn't."

Pulling her in tighter, I noticed she lost her shift, skin replacing shadows wherever I touched her. As we approached the next ship, I demanded, "Promise me. That you will never do that again. A blood oath vow."

"Any type of blood thing with you is a no. I'm aware that exchanging blood is called bonded for an angel marriage. Speaking of a wife, did you know Zehra disliked Lilith? She didn't know how to stop her. I do. Why didn't you explain it to her?"

I sighed as Bram's dragon annihilated the next target. "I guaranteed Lilith could not enter her home. Yet when Zehra persisted, I told her not to worry her small human mind over what Lilith told her." I grunted. "Of course, Zehra said the baby spitting up on me saved me from bread to the face."

Zadie laughed, on a magical high like Bram, her shape slowly solidifying into flesh. "I would have liked Zehra."

Her smile flipped, lips tipped downward when I opened a portal and flew through to Arcadia, leaving it open for them to follow or not. Oh, Zadie was downright scowling when I dropped her on the bed.

"Show me," I demanded. Then, picking up her thought, I answered, "The color of your underwear."

She jumped off the bed. "What!"

"Show me the henna runes. Your panty color is just a bonus as I suspect the symbols need to be reapplied, and you did not say so."

When Zadie made no move to heed my instruction, I breathed a word of power over her, sweeping along the outside of her jeans, sweeping them away with magic.

She no sooner shrieked than I stood in front of her, cupping her beautiful face. "The next time you do not tell me you scrubbed an opening in the rune pattern—and I have to discover it by Lilith finding you—I will have no choice but to keep you in my realm. Where nothing can get to you…and you can get to nothing. Now lie down so I can redo the one on your thigh. If you break one line, then you might as well not have any runes because you are *not* shielded from her."

Was it wrong to be delighted by learning the color of her underwear? She lay on her stomach, head turned the other way while I stared at her backside, sheathed in little black panties with red lace edging. Complete with an embroidered rune. I wasn't sure how many minutes had passed before she turned to look at me with one dark eyebrow hitched. Basically, she caught me cataloging her flesh.

I muttered, "I don't have any henna. You are on blessed land. Do you want me to put you to sleep and repair the markings? Or wait until morning?"

"Ha! It was a ploy to learn the color of my panties. Why are you so angry?"

"There is only one, Zadie. That's you on a team with me. You have no idea how significant that is. I don't mind reapplying the runes; I mind that you didn't tell me. I mind you risked your life.

Don't do stupid things to increase the likelihood of me reaping your soul."

Frown worthy. Her thought flitted into my mind.

Then she sighed and lit a candle. "Since you can see in the dark, please fetch henna tonight. It's not good to sleep on anger."

"I don't sleep."

"Right now, a deep scowl is marring your sublime beauty. Please repair my tattoos? I used sand to de-stink the dino pee."

Still, the emotions swirling through me did not taper off. Finally, I managed to drag my stare away from her flesh. Wobbly. Unsteady. The woman made me bockety!

When I returned with the henna and my silver feather, Zadie was propped on her elbows, stomach down, reading her book. Then, frowning, she read, "Charon, as recorded by Zetta. Pay the ferryman's toll. He never forgets."

"Lie flat and still."

"What do I pay Charon? And the blacksmith?"

"I will take care of Charon *and* the blacksmith. If we want bulk demon blades, the agreement to free him will guarantee it. But we will all have to carry his supplies. The enchanted daggers are not made from metals available on earth. The more we carry, the higher the finite number will be."

Sitting on the floor beside the bed, I exhaled slowly. I lowered a finger to trace where a tiny break disconnected rune lines, nullifying all the runes to hide Zadie from Lilith. Before I touched the wet feather to her skin, she shivered. It wouldn't take long to repair this portion, but I needed to inspect the other tattoos for similar damage.

"You say," she cleared her throat, still sounding breathless. "You are in no hurry to end the world; that Hades has struck and is done. Suppose you stay shifted incorporeal, meaning no one can die. That would prevent you from reaping a fourth of souls. You could stop the world's end, the coming chaos war. Freeze it as it is. Then humans can start over and repopulate the planet!"

Leaning in, I blew on the wet henna. She shivered as I stood to inspect the other side. Then, waving my hand, I created a magical aurora to hopefully sidetrack her train of thought.

Yet she added, "That's what a hero would do."

No lines were broken on this rune tattoo, so I sat beside her on the bed. "I told you; Death is a villain." With that, I pulled the end of her shirt up to her shoulders, inspecting the rune. I suppose she could not scrub as hard on her back as it was fine. "Turn over so I can see the last tattoo."

She closed the book, flopped around, but rested one palm on the bottom of her shirt instead of raising it. Shadows danced across her face as the candle flame flickered in the breeze. "I am your teammate. Tell me why you don't resist your final destination? The pit. With Lilith? I agree with Zehra! You don't belong there like Lilith, Hades, and the Fallen. There is no way God would reward your entire faithful existence like that!"

"Don't worry your pretty little head—"

"Tell me," Zadie demanded as she sat and cupped my cheek.

Returning her gaze, as the darker green circling her irises flashed darker still, I handed her the truth. "Who I am now is not who I will be after final judgment." Then I lifted the wet feather. "Lift your shirt."

After she complied, I sighed. This sizeable intricate tattoo had numerous scrubbed-off lines. Yet her stomach jumped under my fingers before the feather followed the same path. Her heartbeat thudded faster, slowly inhaling, holding it, then exhaling. A countdown in her mind to distract her.

Her eyes closed while her abdomen clenched and unclenched. The scent of sweet peas and honey thickened.

She likes my feather on her skin.

I heard that.

Yet she did not attempt to lie, to deny it. Instead, her full lips parted as she wriggled, slightly panting. Bright green eyes opened; pupils dilated, her gaze smoldering.

Heated embers sparked in my chest; I put aside the henna bowl and feather to bend lower and slowly blow on her wet tattoo. I had the foresight to rest one hand on her shoulder so she couldn't bolt upright out of bed like last time.

Once the tattoo dried, I tugged down her shirt to hide her luscious flesh, which I definitely should not be noticing since my species was an angel.

My thumb brushed over her lower lip as if my hand operated independently of my brain. Her tongue slicked over the same track. Before I lost my concentration, I told her, "You did wonderfully tonight, excelling when wielding your power. Keep it up, and we won't have long before leaving for Tartarus. As a sign of my pleasure, I would reward you. As you are *my* team, teaching magic is allowed. Ready?"

I didn't ask, didn't give her a choice of what magic, before touching her forehead, funneling knowledge for the simple spell.

Zadie bolted off the bed after the magical blast into her brain. Then, with a giant goofy smile, she lifted a palm and triggered her newly learned spell.

Her smile melted when a glowing ball of golden light appeared in her palm. She tossed the glowing orb at the ceiling, where it stuck and glowed like the magical fireflies.

Apparently, she was less than pleased with her first magical spell. Though she added, "Thank you," she cast it over and over, pummeling me with the glowing orbs that simply popped when hitting me. Then she grumbled, "I might as well be trying to batter you by blowing bubbles."

I stood, but she quickly wrapped her arms around my waist and squeezed. "Thank you. Good night, Death."

Chapter Eighteen

From outside the cottage, where white sand glittered tangerine and gold, Death called, "Is the ferret feral again? I heard it hiss, saw it running off with an arched back."

Standing under my magical golden light orbs in the cottage, I sniffled. While fighting tears, I stared at the most hideously ugly yak sweater ever knitted—despite trying to make it classy! The arms were not even the same length. Yippee hissed at it and ran.

Yes, initially, I wanted to attack Death's vanity. Until he helped me resolve the Lilith issue. To insist upon him wearing it, repayment for landing on Lilith's radar. But after his plan to find the blacksmith and acquire demon blades—he was working on a solution. His hand-painted tattoos worked as a temporary fix. Then the fact he did not read the book, merely curious if I would share it with him. After two months of training, he deserved something elegant, not this mishappen monstrosity.

I crammed it under the pillow and blanket, leaving the cottage as Death asked, "Did you hear me?"

Since my best-knitted version of the sweater was disaster enough to scare ferrets, I admitted, "Yippee is fine."

I couldn't give him the ugliest sweater ever created, so I presented him with the next best thing I had to offer. "You'll tire when fighting all those Fallen. I know a guy who sells—what he calls—potions, elixirs, and teas. He was my dad's friend, a chemist before the world ended. Maybe I'll see if he's interested in finding a way to regenerate magic or stamina. If it's doable… it's not candles, not soap. Magic cheese! From Chuckles! For the chaos war!"

Death held up one finger and pivoted a few steps away as if

I didn't hear his huff of laughter. A blindingly bright, gorgeous smile replaced his usually controlled expression when he turned around. "We can look into alchemy if you wish, though eating magical cheese is asking a lot from an angel who doesn't need sustenance."

"Hmph. I can't promise bacon-flavored, but you'll see. Yak cheese will save the day! Maybe for your uber pale horse, too! Carrots aren't helping him. Let's find Keith, the chemist. Next stop, Seattle."

"Ah, you meant immediately." He flicked one finger my way, his other hand holding a henna bowl and his feather. "It's been seven days."

I'd sworn off sand-scrubbing. The reapplications of the tattoos were nearly intolerable. Not every ten days but once a week; he insisted on being on the safe side. And it was all on me, as inappropriate as it could get with a hands-off hero—one with an entire book devoted to him. My *teammate.* Lilith hadn't found me again as we trained. When she tried to hone in on Death, he sensed her, and we left before she arrived.

This would be the ninth time he reapplied all four. Every time seemed a little worse, trying to disregard his finger tracing my flesh. Followed by the whisper-soft wetness of his silver feather applying henna. I'd come out of my skin the next time he blew on it.

Mind blank, I parroted him, "Ah, you meant immediately."

"I'll take you after this. Tomorrow the triplets turn three and their birthday party. We could leave afterward without mentioning it. That way, the family is not thrown off-kilter by the news; it's not like my holy angel brothers can come along. Or, more training is never an unwise move; then we'd clue them in before we go. I'm in no hurry to end the world."

We were really doing it, venturing into hell, then its basement for the blacksmith.

Death added, "You've worked hard every day; better than my sanguine hopes. Huh. There, I used your word for today. You can sense the unholy and control your shift, which makes you invulnerable. That combined with the healing and protection runes…you are ready, Zadie."

And the scenarios started spinning, the what-ifs of something going wrong. Like touching Death… contact would undo his incorporeal form. Then his flesh would melt off!

"Hey," Death moved close enough to rub his thumb over my cheek. "If ever a time comes when I die, like in the chaos war, it is nothing more than sleeping and waking. I'm immortal; I'll return."

My emotions, out of whack since finishing his sweater, took over. I speed-retreated, struck mute, all but snatching the dull-witted award out of the air. Two months ago, I wanted to figure out how to control shifting. Now I could. But I wasn't in emotional turmoil during those exercises. It would be much safer for Death if I made the trip with Hades.

Right now, shadows streamed off me, waving like long banners. My body flickered, shifting, smoke replacing my physical form. I wasn't trying to transform, I was trying *not* to, but now I couldn't exit my shapeshift!

Thump. Thump. Thump.

Although I darted to the privacy of the cliff, Death stalked after me while his scythe thudded. He spoke before I saw him, only not aloud. *Why are your thoughts spinning too fast to grab one?*

In control of neither my emotions nor the gifted power, I jumped from ledge to ledge, dropping farther than my bones could have handled. Basically, I was impervious to everything like this. I assuredly didn't want Death to realize I was this out of control. We were about to leave for the underworld!

He'd taught me to stay shifted for hours, easier than multi-shifting in and out, which exhausted my stamina. Still, this loss of all physical sensation surpassed bizarreness. The disconnectedness of it all. Was it like this for Death when he shifted, able to feel nothing? And I'd suggested he stay like that always to save the world!

Death didn't take the hint after not answering him. Instead, he flew to land by the waves, where I finally stopped on the island's backside. Oh great, he had that look on his devastatingly handsome face again, arrogant, the oh so vain angel's—

"What is resting bitch face?" Death interrupted my thoughts, picking them up as if I spoke.

"Your face right now."

Thud. Thud. The razor edge of his shiny curved sickle glittered with otherworldly light. Death unsummoned his scythe.

I sniffled, wishing my emotions were impossible to feel in my smoke and shadow body.

Death stepped in closer; heat and strength surrounded me. His large hands rested on my shoulders. He was the only thing I could feel as a smoke monster—a destroying angel. His beautifully sculpted face lifted to the sun. Nevertheless, I couldn't sense the sun or the sea breeze that lifted his long black hair.

When his gaze lowered to me, his green eyes darkened, pupils dilated, mouth parting. His smoldering gaze raked down my shadowy body. "Emotions are a powder keg when mixed with magic. I saw it firsthand with Ashi and Serenity. But, thus far, I hadn't seen you mix the two."

His large hands smoothed down my arms and back up. He was returning sensation wherever he touched me as he queried, "Why are you upset, emotions spiraling?"

His hands shifted around my waist, stroking up my spine and into my hair. Then, bending, his soft lips brushed my neck before murmuring against my throat. "I sensed it before you stepped out of the cottage."

I shivered, slowly shifting away from smoke and shadow where his fingers and lips roamed.

Death lifted his lips from my neck, over my ear, his thumb stroking my cheek. If he meant to help me shift, he succeeded. His groan was inaudible, but it flitted from his mind to mine. *Ugh. My territorial male is waking.* Yet he whispered, "Tell your teammate."

Fine. I exposed the ugly truth. "I knitted you a sweater with yak yarn. At first, it was supposed to be the king contender for an ugly sweater contest. Wearing it would be the least you could do as repayment for Lilith noticing me. But then…after everything you've done, I wanted it to be classy, masculine, worthy of you." I sniffled again. "Yippee hissed at it and ran. It's that bad!"

"Pfft. Is that all? Give it to me. I'll wear it for the birthday party with our entire family. See how easy that was?"

I laughed; no way he would. Yet it was kind to call everyone *our* family. They acted like it when I joined his team, so what was the difference with bonded? Marriage. Sex.

Moving on, feeling better, I said, "Thank you. My tattoos are fine. Let's visit the chemist, then wait until bedtime for the henna. There's a way to replenish what is lost when fighting; I know it will work like I knew I would one day have a yak."

The image in his mind slid into my temple. It flashed and was gone, but…? "Death? What was that flash of your fingers pointing from your forehead?"

He summoned his scythe. With his shield in place, he tapped his temple. "Show me. I'll take us now."

I bit my lower lip, contemplating how to tell him. Although the chemist valued knowledge above all else, Keith had hippy-like standards.

"What?"

"You have to be cool."

"I am always cool."

"Put away your scythe. That's the wrong impression to give the chemist. Keith will think you're a villain and won't do business."

He grunted. *Death is a villain.*

I propped my fists on my hips. "If you insist upon looking like the head of the angel mafia—"

"Like a dangerous horseman?"

That was the first time I had associated 'dangerous' with my family hero. Pfft. I agreed with that about as much as I believed he was a scary villain. Not at all. "Let me do the talking. Just stand there and be your awesome self, living your best life."

Closing my eyes, I pictured where the chemist lived, envisioning outside the underground bunker's locked door.

Except when we stepped through the magical doorway, the bunker door stood open.

A burly guy, looking like an old hippie, rounded the corner; sky blue eyes widened. Keith blinked at me. "What kind of voodoo allowed you to appear like that? That was nothing I taught the communal child needing parents."

"If you for real had blood samples containing magic—"

"You've never been a bullshitter; you had me at for real."

Although Keith waved me inside, he smirked and lifted one pale brow. "Password?"

"Sanguine."

"Not bad." Keith noticed Death. "Who's that?"

"My teammate, the Angel of Death." Then I thumbed toward the overly tall Scandinavian with a long ponytail. "That's Keith."

Keith gaped at Death.

I pulled out my notes. Basically, a wish list to incorporate magical potions into yak cheese because this guy was a genius; fond of me because he was close with my dad. Then I waited for him to pull several vials of my blood.

Afterward, I added, "We'll be back in…?" I didn't know how long for a trip to hell, then beyond to spelunk its basement, find the blacksmith, then smuggle out him and supplies.

Death nodded. "A week."

Keith shook his head, blue eyes bright. "Magic?" He grinned. "I have sanguine expectations. Thanks for thinking of me, Zadie."

And just that fast, Keith was off, exuberant with possibilities.

I grinned at Death and moseyed into a knee-high meadow. After he joined me, I whispered, "Thank you. Very cool."

Lifting my index finger, I added, "One more stop. My sinkhole home. I have gold. I doubt anyone else ventured into it."

"You don't need gold."

"I do. Suppose we leave after the party? Now or never. I will pay my own toll to the ferryman. It's in the book! Charon never forgets."

"I will never be far from you, but I cannot touch you. Or vice versa. You aren't going in to fight. It's more like passing through less populated hellscapes. No fighting. It's full of the dead and demons, so shift and drift. Perhaps float. Worst case, trigger a rune with blood if you need additional protection or healing. We aren't marching down hell's main street; we pass undetected through the alleys."

While apex predator scented?

With that, Death's silver wings flared fully extended. A steely band of muscle hooked onto my waist, flying through the portal to the sinkhole's floor. The base had widened, eaten the area where I used to live; it was no longer there. The stone walls and metal tub were now sinkhole fodder. Like my soap-making supplies, the box was buried under a building that dropped from the street above. It was how a beam cracked Death's skull.

Yet he found it! The metal box with gold! I was so relieved and thankful that I tipped onto my toes and brushed a kiss across his cheek. "Thank you!"

Ice, that was what I saw in his green eyes. Like he was frozen in place.

Patting the dented metal box, I grinned. "Let's shop. What are we getting the triplets for birthday presents?"

Since Death still had not unfrozen, I covered the uncomfortable scene for him by gasping. "Oh! You didn't think about presents! *Bad uncle.*"

He blinked at me when I hooked one arm through his. "I know just the spot. She makes bouncy horses!"

Chapter Nineteen

Death

We no sooner parked three bouncy horses and walked into her cottage than I breathed horseman power to slide down her jeans. Now disappeared.

"Eek!" Zadie shrieked. "I wasn't ready!" She huffed. *Too late now.* Then she plopped on her stomach in the middle of the small bed.

Knowing the color of her panties and seeing them on her were two different things. I'd seen six of seven on Zadie the last eight times I'd reapplied the rune markings. These were so skimpy! Was this why she never wore them in front of me? A scant triangle with red and pink roses in front; otherwise held together with purple lace.

I settled on the floor beside her hip; as far as she knew, I didn't care about flesh. But those panties exposed her entire derriere. Her honey and sweat pea scent intensified as my finger started the path my feather would follow. My tracing finger didn't need her little sounds and shivers to encourage how much I wanted to veer off the lines to her exposed backside.

We were not falling into the mate trap! I decided to put her to sleep after settling up the last of today's business. "You need a good sleep if we leave tomorrow night after the triplet's birthday party."

Her sigh sounded almost relieved. "Deep sleep before breaking into hell sounds good. I'm ready."

"First, hand over the sweater, so I'll have it to wear like I promised."

"Oh, Death, no. It scared Yippee. And he is best friends with a yak!"

"Did you make it for me?" At her nod, I said, "Thank you. No one has done that before."

"You don't have to wear it." She rolled to sit, reached under the blanket and pillow, then handed the sweater to me. Zadie blinked big bright eyes, shiny with unshed tears, before a long dark curtain of spirally curls hid her face.

She must really hate me. It was no more artistic than her caveman painting. "It's...." As angels couldn't lie, I waited for something kind to say, something true, to fill in the blank. Yet nothing did, so I added, "Made from Chuckles' fur."

"Yeah." Zadie lifted her head slightly, peeking from under her hair. She'd never looked this vulnerable. Then green eyes blinked, no longer glassy, her vulnerability hidden again.

The territorial male in me surged; she was mine to protect. That surge was enough to repeat what she had done earlier. I leaned over, lightly kissing her cheek. "Thank you, beautiful."

Her sharp intake of breath forced my muscles to flex. Her thought of *forbidden* sounded as breathless as if spoken aloud. *Move away from the family hero.*

She stretched out, stomach down. "Good night; now, please?"

"Good night." *Sleep!*

The trip to hell and below couldn't come fast enough. I would feel nothing after shifting. The territorial male she awakened in me would go dormant.

I wasted no time reapplying her runes, yet then, in contrast, I dawdled to keep touching her. Finally, after rolling her, painting over the intricacies of the rune on her abdomen, I had no doubt she was safe from Lilith on the upcoming journey.

After pulling the threadbare quilt over her, I stared at her while thinking about us leaving tomorrow. If Zadie were anyone else, I'd not contemplate taking them on my quest. My Zadie wasn't a frail little flower needing to hide behind me. I believed she was capable of standing by my side during this journey.

She didn't need to fight; she'd mastered sensing the unholy and shifting to invulnerable when around wicked souls. I knew she would be fine between that and the protection and healing runes.

Famine waited for me to join him, then he pointed toward the bouncy horse presents for the kids. "That is kind. Thank you. Zadie's idea?"

"Her gold, too." As we walked the mountain path, I nodded toward the latest risen ship floating under an alabaster moon. "How long has Morningstar been waiting out there?"

"Lucifer comes and goes. He guaranteed that you would be on his side in the chaos war. Yet he hasn't come straight at you since his corrupted keeper plan failed." Long dark curls shaking, my brother muttered, "You better work on making Zadie immortal."

"We're not mating. We're teammates. It works."

"Brother," Famine sighed. Then he lifted his index fingers to his forehead like horns. "You are long gone. Honestly, the tongue lolling? I pull up the image when I need a laugh. How did your reapers take it?" But he shoulder-bumped me. "She is good for you."

"I'll be back for the party; I need to visit my realm and make changes to accommodate Zadie's human needs. Join me? You can ensure I don't forget anything."

"Sure." He followed me through the portal. "The Fallen's prophecy cloak is officially aggressive in stalking Ashi now."

I nodded. "Like you, I destroy it daily, though it comes back faster. Fortunately, it can't attach to Kobayashi Maru, or it would have done so years ago."

After completing the first additions to my realm since I created it, I nodded. "If ever she needs to be here, it's ready."

Famine crossed his arms over his chest. "You won't do something stupid like War did, locking Serenity in a tower?"

"This is completely different...a realm."

He snorted. "If the territorial male in you is not awake yet...?" Famine pointed past the doorless entrance to the genuinely ginormous bed. "It soon will burst out of you."

"We are not falling into the mate trap. You know I will split, so which part was she mated to? The one separated from her? Suppose it's not, but who I am after dividing won't be the same me I am right now. Either way would hurt a mate. You know there's no recovering from losing a mate."

Pulling his gaze from the glittering reaper-filled sky, solemn gray eyes turned my way. "It won't happen until the very end, final judgment. Meaning that once she's in heaven, there will be no pain and sadness, no losing your mind caused by losing a mate. Could be...you are trying to protect the part of you that will forever be parted from her?"

His lips tipped up on one side. "Think about that. Let's get back; the triplets will wake soon."

I entered Zadie's cottage, pulled off my black t-shirt, and dropped it on her bed. Then I pulled on the mostly white sweater, streaked with black and some gray, where she mixed the black and white fur into yarn.

My brothers would view me wearing this yak sweater in the same light as running in circles, tongue lolling, and finger forehead horns. But her knitted creation was silky soft, likely warm, not like temperatures affected angels. And when I pushed the sleeves to my elbows, it fixed the different arm lengths. It was actually comfortable. She had meant to be kind instead of a hate display.

The sun would rise soon, and so too would Zadie. She'd know I wore the sweater she worked so hard and long on, having left my t-shirt.

The sky lightened to periwinkle as I sauntered toward the beach's snowy portion to see if the sweater would make the ferret hiss again. Yep, Yippee hissed and ran away with an arched back.

Famine came up behind me. "Ha! Ha! Ha! Is she trying to knock your vanity down a few stories?"

"She knitted it. Chuckles' fur into yarn. An efficient pet. Also, supplies a base for candles and soap. I can't wait to see what Zadie does with magical cheese."

Famine grinned. "Magical cheese? You haven't been this optimistic since Mesopotamia."

I laughed. "That was the poppy fields. I have not ridden through them again."

The rising sun blushed with a pink glow, climbing and stretching its golden arms to greet the day.

A portal spun open; Pestilence, Ashi, Zed, and Zoe joined us.

Ashi immediately laughed, pointing. "Baby horses for horseman babies." She said nothing about my sweater, acting like it was my everyday attire. "Cute! Zadie?"

I nodded. Kobayashi Maru's cobalt eyes glowed with supernatural power as brightly as when she had been struck with the fated role. She slipped on her shades, a relic treasure, mirrored sunglasses hiding those eyes. The chaos rolling over the planet, seeding more chaos, fed her magic, never shutting off.

Zadie rounded the path, letting everyone know her word for today. "Let the jollification begin!" Her smile grew more substantial when she spotted me in the sweater.

I, in turn, smiled because she wore the black t-shirt I had left on her bed. It swallowed her. Hmph. The last time she took my shirt, she claimed it smelled.

My smile never wavered as I watched Zadie with my family. "That's some jollification," I uttered within her hearing. Pestilence's crew of four. Serenity and War. Of course, Bram. Famine and Eden, as well as the little stars, three-year-old triplets. It was the right thing not to tell them we were leaving. Instead, I enjoyed how happy and relaxed everyone was; besides, it wasn't like my brothers could come along.

That night, I waited with one shoulder leaning against the cottage doorframe. I'd asked Zadie to wear jeans, but who knew what all was in that backpack? It wasn't until she returned from the snowy beach section, holding two sets of foil-wrapped apex predator stench, that I groaned.

"Leave your sweater on my bed. You totally rocked it. Hella cool to wear it. Gotta say, your kindness is more potent than your vanity. Thank you."

I might have hoped she wanted me shirtless if we weren't leaving. Still, I left the sweater on her bed, then grinned and pointed at the black t-shirt she was wearing, the one I left when

I changed.

Zadie winked, then unwrapped highly toxic-smelling foil packages. "I'm returning the t-shirt I borrowed; yes, to mask your angel scent. Holiness? In hell? Yeah, no. You said hellhounds are a real thing, so…?"

She pulled out the one she was wearing when T-Rex bones urinated on it, nearly strong enough to make my eyes water, saying, "Turn around so I can change."

Exiting the cottage with her stink shirt and backpack on, holding one foil package, she nodded. "Let's save the world."

I ushered her through the dimensional portal while no one was around. The massive rock-maze underground smelled damp; it would look utterly black for Zadie.

She blew a steadying breath into the dank, dark cavern. I reached for her hand but spoke into her mind. *Cast your light spell.* I didn't need it, but she did. *It's holy light, to be specific.*

After she did, I pointed toward an intersection of four stone tunnels, where the Fallen's painted art featured the prophecy cloak and a redheaded Nephilim. "Allegedly Ashi, but all four paintings show from the back of the cloak, long red hair blowing from the hood. What the person is staring at beyond are the chains, which bind two mountains, exploding open, setting the Fallen free from Sheol."

Zadie shivered. "This is a creepy place."

"This was once the locked underground lair of Gogmagog, the demon-spawn giant who snatched Ashi. The demon opened the doorway, but my brother ended him before the foul creature could escape. That's how I know about it. Pestilence nearly melted his hand and forearm when he reached into the demon's doorway to hell." I shrugged. "The charm he retrieved broke the spell on Ashi."

Zadie pointed toward the shimmering magical doorway to the underworld. "I, uh, sort of, kind of, told Eden. Not yet, but she will find the note I left for her. Someone needs to take care of Chuckles for a week! I imagine she will tell all of them."

She gazed at the glimmering doorway, gloomy for the short

distance visible on the other side. Zadie's mental image hit me when distant screams escaped the portal. Her mind confetti blew out the back of her ponytail, followed by facing-melting scenarios spinning in her head.

I pulled one long, soft corkscrew. "We covered this." She stopped spinning unwinnable situations after I released the spring to pop back in place. "There are other doorways and exits when you need sleep. Food. Other demon lairs; at least Lilith was good for that, describing hell. She believed I'd never see it since entering is deadly to holy angels. Mostly, you'll ghost along with me, going around them until we reach Charon, then Tartarus."

Zadie unwrapped the foil to retrieve the black t-shirt she'd borrowed. After she lifted it my way, the darker circle of green in her eyes darkened. Great. Her stubborn streak. "I insist. It will, by default, urge all kinds of nasties not to come too near us. No, if they approach us? They'll catch a big sniffy whiff of an apex predator, then tuck tails and run. Look for easier prey."

As foul as it was, her plan was sound. Hellhounds were no joke. And I hadn't told her about hellcats. "And what do I get if I do this to appease you…?" I braced my arm against the stone, lifting one eyebrow. I believe she previously dared to call it my resting bitch face.

"I know it's worse than the sweater, so what do you want, Death?"

"Phew! It's a big ask. Unlike when you shift, my sense of smell stays intact." Currently shirtless, I had been reasonably sure she would insist upon it. After all, she sought out and saved predator deterrent.

I pulled on the foul-smelling dry shirt, then leaned in. Bracing my hands against the damp stone on either side of her shoulders, I bent until my lips nearly touched hers. "I want this."

Zadie lifted on her toes, arms sliding around my neck, her soft lips brushed lightly against mine.

Cupping her cheeks, I whispered against her mouth. "You are mine."

By her next blink, I zoomed meters ahead of her and nodded.

Then, summoning my scythe, I exhaled and shifted. Instantly, the wanting, the spinning of my mind, the spinning of my newly found emotions…all stilled. I felt nothing, shimmery, nearly transparent. And. Oh. So. Powerful! Like god-mode.

"Come. Talk with your mind until we exit again. You can do this, Zadie. I believe in you." I couldn't take her hand, couldn't touch her at all. Or her me, so I walked into the shimmering doorway where wails keened in the fast wind.

Thankfully, the woman with moxie shifted, then stepped out into the gloom behind me. *Here we go.*

The red dust storm ahead ate into the horizon, yet the pull of vileness seemed to come from all around us. We stopped behind a monolith, stained copper in the surreal light, studying the rocky desert in front of us. No unholy souls were near this border. *It looks clear to proceed.*

However, Zadie shrieked. Her eyes rounded as if with horror. She confirmed it when her agonized whisper flowed into my mind. *All those dead yaks! What happened? Oh, this is too sad!*

Yet nothing existed on the red rocky dust-scape! *There are no yaks. This must be a horror or heartbreak zone. We talked about spinning zones, the rotating of hell's prison to torture unholy souls. Come. Let's get you out of this zone.*

Chapter Twenty

Zadie

"Whoa, partner!" Death whispered. *Open your eyes.*

Shifted into smoky shadows, I was neither thirsty nor roasting, gliding behind Death. I almost bumped into him, eyes closed past all the dead yaks he said weren't littering the barren pumpkin-stained wasteland.

The intermingled wailing of male and female unholy souls sounded from every direction, always someone screaming, hell's opera. No one in sight. On the other side of the red dust storm, the rocky desert gave way to a river that looked like lava, stretching as far as I could see in the scarlet sky.

Death shimmered beside me; if he were any more translucent, he'd be transparent. Then I'd see the lava through his ghostly form.

I winked. *If only I could fly. But you decided females could perhaps work up to a float.* Then I shrugged. *Honestly, I wish I could float over that hell lava.*

We'll go around. Death pointed in the opposite direction, moving that way. *Not toward the city gates.*

He'd warned me about hell's vastness; it was huge and filled with different torture zones. The torment sectors spun like a spinner on a board game, except beneath prisoners, rotating them from one form of punishment to another without needing to physically move them. Of course, the misery zones didn't affect the angel horseman. Still, I hoped we didn't run into any more agonizing dead yak areas. The endless screams were abysmal enough.

A raisin-tinted cloud drifted like dark fog to encompass this side of the lava river. If it were windy or wet, I wouldn't know as I had no physical sensations. The same as Death. It's why I couldn't touch him in here. He'd melt.

The cloud grew darker, blocking screams, thicker fog, easy to hide. Yet I sniffled. Suddenly overcome by deep remorse, my sniffle turned into a sob.

What is happening with you? He pivoted my way.

I am so sorry I knitted you that sweater. I tried to make it classy like you, but it was spectacularly hideous—better than I could have hoped for when I wanted it to be. And you wore it. Another sob escaped. *There is no way you still think I'm kind?*

Death waved for me to follow out of the cloud. *It's another zone. You have no reason to feel remorseful.*

As soon as we passed through the dark fog into a pink blushing sky, my remorse faded. Death could feel nothing, not so much as an emotion. He'd warned me about how he would seem different because of it.

Lopsided obsidian dwellings dotted the sienna-stained ground. In the distance, the lava river funneled through a massive macabre bone mouth. Molten lava streamed through a colossal dragon skull, jaw wide open, magma not orange but blood red.

Hellmouth. Death supplied. *The damned drop into it from the sky. Morningstar moves them to different prisons every thousand years.*

An unearthly howl rose from a rock-hewn building ahead. Shiver-worthy! Seconds later, it was joined by other menacing yowls.

Death pointed to a narrow alleyway. *Shifted or not, the hellhounds are howling like dogs when I enter a city. Get behind the buildings. Keep to the shadows.*

Shadowing him, only this time as an actual smoky shadow, we slid between the slummy buildings. Thankfully, I couldn't smell the dark rubble-filled alleys. The unseen hellhounds closing in suddenly whimpered, some yelping. Then their barks grew farther away. They ran!

I smiled and pumped one fist. *See! Apex predator. It worked!*

As we weaved like phantoms passing through one alleyway to the next, I caught a flash of burnt orange above the buildings. Batlike wings? *Did you see that?*

Hit it with your bubble of holy light. Then you won't think it is so worthless.

Yet when I slowed to summon it, Death growled. *I meant if you wanted to play with one imp, not four. Let's move. We'll stop after we pass this hub town.*

I gasped, stopping again. Maybe I was a smoke monster wearing apex deterrent, but hopefully not too scary. I moved closer. Hell or not, that was *the* cutest puppy I'd ever seen! Oh, blue-gray, huge paws for a pup; he would be a big boy someday. A good-sized buddy for Chuckles. But he was terrified of us!

No making a pet of a hellhound. Death stopped, going unnaturally still. He'd admitted he could smell in his shifted form. But my guess was completely wrong; it wasn't supernatural sniffing but his preternatural hearing. *Let's go. The chatty demons moved on.*

By remaining shifted, nothing could harm me. I didn't know if hell were hot or not. Though it may look like my smoky shadow body glided or hovered, it required leg muscles as if we had been moving at a run.

Death veered away from the lava and town, leading toward a landscape of smoldering black trees. It appeared as if an inferno swept through.

Again, I caught a flash of batlike wings. Now out of the town and into the smoldering hellscape, I saw the winged monster circle back around. I pivoted, using the spell he taught me.

The dark gray imp with orange wings hovered. It couldn't see us until I cast my spell and threw a softball-sized, glowing golden orb. Then I squealed with delight. Holy balls! It splatted like a water balloon, bursting sacred light liquid onto the evil darkness. The creature crashed, dead before landing, and melted away like peroxide bubbling down Halloween's colors.

Hmph. Thank you, Death.

What would you think about calling me…Thanatos?

Like in the book?

You tell me. I haven't seen it.

Why?

Then he pointed toward the ember forest of death. *We'll stop there. Time moves differently here, dragging out prisoners' agony. It's been a complete human day; we haven't stopped. I will go through the doorway first to see if the demon lair is occupied.*

Although the yellow-green glow of his eyes was now the brightest part of him, I still recognized that authoritative expression in his shifted form. At least he didn't say 'stay.'

I waited outside the shimmery purple doorway. Why did Death mention Thanatos?

But I didn't have long to ruminate as Death exited. His scythe dripped blue-black blood on the scorched forest floor. Three dark hearts decorated its arch. He tilted his head. *Come.*

Yet I no sooner entered the dimly lit room, a library with yellow couches, than Death spoke. "Shift. Eat. Drink. Rest."

Three slate gray demons slowly bubbled away to goop in the far reading section, as disgusting as the demon hearts skewered on Death's scythe. But, he added, "I'll watch out for you."

Shifting, my tired legs clumsily galumphed before I collapsed into a large blue armchair. "Wow. I am tired."

I dug through my pack for supplies. Knowing Death had no emotions when shifted implied he wouldn't care to explain the name change request. "Why ask about Thanatos?"

Indeed, he didn't pause before answering. "Unlike my angel horsemen brothers, God gave me a name in addition to my purpose. And I believe that will be the part of me that isn't cast into the pit."

"So you'll split in half? Like toddler-sized versions? Or like *pop —*"

"Hero and villain separate."

I shrugged. "Meaning, nothing changes. I've always known. Thanks to a thick leather book. Hero."

After eating a packed sandwich and drinking plenty of water, I pulled out a pen and blank paper. Then I drew a map of where we'd traveled today, something I could clean up later and contribute to the book. Finally, I tucked it into the pack.

Although I wanted to peruse the books on shelves, I lost the battle of heavy eyelids slamming shut after a quick trip to the scroungy toilet. The bare minimum for any possessed human passing by hell. My body, stamina exhausted from the long shift, dropped back in the armchair. I was on the struggle bus, closing my eyes for the ride. Then I whispered, "If that's what you want me to call you, Death, then good night, Thanatos."

Though it seemed like I hovered in a void, cocooned in velvet shadows of deep slumber, it had to be a dream that sent me gasping to wakefulness.

Or perhaps the warning came over the new Team Horseman sense? Death stood nearby, black goo dripping from his scythe—now decorated with ten demon hearts. "We need to leave before more demons visit. There can be no survivors if they see us. We cannot risk them getting word to Lilith or Lucifer. Sooner or later, one of the demons will be missed."

"Even ethereal, you look angeliferous. So don't you think all the hearts trophies are overkill?"

"Not at all." Immediately, he tossed my word for today back at me. "I am always angeliferous. I am Death."

Walking among the book racks, he pointed. "You might like this alchemy book, though I'm sure you will succeed at magical cheese without it."

I tucked the book into my backpack. Although Death stepped outside, I paused, looking at what appeared to be a water fountain. Yeah, I didn't imagine those were common in hell. After it looked the same as regular water, with no smell, I topped off my canteen. Then, I shifted, charging outside behind him into the desolate smoldering forest.

Like yesterday, Death moved fast but not too fast for me to stay close behind him. Also repeating, I nearly rammed into him after we topped a steep hill; he stopped, holding unnaturally still. His stare riveted on the now-visible massive mountain ahead of us.

Dozens of lava rivulets drizzled from thin cracks down the midnight-colored mountainside. Mammoth chains, each link the size of a car, surrounded the mountain. I spotted gaps in every sixth chain link. Not broken, but pulled slightly apart as if the links were failing around the swelling mountain.

What is that?

Death sighed. *That is not good news. The chained mountain over another mountain containing Sheol and the lesser Fallen below. The generations for the Grigori to be bound are nearly ended; they will break out eventually without help from the prophecy cloak wearer.*

The smoldering forest stopped atop a hill. Beyond, the fiery orange glare, like a brilliant spotlight, was almost too bright to behold. Yet it surrounded everything now, including the nearly bursting black mountain.

Onyx-stained cliffs, carved from top to bottom, boasted four distinct sculptures of colossal gargoyles. Small stacked cages, grouped in four separate squares, filled the valley between the enormous figures. Four different overcrowded outdoor prisons? Tiny cells, one person wedged into each pen, lying atop another. I shivered to the accompaniment of hell's opera.

Death rotated his finger to encompass everything around us. *There is no shade to be had. This is a burn zone, another layer of scorching anguish onto the outdoor cages. The smoky shadow of your destroying angel will stand out in the bright light.*

Then he pointed dead ahead toward the lava-leaking, chain-breaking mountain. *There is where we are headed, the fastest path down to reach Charon.* His finger circled again. *These torture sectors are heavily infested with torment demons.*

He was making me nervous.

Don't be nervous, Zadie. I'm alerting you, so you will know what is happening as you go through the zones. Don't stop. Whatever you see or feel, it's not real.

He waved for me to walk beside him. *Keep going if I stop to fight.*

When a wave of anxiousness swept through me, his soothing baritone whispered through Team Horseman telepathy communications. *Nothing can harm me.*

Yeah, except me. I could pull him out of his shift and melt his holy skin off if I touched him.

Within three minutes of entering the fiery orange glare, motorcycle-sized, scaly green cats charged from the prison sectors. One roared like a lion, except fire blasted out of its mouth.

Hellcats! Go! It was a command.

Trust in the predator pee. Go together!

Although a growl rumbled from him, I didn't mistake it for emotion. He had none like this; he felt nothing like the angel who made a deal with Zehra.

Suddenly, shadows around my smoky body whipped longer, lashing at the bright orange spotlight over this land. I growled, true destroying angel power flooding, then overtaking me. Not the dead or the demons, but a living, breathing, unholy soul was near. A human abandoned by a guardian angel. My body pivoted like a compass until the pull was the strongest for a Grigori-possessed person.

Zadie, no!

He, of all people, should understand that it wasn't a choice!

A ginger-haired man ahead, wearing a gray suit, stood with his back toward me beside a stack of cages. A dozen high, each held a single individual lying down, cages smooshing them like they were inside barbeque grill baskets.

A blast of death magic burst from my palm into his throat. I ended his tormenting taunts to the caged woman—her soul's residual appearance.

Yet a humpback creature, tinted eggshell to blend with the seared salt desert, rose from the ground in a dusty swirl. Its body reflected the glaring orange glow overhead, skin sagging and bagging like wrinkles made from sand. Leathery reptilian wings and pointy horns burned with rusty corrosion as it bellowed, "Destroyer!"

Another guttural cry pierced through the anguished screams of the caged damned. "Slayer!"

Death immediately engaged the foes, moving like a blur from one to the next, glinting scythe collecting more hearts before the bodies could fall. His cannot-die-power didn't apply to hell and its minions. Several rust-stained talons made contact with his ghostly body. Not through him like when the man swung through my face, but claws striking him.

As he said, nothing could hurt him. Yet how was it that other hands could touch him without him melting? Even people's fingers jutting from pens brushed him. Why could they touch his wraithlike form but not me?

Gliding, continuing to turn my head to watch him, I faced forward again, only to freeze. The white patio wall from my house in Jerusalem appeared directly in front of me. I jumped back, lifting my hand, which was now filled with a can of neon orange spray paint.

Mom stepped out the patio door, hands on her hips, long black hair swaying as she shook her head. Yet now, the white wall dripped with fresh neon orange like my finger on the spray nozzle. Mom was so mad, *so* disappointed in me.

I dropped the can and swiveled. My pivot landed me in front of the blank white wall with a spray can in hand. Again, I heard Mom call me before the door swung open to a neon orange drawing on the wall.

While I was stuck in a loop of my actions hurting my mom, Death's command roared through telepathy. *Go! It's not real. Keep going.*

I flung the can against the all-in-my-head wall; after it flew through the illusion, I dashed through. Then I sighed shakily, hover running, Death not far behind me. Nothing but demon hearts showed along the curve of his sharp scythe.

After making it past the first outdoor prison, I darted past the next gargantuan gargoyle shaped into the tall onyx cliffs. The burnt orange spotlight blazed so brightly that I shielded my eyes as I ran. Then, with a glance over my shoulder, reassured that he was nearly beside me, I faced forward again.

Yet it wasn't hell; it was one of many hellish nights. Seattle, rain falling in earnest, a dozen men systematically searching for any people living outdoors. Or in common areas…like soup kitchens and shelters.

As one man tossed a bola, I dropped to my knees behind a trash bin. The cord caught my best friend's legs, weights on the ends wrapping around tight. He fell and banged his head, not getting up.

When I cried out, another man ran in my direction. I hastily twirled away from the dumpster to run out of the rain and into the underground. Ahead, a blond man waved me forward. I'd spotted him off and on in the past when experiencing a sketchy moment. He turned on the underground path toward a loosely chained door.

When the trafficker's pounding footfalls followed me, I stepped off the main walkway and squeezed through in pitch blackness. Alone. I covered one hand over my mouth to stifle my breathing, waiting to see if the flesh trader would keep running or turn toward the chained but not fully sealed door.

As my eyes adjusted, I couldn't imagine where the blond had gone. But I noticed an old metal tub, then hid in it. The trafficker made several trips back and forth on the main path, his flashlight passing by repeatedly. Yet he did not veer off to the room that was not open to the public when there had been tours. He glanced my way, but entirely too big to fit through, it didn't dawn on him to break the chains and enter. God was watching out for me.

Zadie, it's not real. Stop shaking and hiding. It's a terror zone. Get up and go. This isn't Seattle; it's hell. Move it.

I shushed him, paralyzed with fear, and scrunched down in the metal tub. *Shh! The trafficker will find me.*

Chapter Twenty-One

Death

Run, Zadie! I couldn't scoop her into my arms, but thanks to Team Horseman, Zadie's terror memory from age eight bloomed in my mind as if it were happening now to me.

Still, she crouched on the desert ground as if hiding in the metal tub within the ebony darkness of an underground room. Her reflection in the smoke showed her trembling, terrified. Mixing emotions and magic was rarely good. She hadn't needed a protection rune for healing, but she would if powerful emotions knocked her out of her shift. If she didn't move before an alarm was raised!

I left a trail of dead demons, melted after cutting out their hearts, but too many not to be missed. *Run through this sector. It's not night. It's bright, and you are a glaringly dark speckle upon the land. I cannot carry you, but I am with you. You can do it; I know it. Come with me now, Zadie.*

Finally, she moved, hover gliding beside me right outside the next prison patch, making our way to the drop chute at the base of the black mountain. Shifted, I thankfully was unable to feel her emotions from that memory. But I had the man's face now; I'd make a point to kill the trafficker.

When I warned her not to attack, I knew she felt a compulsion to heed my words due to Team Horseman. If I could feel emotions in this state, what would be the point of being mad over her memitim power triggering? It was my gift of power; it activated automatically. Yet it resulted in another forty-seven demon hearts on my scythe. Not opportune, considering we still needed to traverse back through hell with supplies and a blacksmith.

There was nowhere in this utter openness to stop for her emotions to settle. Furthermore, the drop from the trapdoor? She absolutely must be shifted to use it *and* survive the landing unscathed.

I reached into the outer pocket of her pack, pulling out a single rune paper. Of course, it wouldn't work without mixing blood with it…and neither of us was in a form capable of being harmed and bleeding. Still, I wanted one handy in case she needed it. *I've got you.* I repeated it like a whispered mantra into her mind.

She shook off the last of her fear. Her thoughts shifted toward crossing the seared salt desert to reach the goal line at the mountain base.

The state of the chains around Sheol, around two mountains, looked no more encouraging up close than when viewed with supernatural sight from a distance. I'd later share the images with my brothers, committing them to memory. Unfortunately, our surface communication link didn't work while I was in the hell dimension.

With the base of my scythe, I bashed the black diamond grate that served as a communication tunnel leading down. It didn't budge. Fastest route; we were sneaking to Charon in hell's basement. *This is it.*

Zadie tore her gaze from the lava drizzles and failing chains to the impossibly narrow chute below. She bent, trying to look through it, but a spiral of rock arms wound around like a broken staircase. I understood why her thought bubbles burst with disbelief again. *That's much smaller than a manhole!*

I nodded. *Not a clear opening; nothing can wedge through the chute. It should never work as a passageway…unless, of course, you squeezed through as smoke. Close your eyes, or your disbelief will kick you out of shift. At the end of this communication tunnel, you will freefall from the cavern ceiling over Styx. And shifted, you won't be injured when you crash land. If I go first, will you follow? Or will something grab hold of you again? Do you wish to go first?*

Zadie blew out a slow breath, her thoughts a mantra of *I can do this.* Then she nodded. *I'm right behind you. I'll count to sixty, then jump with my eyes closed. Otherwise, my brain says I won't fit. Blown-mind confetti will clog the tube.*

Try not to scream. I'd rather not awaken any sleeping Fallen. With that, I dropped through the chute, landing on the outskirts of Hades and the underground mountain, the second mountain that bound Sheol and the lesser Fallen.

Charon waited on the black bone dock. A lantern hung from the front of his unoccupied skiff adorned with white skulls. A child of night and darkness, his black-boned demon form was shrouded by a long cloak pulled to hang over his face, showing only glowing orange eyes. Charon's appearance most closely resembled human simulacrums of me.

"Death!" His voice was the same, like ground glass going down with a draught of vinegar. "What brings you to my domain? And how did a holy angel survive hell? As you know, Hades is not home; he's topside."

A squeak came over mental communications, but Zadie held her silence as she dropped and dropped, landing in a crouch along the dark river's bank. Long shadows whipping from her smoky form blended nicely in this gloomy domain.

If my emotions were not cut off from my shift, I knew I'd be bursting with pride. I knew she could do it!

Yet Charon let out a low growl, his glowing eyes brightening from pumpkin to tiger. "Memitim."

Zadie took in Charon's appearance and the bone-littered land next to the black river; she ignored the menace dripping from the ferryman's tone. Again, my pride would have erupted if I were capable of it as she immediately held one smoky hand toward his skeletal one. "I'm Zadie. It is a pleasure to meet you, Charon!"

No one except his parents would be glad to see Charon; she disarmed him. Those orange eyes widened, then narrowed before he attempted to shake her shadowy hand. "As a destroyer angel, you can float across."

"I wouldn't dream of it!" *Zetta said to pay him; he never forgets.*

She pulled out two gold coins, dropping them into his black

bony hand. *Do you trust him if I were to mention the blacksmith and supplies for the way back?*

No.

She pulled out three more gold coins, explaining, "Here's an advance for the return trip; please and thank you. And a tip."

Yet Charon flicked one black bony finger toward her. "You must each remove those shirts; the stench would seep into my skiff."

Although only his orange glowing eyes were visible, I was sure I'd see his leer if more of his face showed. *If* my emotions worked, I'd growl. Charon was not holy; he definitely noticed flesh.

Zadie appeared much less enthusiastic, but she didn't show the panic swirling in her mind as she stripped the t-shirt over her head and dropped it on the shore. Then, after slipping on a shirt from her backpack, she added another two coins to his palm. "Save them for us. We'll need them going back."

She was likely the first to ever tip the ferryman.

Charon stepped down into his skiff, midnight skeletal hand waving Zadie into his boat. Once we sat, the green-glowing lantern flickered brighter, hanging from the mouth of a giant's skull. Charon dipped his oar into the turbulent black water, asking, "Where to?"

"Bottom level," I said with authority. "Take Styx to Acheron. We need transport to the lower world below Hades."

His gasp sounded like he had swallowed another bucket of glass. Zadie had so disarmed him, apparently very different from Zetta, that the ferryman had accepted payment before asking our destination. Charon was bound to comply. Only Zadie, no one else, could have handled him better.

Zadie broke the silence. "Do you wait at the shore for our return trip?"

"Whisper for me from the shore; I will appear." Charon pushed his oar to steer around vortexes within the infernal river; the gray swirl filled with ancient Greek souls too poor to pay the ferryman. Stuck, they never left Styx. So this was where they spent their time in Hades, awaiting the very end.

The sight sent Zadie into picturing blown-mind confetti, but Charon continued. "No one has paid in advance for a return trip. But, I will come if you survive and call for me."

Although I didn't trust Charon—only a fool would—I wasn't concerned about him blabbing to Lucifer. They were not friends, each player hoarding their own power. Hades, who wanted more authority than Satan, was topside, so Charon had no way to contact him.

The currents grew swifter, more turbulent. Then, dead ahead, the churning Styx intersected the river of misery—Acheron.

"Who is that?" Zadie whispered after spying the nearly petrified woman on the bone-littered shore.

"The oracle of the dead," the ferryman replied.

She shivered, still smoke and shadow, but unsettled; her gaze stuck on the verdant luminance from a small tree-bodied woman.

Charon angled the boat into an offshoot of Acheron. Not fast-flowing, but a bubbling swamp. He laughed wildly. "Going down."

The skiff spun slowly as a dimensional doorway opened beneath us.

I've got you. I repeated into Zadie's mind before and after the bottom opened under us. The skiff spun and fell.

The impervious boat landed in a hellfire lake deep in an abyss. One similar to where I would dwell after final judgment. Even in god-like mode, the oppression was nearly crushing as we neared the entrance to hell's basement, where the Titans and most wicked monsters were banished and imprisoned. It was here where Lilith's endless pit of information stopped. From here, it was only what I'd been told by Michael so long ago after helping imprison the Titans.

Charon escorted Zadie onto the rock dock. "Call for me. I'm rooting for you, Zadie."

As soon as I joined her, I inclined my head so she would follow. Charon didn't know how to open the dungeon under Hades—

Tartarus, the bottom-most level of hell. We most assuredly were not showing him. We disappeared into a dense forest composed of sharp stone hedges grown into a maze, trees as tall as the cavern.

After the whoosh of Charon's gateway closing, I praised her. *I'm proud of you, my Zadie. We will stop for you to rest before proceeding.*

In the next instant, the ground slightly thudded. Not my scythe, but footfalls. I hadn't warned Zadie about the beast winding through the stone forest maze. *Roar! Hiss! Bleat!*

Chimera, I supplied as the beast came into view. A black lion body the size of an elephant, a long black anaconda tail whipping and hissing, and a massive bleating goat's head centered on its back. The lion's face, surrounded by a shaggy mane, opened to release another mighty roar.

Seeing it was one shock too many as Zadie's smoky body shimmered, shadows around her lessening like she might shift. Yet she held out both cupped palms, double casting the golden light bubbles. Holy light. Perfect for fighting this beast. Which she wouldn't need to do if she stayed shifted.

Throw them, then run through the trees beside me. Don't lose your shift, or the razor-sharp thorns will shred you.

No pressure! She tossed the holy orbs, then ran beside me, phasing through solid mass. The colossal chimera's bulky figure could not cut through.

We stopped at the base of a dark cliff serving as a dungeon wall for Tartarus. Intricately carved markings adorned every section, rune symbols slightly pulsing with an orange-gold light. From here on, I knew only what Michael had long ago confided. An angel entered his name as the password. It would open for the worthy. Wielding my scythe, I hit the correct sequence of runes with holy light.

A vertical crack in the air settled against the wall, stone sliding open like elevator doors. As we passed, sconces flared with blue fire. No comforts in this large stone room, no ledges, no chairs, nothing angels fighting Titans had needed.

Immediately shifting, Zadie shoved the backpack off her shoulders. She dropped to the stone floor, then fished out her canteen.

While she drank deeply, I dropped telepathy. "Are you alright?"

"Yep." She pulled out her map and updated it.

A big silly smile spread across her oval face when she tucked away her supplies. "How come others can touch you, and you don't melt?"

Suddenly she stood, coming closer but not touching me. Then, she lurched to the side, quickstepped beside me, and giggled. Yes, something was definitely wrong.

"You topped off your canteen in the library, didn't you?" At her grin, I growled. "Demon water is like high-octane *moonshine* to humans."

She inhaled deeply, following my retreat. "Why can't I touch you, but everyone else can?"

I lifted both hands, running out of room to back up unless I walked in circles. "Because your touch alone changes me, transforming me to corporeal."

"Why?" She stopped, swaying in front of me before her legs gave out to seat her. It should not be much longer before she passed out.

"Because you, Zadie Grace, are meant to be my mate."

Her wide green eyes fluttered shut. *Mate* bounced around in her brain as sleep claimed her.

Chapter Twenty-Two

Zadie

"**G**ood morning, beautiful," Death said with a smile when my eyes opened. He sat leaning against the dark stone wall, still wraithlike in the flickering blue torchlight, long legs stretched out and crossed at the ankle. Still with no shirt, thanks to the predator deterrent versions waiting on the Styx riverbank. Long hair swayed as he nodded. "Congratulations for delving deeper than any human has gone before you."

If he hoped I would be slow-witted upon waking, he had another thing coming. "Mate? That was not mentioned when I joined the team! I specified nothing involving blood like for an angel marriage."

"There won't be. It's a trap we won't fall into; meant to be mates and actually being them are two very different things. And being teammates works for us, right?"

I sighed, nodded, and sat, head pounding from my spiked canteen. Although parched and thirstier than last night, I didn't dip into the moonshine.

Shirtless and chiseled, seemingly relaxed, Death's glowing yellow-green eyes stared directly at me. "I killed the chimera while you slept. Get ready."

I shifted, joining Death outside in the stone forest maze. *How are you holding up shifted? Still no emotions?*

A bronzish haze stained the air. Tall, dark gray, razor-sharp rock trees served as maze walls, shot through with large charcoal thorns.

Death followed the path, not cutting directly through like last night. He shrugged one broad shoulder, his translucence otherworldly. *The detachment is welcomed here, unlike on the surface, where I know I miss the feel of the wind and the sun. Morningstar wants me to covet the excessive power, so it corrupts me as Death. That refusing to give up the power causes me to fall. Otherwise, I'd consider your solution; stay shifted to avoid reaping a fourth of souls.*

Perhaps he picked up my accelerated heartbeat or my hopeful thoughts that he might be able to stop the world's end because he grunted. *But, not feeling anything would further the detachment from Thanatos until, eventually, I'd drift far away from Bram, my brothers, and my entire family. Back to how I was when I was first sent here. Like I was when I knew Zehra.*

Zehra wrote that she prayed for the last Grace to find the man behind the angel. Back then, he doubtfully had the humanlike body nuances and inflected tones down to a fine art. Now he played the part, but I could sense that he was far away, cut off from everything. Was that utterly emotionless part of him Death?

Suddenly, he accelerated and plowed through the stone forest, phasing through the trees. *To prepare you...one of the worst anguishes for angels is to be cut off from the light. We don't fear darkness, for we can see fine and far in the dark. But the complete absence of light would be an endless torment. So expect Tartarus to be a gloomy dungeon dimension—perfect for your shifted smoke and shadows.*

It might be perfect, but it sounds dreadful.

As dark as it will be, the utter blackness of a black hole is the sentence imposed on the Fallen leaders. Each individual is chained and utterly isolated in a black void, a complete absence of light, chains eternally pulling them through the black hole like constantly falling with no wings.

Like in the pit?

Death sighed. *The lake of fire is plenty bright. As are your orbs. So don't cast; stay shifted and hold the end of my scythe as I lead you through. With the condition of the failing chains around Sheol, I do not know if their shackles are sempiternal—your word for today.*

He stopped along a black rock wall that extended to the

mountainous ceiling, the entire surface coated in rune symbols. The mountain under the chained mountain.

He shrugged one broad shoulder. *With the state of the chains binding the mountains, I do not know if the Fallen are still shackled to the wall. Magical shackles blocking theirs. Otherwise, I'd imagine all bound angels would gather around the blacksmith's forge…for the light. Put another way, speak to none; they are wicked and imprisoned for a reason. We're heading straight to Hephaestus.*

I'll call him Heph.

Immediately, Death gripped the demon-hearted scythe blade with two fingers, holding out the handle base for me. *Close your eyes and follow along. Despite the sulfur-scented humid air, I will paint a lovely picture in your mind.*

At least I couldn't smell that while I was shifted. As soon as I complied, a thundering waterfall blossomed to life behind my closed eyes. Dark green moss coated the rocky ledges on either side. I watched it tumble and foam, feeding into a pool in front of me. *That's nice. Thank you. Complete with sound effects!*

The crashing *pound* of a cascading waterfall blended with whispered musical-sounding words, beautiful Angelic. A spinning pinwheel of stone opened in the mountain. Then, with a deep rumbling, a new path that led behind the falls spread in front of me.

Step through the prison portal.

Happy his illusions for me didn't include our actual surroundings, I continued along the path he painted in my mind. Then he took the stairs that grew in front of me, leading down.

I grunted. *That was smart. The slant on the handle fits the path I see. Thank you.*

Of course, it was smart. I am Death.

Are you? Or are you Thanatos?

The perfect illusion stuttered before continuing on a downward spiral path. He held his scythe blade between ghostly fingers, vision including a lantern but no demon hearts.

With no answer forthcoming, I poked a bit more. *So your soft, gushy center is Thanatos? And the vain one is Death? Which one values kindness? Which one wears jeans, a t-shirt, and tennis shoes to blend?*

I don't know, Zadie. The villainous side is death. Still, it's not like I'm two separate supernatural entities now. I haven't been divinely split; the angel horseman I am now is both. A villain. A nightmare.

Mofubushi.

I don't know that word.

"You never will." I was so aggravated that I growled it aloud. We were here to retrieve the blacksmith, for daggers to help save mankind—no way I'd believe he was a villain.

Team Horseman comms only. They know your language now.

Death showed me a colossal cavern but didn't blot out a rumbling male voice in the distance. "What *is* that smell?"

A snarl followed as a different raspy growl replied. "Apex predator piss and pussy."

Rude. I mind-mumbled. *But good alliteration!*

Death's tug on the scythe increased, moving us along faster, so I thought-whispered to him. *Are they shackled along the base wall? Sempiternal, still chained and unmagical?*

Yes.

Which meant we were safe enough for me to push on. *Tell me more about the divine split.*

Yet I opened my eyes to darkness so deeply oppressive, it sprung a slow leak, siphoning my hope, immediately sucking it from me. Fallen angels tossed words back and forth, hidden by an ebony curtain of despondency too thick and dark to peer past. I didn't understand the language bouncing between them, not beautiful like Death's, but slithery discordant notes. The jarring sound seemed to feed me discontent while the darkness slurped my hopefulness.

We are in the center of the dungeon. The gargantuan forge is not lit, but the fettered Fallen all face it. The blacksmith is chained to it.

Despite the heads-up, my heart skidded past a beat when chains rattled nearby, and I could see nothing with my eyes open.

Filthy whispers flew into my head, a sudden slew of male voices. Death's presence surrounded my mind. He created a barrier, relieved for once with him in my head; the Fallen couldn't mind-voodoo me. I would have hugged him, but...he'd melt.

Under my temples, I felt another presence join us...the unseen Olympian Hephaestus. Then two male voices bloomed in my head. Sadly, I didn't understand what Hephaestus said or what Death replied. To top that off, Death mentally handed me a bronze dimwitted trophy award.

A blindingly bright light flashed, a spell from Death's scythe, illuminating the chain as it broke, freeing the blacksmith. Curly blond hair, long beard, golden pegleg, the Tartarus captive stood as tall as Death.

Blinded again by the soul-siphoning blackness, I still held out my hand. *Heph. I'm Zadie. I'd like to commission a mindreading blockade helmet and demon—*

Yes. Hephaestus interrupted. *Death told me.*

Either he couldn't see, like me, or he ignored my outstretched hand since I kept forgetting no one but Thanatos could touch me. Then he went back to talking in the language I didn't know!

Rude!

Death, sensing his teammate was losing her cool, switched to English. *Let's move to the dungeon's attic, where the magical metal infused with adamite is stored. Hephaestus said it was the route the Titans used to chain him here, where it was stored when they had him working the forge. We'll hunt more demon hearts on the way out of hell, one of the components.*

Although Death and I glided silently as I held the scythe handle, Hephaestus loudly thumped on the rocky floor. Who knew how long he was chained and couldn't move around? He grunted, then muttered, *I fell. I'm bleeding.*

Immediately, Death used the protection and healing rune he'd pocketed. Around the blacksmith, a golden orb bloomed bright, nearly like the sun.

"Whose child," a gravelly voice beseeched, "holds the

prophecy cloak?"

"None of yours," Death replied. It reverberated in a supernatural echo like the tapping of his scythe.

To me, he added, *It's true. Though I won't encourage them to know so many of their heavy-hitting leaders are in the game. Ashi's father, Amaros, is in a space prison. As are the two DNA donors for Serenity; Tamiel and Azazel. Also, Eden has four imprisoned grandfathers in her lineage. Yeqon, Samyaza, Shamsiel, and Penemue.*

We continued up a long, winding, steep incline, heading toward an upper cave. Hephaestus glowed brightly, safely bubbled, though his breaths heaved heavily. We nearly reached the top when the healing orb ended, suddenly tossing us into the hope-slurping, stygian blackness again.

I caught a flash of green light ahead, a cavern around another black-runed corner. Then it was gone.

A flash again showed we were getting closer. When we stopped, we stood in a large rectangular rock room filled with chest after chest of pale-yellow metal. It flashed with a vibrant emerald fluorescence every few seconds. Practically a green strobe light in the attic's gloom. My heart sank; how would we transport tons of loud glowy metal?

"You may speak now, human," Hephaestus announced in the pulsing unearthly light. "The Fallen cannot hear."

He tugged on his long curly beard before raking a hand through matching blond hair. "I can make anything. I created Pandora for Zeus. Get me out of here, and I will make your helmet; my wife may show her appreciation, too."

"Is there a style other than a helmet? And who is your wife?"

"Aphrodite."

As my blown-mind confetti streamed from my ponytail, Death sighed. "Stay here while I work on collecting components, smoke feathers from my lost dark brothers."

"What else?"

"Smoky feathers from the Fallen," the bearded blacksmith whispered. "Tears from holy angels. Nephilim blood. All mixed with adamite, smithing-magic, and alchemy performed under a full moon."

I frowned at Death. "Why would they give you feathers?"

Just as the Fallen count on the prophecy cloak, they, like Morningstar, are convinced I will fall and join them, earning my destination in the hellfire pit. "They can give their feathers, or I will take them."

In a sudden burst of movement, Death lifted one metal-filled chest out of a minecart. He spread it into another eighteen connecting cars. Then he disappeared out of the pulsing green glow into the soul-eating darkness.

Hephaestus nodded and settled against a wall. "How much metal we bring depends upon how many feathers he collects."

I frowned, fully aware the Fallen would not help create daggers to end Grigori. Further frown-worthy was their certainty that Death would covet his magical power. So much so that he'd refuse to give it up, fall, and join them. But Death wasn't a villain, or we'd not be here on a mission for daggers to save mankind. "How many demon blades can you make with that metal if you have all the components?"

"Thousands, but we will be lucky to collect the other elements."

"We take it all," I ordered, fully convinced the daggers would make the difference in humans surviving the angel war. Ending Lilith was a bonus.

I lifted a piece of heavy metal, which appeared more like a crystallized jewel than metallic. The pulsing green mineral running through it was mesmerizing. I didn't know how we would transport a long train of minecarts carrying chests, but we weren't leaving any behind. Then, emphasizing my demand, my smoky shadow billowed behind me into pseudo wings.

Nevertheless, I didn't care for the look the blond, curly-haired Olympian shot me; it was like that race's dimwit award. "It's heavy, human."

Animated now, Hephaestus pointed toward the colossal crystal cavern outside this room. Giant underground white crystals jutted at bizarre angles between here and the far mountain wall. "We will be fortunate to make it through the next section, past Leviathan, before entering hell. When the Titans brought me on this path, the primordial beast was feeding on souls in the River Styx."

Hephaestus rose and stumbled, blood welling on his arm where it connected with a minecart. The Olympian seemed all but fragile. Wow.

I dug out another healing rune, placing it over the wound. A bright bubble swelled around the blacksmith, mending his cut. His new golden bubble glowed brighter than anything.

Hours later, I reread the section in my alchemy book from the demon's library. "Hey, Heph?" I smiled at him, unsure if he could see me as anything other than a smoke monster. "My book suggests my backpack could be infused with a rune to enchant it into a dimensional pack. A dimension capable of condensing size and weight as if sent to an entirely different location. *You*, the blacksmith, first came up with the infusing spell for an Olympian pocket dimension."

Then I handed my backpack to him. "Please. And thank you!"

When Death finally walked out of the darkness, he appeared burdened, muscles bulging under the weight. Then he confirmed it. *Black smoky Fallen feathers are very heavy. Time to go.*

He blinked, released the chest, and then summoned his scythe. Death growled, pointing the sickle decorated in demon hearts at the empty minecarts. "Where did all the magical metal go?"

Hephaestus pointed at my backpack on the ground. "To another dimension. Your human pet is pushy. Put the heavy feathers in the dimensional pack."

"She's not my pet; she's my partner." Then Death held his scythe straight out; with a flash of light, rune symbols on the far wall shimmered. "To there."

A glimmery spiral coiled around one ginormous white crystal in-between here and there. "But watch out for—"

"Is that a snake?" I gasped.

Heph sighed. "No, a primordial monster. Leviathan is a chaotic creature capable of camouflage. That's why the seven-headed beast blinks in and out of view. Wait and watch for the smoke to rise from its nostrils, flames from its mouth, blindingly bright eyes like the dawn. Then you'll realize its size."

This massive rectangular room paled in comparison to the crystal-filled cavern. Eventually, I spotted all seven heads of the serpent, which otherwise looked like a dragon. Each red and gold striped head was coiled like individual snakes around skyscraper-tall crystals. Its eyes glowed like hot coral coals, helping to show behemoth black wings.

The Olympian had needed two protection and healing bubbles while still in Tartarus. Although Death and I were basically smoke, I didn't care for Heph's odds if we entered the colossal beast's lair.

I hear you. Death added, "God killed the female Leviathan so the two would not eat the world. A sea dragon, but not bound to it. We leave when the creature does, using its summoned doorway. Hephaestus is solid; that's the only way the blacksmith can leave the dungeon of Tartarus. We'll exit directly behind it before the gateway closes. Leviathan will return to Styx to feed on the damned souls stuck there."

Chapter Twenty-Three

Death

I poured on a burst of supernatural speed, propelling the blacksmith from Tartarus's attic into the chaos monster's gateway. Zadie's smoke and shadows glided on the current behind me.

Air turned to black water as the portal dumped us into Styx; trapped souls grabbed for us as if they were drowning. We exited right into Leviathan's feeding zone!

No choice but to summon my wings, flying the Olympian out of the water and onto the opposite shore. Slightly less harsh than a slap, I splatted another healing rune on one of his many scratch wounds.

Zadie! Tormented souls lashed at her, beleaguered by anguished cries begging a memitim for help. None ripped into her, none connected, thanks to her shift. Yet she stayed in the vortex among the damned, surrounded by terrified souls and desperate wails for help. Horror reflected in her glazed green eyes. She needed to reach the bank before one of the sea dragon's seven heads spotted and ate her. That would knock her out of her shift.

I couldn't touch her; if I lost any of my incorporeal shift, then I'd trap her here when I died…until I could come back for her.

Zadie, float! I commanded it; our team bond boosted the telepathy channel required.

Smoky wings billowed behind her as she rose above the Styx. Yet frost coated her green eyes as she floated, immediately calling, "Charon."

As promised, the ferryman appeared. The Leviathan swam further from Charon, whose glowing orange eyes widened as he took in the Olympian. "Hephaestus?"

The curly-headed blond grinned and tapped his golden pegleg. "I go by Heph now."

Zadie did not smile, not snapping out of it. A part of her destroying angel power was to protect souls from monsters feeding on them. And monsters preventing them from moving on.

The Olympian, ankle-high in the Styx, made his oath to smith the blades. Now he was bound to it on more than his desperate word when he wanted freedom.

Levitating, Zadie's thought bubbles popped with how much she wanted to be done with Charon, who left the souls to suffer in Styx. She showed no excitement about floating. After her feet touched the ground, she dug through her backpack. Then she held out three coins to Charon. "We're excited to return to hell. Please and thank you?"

If I were capable of emotions, I'd likely be bursting with pride over Zadie's dimensional pack solution. Instead, I realized the little nuances to mock the sentiment but couldn't feel it. In the same way, I knew I should be concerned when she pulled further away into her shift.

She froze me with the silent treatment after Charon blasted us up through the river of misery's geyser. Wordless, too, while the ferryman steered toward a hidden dark doorway. Only Charon held the key to this private magical gateway that connected Hades and hell. Though untalkative now, she'd clearly impressed him. In fact, our predator-stench t-shirts awaited us on the riverbank. Still, her ice didn't melt.

I sighed. Finally, it clicked for her. Thanks to her destroying angel power, she understood how monstrous I was.

The blacksmith constantly complained about our stinking shirts as we wound around crumbling obsidian temple ruins built into the mountain, a treacherous path from the magical exit. The collapsed temples were an area Lilith referred to as a shady side of hell. That would take something.

Thanks to Charon, we exited farther from Sheol. Still, the damaged chains and lava dripping through cracks looked no better from a distance. Both companions needed rest, but only one of them used another two protection and healing runes on the way to the closest demon lair.

Hephaestus sighed. "It was the zones, one of hesitation, the next lament."

Ah, the affliction of lamenting explained why Zadie hummed a dirge. The same one she whisper-sang the first night underground, resting in a metal tub beside a sinkhole. Before I learned her name and ruined her life.

Hovering around huge stones that crumbled from a temple cave-in, she barreled forward, fully aware of her invulnerability. The strong pull of the demon lair represented many unholy souls inside. Yet she charged through the shimmering portal doorway.

Oh, hell no! The demon lair—not a library this time—but an entry for Are. You. Kidding. Me? Zadie surged into a packed demon nightclub!

She wasn't done, both hands up, casting light orbs and tossing them supernaturally fast. Holy liquid hit evil, sizzling, so I moved quickly to harvest the hearts before the bodies melted.

Hephaestus dropped onto a bench behind the bar, watching the kerfuffle, not bothering to offer assistance during the commotion. He was the first, however, to pour himself a drink.

With the dimly lit demon nightclub now a mess of melting lumpy gray corpses, I approached Zadie. "Give me your pack; I'll add these and more demon hearts. Shift. Eat. Drink. Sleep. I will protect you."

I tried a grin, but she wouldn't have it. Her smoke and shadows dissolved as she reached for a drink the blacksmith poured her. She downed it fast. Dull-witted like that, not stopping to wonder how much harder the demon liquor would hit her.

Zadie stretched out in a booth, using the table to update her map. Then, wobbly while tucking it away, she finally laid back and directed her full attention on me. Her anger, thrumming through Team Horseman, now pointed at me.

"I couldn't see it, grasping too tightly to the hero legend from my family book. But you *are* a villain. When shifted, you stop death. You prevent souls from passing on like those tortured and stuck in Styx! And I wanted you to do that to save the world; I was so wrong! Across the globe, people can't die, just endlessly suffer."

I nodded. "It's part of being a memitim, wanting to help and protect those souls that swarmed you in Styx. It will trigger over the battlefield during the chaos war as well."

Her green eyes narrowed. "And when you're not shifted, Death busy reaping souls, you're tearing loved ones away from each other. Lastly, as the final horseman, you'll end the world. Congratulations. You've convinced me that you are a *villainous nightmare.*"

"Finally. Yes. And we are teammates."

"Where is Thanatos in any of that? The mushy guy who helped pick out bouncy horses for triplets? Who asked Famine to make a snowy area for Chuckles and Yippee? Who appeared immediately when Bram needed him? Or the utterly emotionless one who saved Zehra? You are both a villain and a hero. How is that?"

Although I opened my mouth, Zadie shook her finger at me. "Meaning shape up, partner. The guy from the book is real, so get with the program!"

I scoffed. "The hero program? You're joking? I. Am. Death!"

She closed her eyes, dismissing me.

I added, "I warned emotions and magic don't play nicely. So will you be a loose cannon like Ashi was early on? Because my realm is ready for you this time, woman."

Her eyes opened, staring into mine. Her look was intense, yet her whisper was so very soft. "You changed your realm for *me?*"

"We'll stay here tonight, a busy spot, plenty of demon hearts to harvest. We need too many to believe the demons won't be missed when thousands don't report to work. So we'll zigzag to stay ahead of search crews and any alarm big enough to raise the attention of Lilith or Lucifer. We're evading his cameras, which cover very little of hell's vastness, unlike those in his dimensional portals for TV."

Zadie's eyes closed before she whispered, "Good night, Thanatos."

As soon as she went out, the Olympian tossed back another drink, muttering, "Lightweight."

"That human? *She* is why we came for you."

Hephaestus narrowed his blue eyes. "Who is her blade for?" Then he blinked at me. "Not Eve? Not still?"

"She goes by Lilith now."

The blacksmith pointed toward the shimmering doorway. "Are you planning to ask me to repair the chains around Sheol? Because they *will* fail sooner rather than later."

"Could you?"

"One chain-link, no more; it would use all our metal."

"No. One link will not stop it. We need the demon daggers."

After he stretched out, ready to sleep on the bench, Hephaestus asked, "Is your mate immortal?"

"No. But as you've benefited, we have eighteen more protection and healing runes. And she is invulnerable shifted." Thankfully, Zadie had one for herself, an embroidered rune sewed into her panties.

I exited, hunting near the doorway as more demons came to the nightclub. By morning, I added another two hundred demon hearts. It was time to go now!

Zadie and I drifted on each side of the blacksmith, who carried the protection runes. The Olympian thumped along with us, slowing our pace considerably. Otherwise, noisy. Verbal grumblings, not telepathy.

Though there were no tulips in hell, I hoped Hephaestus didn't find one to trip over...or anything else to drain his health and the rune supply. Of course, by now, he could apply his own healing runes. Like when he fell within the zone of woe and again in a section amping up apprehension.

As we neared a red dust storm hiding a ramshackle town, Hephaestus need not explain why he fell to his knees, skinning them, crying. The gritty hot wind chafed his skin before he triggered another rune to heal. I knew it was a zone of remorse because Zadie sniffled. Her thought bubbles popped over her knitted yak sweater.

Why was she trying to confuse me? Because I was no different than when we started this quest; shift, free the blacksmith, arm humans. I told her the truth about being a villain. The hated grandpappy would be better than this, feeling like I fell off her damned pedestal.

With my head bogged down, I poured on the speed, zooming ahead of them into the magical doorway to see what the lair held.

Zadie didn't dare leave the blacksmith unattended, so the workshop was cleared when they arrived. Not a forge, but an alchemy shop. Hopefully, that surprise would pull her back from how deeply she'd shifted. Finding herself surrounded by wailing trapped souls? Only her body had been immune to it, apparently.

Within an hour, another wave of fiends appeared. When demons arrived, Zadie attacked with holy balls, then returned to tinkering at the station with her alchemy book open. Who knew alchemy was such a busy pastime? Out in the middle of nowhere? Likely a demon terror lab, cooking up new torments.

Hephaestus infused the backpack's dimensional pocket for additional weight, improving it while Zadie and I wiped out demons.

After the fifth wave, Zadie lifted a corked vial filled with a nearly neon green liquid. "For your horse."

It disappeared into her backpack, along with hundreds of demon hearts. Then we were off into the dust storm hellscape.

I steered us south, closer to Sheol, a zigzag, looking for a quiet place for them to sleep. Far, far from the murder zone earlier at the shady lab. We still needed thousands of demon hearts. Plus, basically, Hephaestus needed to be bubbled at all times. It protected him, so he didn't bleed to need the healing.

The next shimmering gateway led to a private lair along Sheol's mountaintop border, currently unoccupied. Perfect for Hephaestus. They both ate, celebrated playing alchemy together…and the many hearts I collected.

Interrupting my vanity celebrating this power—a holy angel in hell— Zadie leveled me with her stare. "Our next zag should be over the lava river. Hellmouth? Because I can float over it now. Fly him over; I'll meet you at the bank."

She shrugged. "Your wings are bright, true, but so are Heph's protection bubbles. Anyone can touch you but me. Fly him before he uses up all the runes." Then Zadie fisted her hands on her hips. "Or don't you think I can?"

"Of course, you can. I've never doubted you. First, though, consider that Morningstar and Lilith know my magical signature without needing to see my wings. If I fly, I can't disguise it. Still, we need to collect the components, the demon hearts. Then leave. This excessive power? I'm starting to like it, more so the immunity to any emotional feelings. I can mimic the emotions, but I feel nothing."

"If you can't feel that you miss Bram when I know he's missing you? And you know it through the soul chain? Then you've been shifted for too long, Thanatos. Now I understand about calling you that, to put the kibosh on you falling."

Chapter Twenty-Four

Zadie

Death raked one hand down his wraithlike face as Hephaestus triggered another healing rune. Yellow-green eyes, a pale eerie glow, narrowed on me. *Do you have on panties?*

We'd covered this, so I lied right to his face. *No. That's why we leave. It's been a week; usually, you'd freak out about reapplying the henna runes. Instead, we have fifty-eight hundred demon hearts. There's one last healing rune. If Heph is hurt after that? It's all for nothing.*

Death stopped mimicking human nuances two days ago. He'd been shifted too long back then. Instead, he seemed to enjoy the murder and mayhem to collect hearts, these next-level hide-and-seek games with Lucifer. No way Lucifer knew a holy angel was in hell. Not yet....

I waved one shadowy arm toward the dust storm and hell's opera where we entered. "Hurry, Heph. We're nearly there. Time to go and then shift, Thanatos."

Death didn't blink, didn't move closer to the magical doorway out of hell where we started the quest.

I hurried the Olympian through the rocky landscape littered with dead yaks, knowing they weren't there. They saddened me, but nothing like the underwater vortex holding trapped souls.

And still, the Angel of Death made no move to leave hell. Fine. Full nuclear option. Glancing back at the final horseman, I added, "When we reach the demon lair, I intend to help you shift. We left off kissing, so I'll start there. But first, you better call your brother to whisk Heph to safety."

A shadow moved overhead, obscured by a red dust storm, yet still imposing, more so when a dragon roared. Lucifer was again looking for the intruder murdering demons.

I didn't dare speak aloud this time. I couldn't take Death's hand, or he'd melt...so close to stepping out of hell. *Get the blacksmith to blessed land, Thanatos, please.*

He sighed, stepping through the demon lair doorway first. Immediately our team connection expanded as Death tapped into communications with his brothers. *Come collect the blacksmith. He's fragile.*

Pestilence and Ashi honed in on our location within seconds. Then, a golden portal opened to blessed land at Famine's; Heph stepped through it while the couple stepped out of it.

I shifted, shedding the cloak of shadows and my smoke monster form. Ready to help Death transform.

Ashi looked like she'd swallowed the sun, cobalt eyes glowing intensely in the lair's gloom. "I worried I'd have to put on that prophecy cloak to open a way out!" She growled. "I hate this place. Gogmagog's. Let's go."

Portal still spinning, gateway to the island, Ashi waved us through.

Goosebumps skittered to life over my arms for about a second before a hard yank on my backpack tugged me back through hell's doorway. The forewarning triggered my shift, yet my pack pulled free of one shoulder. Whatever it was didn't have me; it had our magical components!

Still shifted, Death stepped back into hell as the ground crumbled like a sinkhole starting. Immediately, he reached for me. "Take my hand!"

Instead, I flung the backpack off my last hold and directly at him. When he caught it, his jerk freed it from an orange claw.

That claw swept through me as Death growled. *Leave hell, Zadie. Now!*

The instant I drifted into the portal, he opened another in front of me. So sudden, in fact, I basically fell through it.

I passed into his realm, the moon still massive, the universe alight with reapers reflecting off shallow water. Except we entered near a barely visible dome building, a mirrored camouflage reflecting the water and stars. He stepped inside the one opening, a doorless entrance, so I followed.

"Wow! From in here, it's like glass!" I was still shifted as I drifted, taking in the gigantic bed, two chairs, and a bathroom around the corner. I grinned. "Is that a disco ball? I've only seen one in a magazine, but it wasn't in a bathroom."

Death stood in the doorway, blocking the exit while being blocked from his reapers' prying eyes. "Do it. You said you'd kiss me, help me shift."

Shedding my smoke monster, I slid my palms over his chiseled chest, to his broad shoulders, then around his neck. Was it wrong to revel in the knowledge that only my touch returned his sensations? On tiptoe, I pressed against him; the more I touched, the stronger he smelled of teakwood and leather with the tiniest hint of smoky amber. Otherwise, we both reeked of predator deterrent. I ran my hands down his back, then back up.

He waited, emotionless pale glowing eyes locked on my lips, but I whispered, "I don't kiss villains."

Nevertheless, my lips hovered in front of his. "I'll kiss Thanatos, though. Shift. I want him to come out and play. I'll kiss the hero."

Long dark hair shook, but before he could argue, I added, "Really, a villain and a heroine—I earned that when we broke into Tartarus—but bad and good don't team up. Good sticks with good; bad with bad."

"Break the mold," he dared me as his thumb lifted to brush over my lower lip.

I couldn't resist a little push; with all his vanity so close to the surface, ready to shift—he knew he was hot. I nodded once at the bed. "That's so big you undoubtedly planned on keeping me company?"

He grunted. "You undoubtedly wanted me to call your bluff. Show me that you have no underwear on."

He wanted a kiss? He didn't deny the bed was made for both of us? He wanted to see my body? "I don't know who this horny guy is." My face burned hot. "I meant hoary, as in your silvery wings.

Word for today."

"You didn't mean hoary." His beautifully sculpted face lowered until he murmured against my throat. "That horny guy is the territorial one who will take over once I shift, the one about to redo your henna runes."

"Um, unless bonded, angels fall if they indulge in carnal delights, right? You claimed no interest in earthly pleasures, but now you're suddenly interested in sex?"

"We are on the same team, yes?"

I nodded.

Death smiled, pulling off his shirt. "There is nothing we can do to cause me to fall."

Just that fast, his wings appeared, flashing red symbols over silver feathers, and he shifted to solidness. He shuttered, feeling who knew how many deaths from a week.

I gave him a moment, no more, before trying to figure out what rules had changed. Sure, he kissed me for the first time right before we stepped into hell, but from no interest in sex to the angel wanting to be kissed? "When you say nothing...?"

"I mean nothing." His wings folded inward, a soft silvery shelter around me. He grinned. His expression, no longer tightly controlled, was now unconstrained. Full of wild heat, green eyes burning brightly like from a divine inner fire. "Bathe. You smell like you've been in hell's basement for a week. I will burn these shirts, but they were smart. Good job."

"Try a bath because it feels great." Yet right before my eyes, it was like a magic cleaning wand ran from his head to his feet in a flash.

He shrugged as his wings disappeared. "My daily regen. I don't need to now. But you stink, woman. And you owe me a kiss."

Around the corner, in the flashing glow of a mirror ball, water lightly steamed from a sunken jacuzzi-like rock tub, one end deep like a pool. "This is really nice. Why a disco ball?"

He shrugged. "Famine said all classy bathrooms have one."

I laughed, but it cut off as his hand moved up my spine to thread into my curls.

Death's eyes blazed forest green, no longer pale like his horse. "There's more to Team Horseman than you know; it doesn't apply to us or didn't, but here's the full truth and where we're at. Not that we are angling toward a more human bond, such as intercourse, but we cannot have sex, Zadie. I would not fall because you joined Team Horseman. But birthing a Nephilim would straight-out kill you."

He turned to go but paused. "Unless we shared blood enough to make you immortal. Then yes, it will kill you to birth our evil Nephilim spawn; but death is to sleep and awaken."

"No to the blood thing. And the 666 child that kills me at birth. I don't want to bring babies into a world experiencing its end."

"Beware, the villain might be willing to risk impregnating you just to take the memory with him when he's cast away. You saw the state of the chains. My angel brothers spend so much time copulating that they obviously enjoy it."

I lifted one hand, repeating what he said after revealing we were supposedly mates. "Teammates, it works for us, right?"

He nodded, long black hair swaying.

"While I bathe, will you take the supplies to the blacksmith? Drop off the alchemy book in my cottage, please, and bring back the family legend book. You should read it to remember who you really are."

"I'll return with your essentials. For the kiss."

"And the book, Thanatos." I entered the bathroom.

"You still think of me as Death. I think you like me as the Angel of Death. I think you may like the villain best?"

I sighed. His conceit was fully restored. Then I tossed all my stench-coated clothes around the corner so he could burn them. "Read the book. Visit Bram. It will take a long time for me to de-stink."

Dismissing him, I sank in the warm water before I heard the *whoosh* of him leaving.

I laughed, head back, staring at the beautiful universe—of um reapers. Famine must be a bit of a troublemaker...a disco ball in the bathroom!

Staying a long time after reaching clean, enough to start pruning, I rose and wrapped an unnaturally fluffy gray towel around me, another around my head. It was all I had to wear for now. Still, my mind spun, stomach flipping, thinking about Death's new sex revelations…about warning that his villain wanted to try it.

Above, a sapphire-like star slowly lowered into the shallow water outside the doorway.

The reaper stared at me, blue light superimposed over a woman, as I said, "I remember you. You took the trafficker."

"I remember you, memitim. You killed him. I'm Rhea."

"I'm Zadie."

"You live here now."

Readjusting my towel wrap, I scoffed. "Nah."

She nodded, blue hair floating behind her like she was underwater. "You do. I heard Death and Famine. We never believed Death would take a mate."

"We're not mates but teammates."

She stepped nearly into the doorway, pointing at the ginormous bed. "You are Death's mate."

I regurgitated Death's phrasing. "Meant to be and actually being are two very different things."

Rhea lifted both index fingers to her forehead, making horns. "Ask him about that. You are his *mate*."

"Okay. But let me ask you about this first." I swept one finger up, indicating the jeweled sky showing through the glass ceiling. "As I understand it, the Four Horsemen are to stand against all the Fallen in a chaos war. Hundreds of thousands. The numbers are horrifically lopsided. Why are the thousands of reapers not helping?"

Rhea blinked at me. "No one asked."

I tossed my arms. "I'm asking!"

"We will follow Death wherever he leads." Rhea nodded. "As will you, destroyer; his mate."

Then she blasted into the air, back into the sky, seconds before

Death stepped through a portal.

He tossed clothes on the bed from the doorway, wearing clean jeans and a t-shirt, black, of course. After swiveling into the magical gateway, he handed me a peanut butter sandwich and milk. Then, pivoting back again, he returned with a henna bowl and feather in hand.

As I sat in the overstuffed gray chair, stuffing my face, his green eyes swept over my towel-clad body again. "Now, you do not have on panties."

I choked, eyes watering by the time milk washed down the bite. He looked at me like I was exquisite...as if Death wanted to see more.

"I want to see you, but then I'd mark you. We can't have sex, but I can give you mind-blowing confetti orgasms when I magically mark you as mine. In case you were curious about Team Horseman rules. And the reason for the colossal bed. So if ever the terms change, if you want that, let me know. That I can do to satisfy you. Without exchanging blood to become mates."

"What do you get out of that?"

He shrugged. "Whatever you do. I'll feel what you do. My brothers spend a lot of time doing it, so they certainly find it pleasurable. I won't make you my mate, won't drag us into that trap, but I won't share you either. Meaning it's me or no one."

"Is that what you want? Friends with benefits?"

"We're deeper than that. You belong at my side. We delved into hell and its basement. Shifted, I couldn't feel it. But I can now. We can reapply the runes or not. You're safe here."

A tiny tendril of unease wound through me. "But not a captive?"

He sighed, long black hair shaking. "You will need the runes to hide from Lilith if you wish to leave."

"I need to see the chemist, then pet Chuckles."

His lips tipped up on one side. "You need sleep."

Who was this guy—*angel*—possessive, guaranteeing magical orgasms if I wanted him to mark me? "You or no one? What if there is someone special to me?"

His smoldering forest green gaze raked over me again. "He can't be too special. You've not thought of him once since I met you." Death sighed. "I know you were making a point. Otherwise, I might have to end him, like I did the trafficker who terrified and hunted you."

"You did?"

Death nodded. "He was living on borrowed time since he did that. He remembered you, so it wasn't the only time he hunted you."

Thank you for murdering the trafficker hardly seemed the way to go. If Death were two entities, then Death, the vain villain part of him, did it. But as Death said, he wasn't two different people smashed into one smoking hot body. So did all of him— did Thanatos—want to mark me? Or was this what he warned, Death wishing to take the memory with him?

Not following the villain or hero line of questioning, I asked, "What's the plan for holy angel tears?"

"War. He cried with relief once for Bram. The Conqueror raged —not cried when Ashi temporarily died. But he did when the twins were born like Famine did for the triplets, so they'll try, too."

Exhausted, clean, and with a full belly, I stretched back dead-center on the bed. "Gonna nap. Read the book, Thanatos. Read Zehra's original words. Now, you have emotions. Maybe you will help your brothers with angel tears?"

My eyes slammed shut repeatedly, crashing fast, so I whispered, "Thank you. For making this place for me. For our trip into the underworld and the future demon blades."

Chapter Twenty-Five

Death

I gently shut the book, swiping at another two tears, adding the wet diamond-like droplets to my front pocket. Book in hand, relieved to hear Ashi's private communication ring, I opened a portal. But when I stepped out, the redheaded Nephilim's thought bubbles popped loudly—a contingency plan to end her, so I ordered, "Kobayashi Maru, do not ask this of me."

Ashi nodded. "I knew you'd understand." We stood alone at the top of Arcadia. "It has to be you. Lance can't cause of the soul chain. War won't—because of Serenity. Famine will never attack me again. It has to be you, Death. And I'm immortal, same as you. If I turn, find a way to keep me down."

"You don't have to fight your father! The Four Horsemen will. This is why you called?"

"No. Don't mention it to upset Lance; he's certain I won't turn. But the cloak seems closer to latching onto me. I didn't think it could settle over me and go against my will, but now I'm suspicious. Since you shared those images of Sheol and the chains, we want you to watch this."

My brother approached, holding the tiara that Ashi despised, which she claimed was a chaos battery; she looked about to blow with magical power. She assuredly didn't need extra, yet Pestilence sat it upon her head.

Glowing cobalt eyes did not dim, the chaos in her swelling too much for the tiara to take the edge off. Her power of lightning, a gift from Zeus, cracked in over a dozen long whips away from her. The wind ferried them in different directions.

I sighed. "What did you do?"

"Lit twenty protection domes around the world. They will

never go out, thanks to the tiara. This is how real the chaos rolling over the planet is right now. If I die, the chaotic power stored in the tiara battery will keep the magical shelters going until I resurrect."

Pestilence pulled her in closer as Ashi wagged a finger my way. "One thing you don't want to miss out on if the world kicks it? That is love. Let's talk about first love."

"Let's not. Zadie and I aren't falling into the mate trap."

The Conqueror snorted.

Ashi grinned, lifting her index fingers to her forehead. "Not even you, Death, are immune to the insanity of first love. You took a long time to return, a week! Did you stay shifted so long to stave off how hard those feelings hit?"

I scoffed. "We were busy! Blacksmith. Metal infused with magic. Fallen's feathers. Demon hearts. Gathering components." Grumbling, I added, "And those feelings are confusing."

Pestilence nodded, long golden hair swaying. "We don't have long, brother. Make her immortal before you are sorry you didn't. It takes time and lots of blood exchanges. Soon, ring first will mean something to you."

Pivoting, walking down the mountain path opposite the dragons, past a new shelter for the blacksmith, I spotted Famine and Hephaestus discussing a forge.

Bending to the backpack, glad they were busy, I pulled eight diamond-like tears from my pocket to dump inside. After the forge was built and lit, once Ashi donated blood, that would fulfill all the component requirements. Then, the first blades could be forged.

I didn't want to admit to donating holy tears, hoping those were my first and last. Still, there was much of the book to go. Once upon a time, Zadie advised me not to read it because it might hurt me. Now she insisted I read it.

Zehra knew me, not in love with me, but she loved me; the best I could do in return was to be fond of her. Little wonder why she prayed for my emotions to awaken so I'd find a real wife. Zehra's faith was so strong that she wanted Grace passed down until the last Grace was there for me when my seal broke. Then, thousands of years later, it came to pass; her prayer was answered. I opened a portal near Zadie minutes after waking.

As I walked the beach onto the snowy cold portion, Chuckles and Yippee ran in circles around me, greeting me. With only animals watching, I took the opportunity to read more of the book.

I pray the last Grace will know how to stop Lilith and unlock Death's emotions. I pray for the man behind the angel to awaken and fight an ending in the pit. There is a way. God would not do that to his loyal angel horseman.

I closed the book, nettled that I never bothered to explain to Zehra. She had nothing but Lilith's truth about an eternity in the lake of fire.

The risen sunken ships kept one stationed off the coast of Arcadia to observe the horsemen. A funnel of ravens announced Hades arriving on the deck; he bellowed my name.

Yet Bram launched into the sky upon Samson, flying toward the ghostly ship.

I joined him on his red dragon as its dragonfire sank the skeletal vessel.

"Look," Bram beamed, forming a fireball between his hands. Ashi's chaos boosted his power, for this was far from one flame on a finger.

"Land, please. Hades fled, but he will take that personally. Stay on blessed land for a few hours. Visit Mission Mankind; let the Titan-child calm down."

Thankfully, Bram didn't argue. In fact, the little zings running through the soul chain indicated excitement about visiting Mission Mankind. *Zing! Zang! Zap!* Ah, he liked a girl there.

Opening a portal for him, I grinned. "Have fun."

I re-entered my realm to find Zadie in the doorway, smelling of sweet pea flowers and honey. She shot me a brilliant smile, declaring, "Good morning! We told Keith a week, so first to see him. Then your horse. Then Chuckles."

Like an inescapable gravitational force pulled me closer to her, my fingers lifted to trace a long springy curl. "How long have you been awake?"

She shrugged. "A couple minutes? Long enough to jump into my clothes."

That ability to think clearly immediately after waking proved how much of a survivor she was. A child molded by a myriad of survivors in a post-apocalyptic world. Think fast. And she could. How had I ever thought she was dull-witted? Shaking my head, I reminded her, "We didn't reapply the runes."

Darker green, circling her irises, darkened more. Great. Her stubborn look.

"I lived as a smoke monster for a week without a physical body unless sleeping. The hide-from-Lilith runes are like new, no wear and tear."

I'd noticed that while she wore a towel. The runes on her thighs looked fresh. Thinking about her soft olive skin, my primal male beast purred; I wanted to mark her with my scent… to claim her as mine.

Unsettled by that realization, I opened a magical doorway outside the chemist's bunker. The tall, middle-aged blond on the other side of the open door waved us inside. He ignored me exclusively, focusing on Zadie.

Keith shot her grin. "You were right. Drinking an elixir won't trigger its properties; it needs a different delivery method. So, congratulations, you'll be the first person to create magical cheese!"

He barked out a laugh. "Your dad didn't foresee that one when he got you a yak. I'm glad I kept her for you until we met. I'm proud of the small part I played in raising you."

My inner male animal pulled at me to keep physical contact with her; the fact revolted me. How primitive. I turned away, zoning out the detailed chatter, watching a looping tube with blue bubbling liquid. Not a single solution to stop the primal male beast's progression occurred to me.

When I glanced back at the blond with the long ponytail, his expression was alarmed, still focused on Zadie. Suddenly, my focus was too; her thoughts seemed shielded; interest peaking the more I heard.

Cocking one dark eyebrow, she nodded. "Because it will kill me. Then the Angel of Death will come looking for you. So, you guarantee your tea?"

"It works! I swear it on your father; God rest his soul. You don't have to threaten me with the Grim Reaper!"

"What tea?" Her thought bubbles didn't broadcast it.

Zadie waved it off, bundle in her hand, telling Keith goodbye. Then, launching into a list of things she needed to make cheese and an alchemy table like in the demon lands, she turned to go. She stopped in the knee-high field. *Can you heat water in your realm?*

Yes. Why?

She stared toward Mount Rainier, nodding. *For tea.*

What is its purpose?

To drink. She dropped telepathy and shot me a grin. "To Chuckles and your horse, please."

"You owe me a kiss." That was unfortunate; the words fell out of my mouth. Yet her sharp intake of breath triggered my muscles to tense.

Trying to cover, I opened a magical gateway to Arcadia and asked, "What is your word for today?"

"Your turn."

"Concupiscent. Lustful, chalked full of sexual desire."

She stopped, pivoted, and placed her hand on my pec. Her palm inflamed my flesh as if I wore no t-shirt. "Are you?"

Bedeviled, I could see my reflection in her eyes, the way I stared at her; she was the most exquisite thing I'd ever seen. And I wanted to see all of her; the territorial male beast might erupt to shred her clothes any minute.

When I didn't answer, she squared her shoulders. "Let's return to your realm. First, I need hot water for tea to prevent pregnancy. Then let's explore Death with benefits? Fair warning; I didn't much enjoy sex. But if you are concupiscent, I'll give it go."

Torn between taking her up on it and erasing anyone who touched her before me, I finally answered, "I told you. If ever you want the terms to change, you let me know, and I'll join you in the enormous bed."

She grinned. "Drinking birth control tea implies a physical union, not a magical one. You let me know if your terms change, and you want that?"

I closed my eyes. I did want that. "Are you sure about the tea?"

"Keith guaranteed it."

After I opened my eyes, her fingers lifted to her forehead like horns. "Did you do that, make like a pet yak?"

I summoned my scythe, thumping it once, but Zadie dashed off for a bucket to milk her yak. The ferret danced in circles around her feet.

War joined me near her cottage, watching her the same as me. "Make her immortal, brother. My Valkyrie wife is traveling, marking people as worthy; her power is triggered, and she's on a mission. The state of Sheol's chains? Amped-up Ashi? The end is closer than we wish."

"I have not come close to reaping a fourth. I'm reaping, but it's a slow drip from Hades spelling the animals to attack mankind. Meaning I've done the bare minimum like Pestilence did when he ended the world's connectedness."

Famine joined us. "I finished building the forge. Stormbringer lit it for the blacksmith. Thank you for making demon blades a possibility and a game-changer."

Then Famine frowned. "Right after I woke, Morningstar said Serenity giving Ashi the cloak was part of his plan. He was not lying. Eden—all the women—are antsy. I think Ashi is the women's commander, as the Conqueror is ours."

I pointed my scythe toward Zadie. "She's safe and busy. Want to come with? She needs supplies for an alchemy lab and to make cheese."

Pestilence joined us. "We'll all go. Between us, maybe we can convince you to listen to one of your brothers about making your mate immortal?"

Although my mouth opened to protest the mate label, it hung open. All of us stared at Zadie hovering on the beach. She laughed while showing Chuckles and Yippee how she could shift and float.

The other women on Team Horsemen slowly made their way down to the beach. The triplets ran circles around them. When they reached the crashing waves, I heard the ladies hammering Zadie with questions about hell and Tartarus.

I reached into Zadie's mind. *The Four Horsemen are riding to slay the risen and collect your components. We will discuss the merits of tea when I return.*

Chapter Twenty-Six

Zadie

"You can float!" Eden cheered when my shadowy form showed off my newest ability.

I air-bowed, happy that I stopped to show them during my tale of hell and its basement. Then, as Ashi wooted and Serenity clapped, I brandished my floating.

I hovered over the beach, then the crashing waves; sharks below kept pace with me. While showing off, a conspiracy of ravens formed over the newest nearby seaweed and rusted skeletal ship.

Mere seconds later, Hades nearly blinded me in his pineapple yellow suit, calling, "Where have you been, pet?"

This was why people shouldn't show off! Death would be ticked. Far from shore, I slowly floated closer as a rowboat, colored like a coral reef, lowered from the deck. Although Hades stood, no oars to be seen, the coral-encrusted liferaft steered my way at high speed. "Where has your master been?"

"Busy." Though true—not the *master* part—I hoped Hades couldn't also read minds since I waggled my eyebrows suggestively. No telling how that came out on a smoke monster.

I heard Serenity's snort from here.

Hades smirked. "Ah! A week holed up to scratch the hot and bothered itch. I told Lucifer that was likely the case. Yet he said no; he'd know."

I neared the white sandy beach, not a fan of Hades and the devil discussing Death's possible sex life. Also wondering if Lilith was in on the discussion.

Hades ignored everyone else, holding one hand toward me, silver eyes shining. The sun glinted nearly blue on his short black spiky hair. "I can't follow on blessed land. However, we have payment terms to discuss if you still want to visit Tartarus to see the blacksmith."

"Nah."

"Why the sudden change of heart?"

"Zadie," growled over the water.

Hades barked out a laugh. "Poor pet. Leash time again." But his smile flipped upside down, ebony brows almost in a V. "Or not."

I spotted Death levitating over the crashing waves halfway between Hades and the shore. He held out a hand. "Move away from Hades."

I frowned, feet about to touch down on blessed land.

Eden sighed. "He looks ticked."

Death waved one arm impatiently for me to come to him.

"You don't want to do that," Hades growled.

Ignoring Hades, Death's weirdness about coming to him, not blessed land like constantly warned, confused me. Although impatience was a trait that Ashi claimed defined Death, I'd not seen much of it. Since his seal broke, Death was in no hurry to end the world. But he certainly displayed it now. So I asked, "Did you change your mind about the terms?"

He raked black hair from his face but didn't summon his scythe as usual when uncomfortable and needing a shield. Instead, his green eyes narrowed, edginess nearly palatable. "Yes."

No doubt, blown-mind confetti streamed out my ponytail. Yet when I reached Death, he sighed. "Shift, so I can catch you."

Shift? But he could touch my physical body while I was a smoke-and-shadows monster; Death was the only thing that didn't pass through me like I was smoke.

"No, pet," Hades growled. "Trust me in this."

Though I didn't correct Hades, I tapped into Team Horseman telepathy under my temples and growled into Death's mind. *I'm not the pet. I'm the damned hero.*

Death's laugh rumbled through my mind. His laughter sounded genuine, but it didn't show on his face. *Yes, you are the hero. Thinking about Hades?*

Of course, Hades was nearby taunting me! *Will you never correct him?*

Death levitated over the water beside me, both arms out to catch me. And was that a leer?

I scoffed. *Good luck slaking your lust if you can't tell Hades.*

Why are you hung up on Hades? What does he have to do with luck and lust?

I demanded, "Tell him that I'm not your pet!"

Finally, he tsked Hades. "She's not Death's pet."

"Hmph." Appeased, I shifted, and he caught me. Senses working again, I immediately noticed Death didn't smell quite right. More smoke, less teakwood, and leather.

Triumph laced his broad smile. The air shimmered around him. "She's my pet," he growled in a different voice, an illusion dissolving to show another face!

"Zadie!" Death, silver wings spread wide, dove through a smoky portal, coming straight at me.

But the blue-eyed blond with brain-melting beauty tightened his hold as he hurtled through a dark purple swirling pinwheel.

Heat seared my skin for a nanosecond; a flash of pain skittered along my flesh like it was on fire before I shifted back to smoke and shadow. My kidnapper's hand passed through me, but the magical gateway closed.

Directly in front of me, azure flames flickered and sputtered from a colossal castle's tower windows. Black and rock-hewn, the same as the small charcoal-tinted buildings around it. I spun, but now dead ahead, lava flowed through the open mouth of a massive dragon skull. I was back in hell but on the city side of Hellmouth! *Thanatos!*

The blond couldn't touch me now, but he laughed, extraordinarily beautiful. "I'm Lucifer Morningstar. Death's buddy. It's how my glamour of him is so spot on."

Death had no way to contact his brothers when we were here together. Hell had an entirely different dimension. I felt the disconnectedness of it immediately. My temples were numb, like a link cut, with no throb of Team Horseman telepathy. That loss ached.

Morningstar inhaled deeply, nostrils expanding. "Welcome back. I knew you were here, smelled both divine and death magic. That's what you wield, *destroyer*. Thousands of demons were slaughtered for their hearts. It should be impossible for a holy angel, but let's see if Death was with you. If he comes now for you."

Floating from him at top speed, I hit a solid wall as a dome suddenly sprung around us. I could not pass through, trapped with Satan on the banks of Hellmouth! Desperate, I banged into the shimmering purple wall again.

"I, too, was once holy, memitim," the devastatingly handsome devil smirked. "Not so much as a drop of holy magic can pass the barrier. Nothing from outside can get to us. We'll stay in here while we better our acquaintance. You won't melt; the cage will protect you. Cooperate? I won't give you to Eve."

I stared at blood-red lava flowing into the massive open Hellmouth skull. I'd drawn a map; I knew the closest lair to reconnect my link to Death. Perhaps I couldn't pass through the barrier right now, but nothing could hurt me if I stayed shifted. Not Eve, not even Satan. They couldn't torture me.

"You can't stay shifted forever." Then, crossing his arms over his chest, still dressed in all black like Death, Lucifer demanded, "Explain your relationship with Death. You are not bonded to him. Or else God would have made it known to me."

I offered no answer. Yet after the briefest flicker of flames flashed in his pupils, I wondered how unwise it was to infuriate the devil in his domain.

The fire disappeared as he growled, "What terms? You asked if I changed my mind about terms."

When I again didn't acknowledge him—it wasn't like he could hurt me—he sighed, "Very well." He waved his arm toward the rocky ground devoid of anything but shades of gray; a grinding noise rumbled beneath my feet. "I'll run you through the zones. Then, we'll see if you feel more talkative after hours of torture."

Floating close to the dome wall, utter despair rolled over me as the landscape changed. Not dead yaks, but a devastated world, mounded piles of human bodies in street sinkholes as angels flew over, tossing spells and clanging swords. I didn't know how long I cried and stood in horror next to the bodies as the world ended, adding my voice to hell's opera. Not knowing if the devil could see what tormented me. Or if he was its author.

The grinding spin of the torture wheel kicked in; seconds later, the scene changed like Lucifer swiped a new one into existence. This time, I stood in the most beautiful garden I'd seen, a flowery path lined by fruit trees.

Ahead, Death stepped out of a portal, approaching a gorgeous brunette in a skimpy fur outfit. He wore a black formal-looking uniform with a cloak. The exact cape he spread over me on his rock throne.

"Death!"

"He can't hear you. A clip of long ago. That's Eve," Satan supplied. "She would not stop sobbing after Death reaped his first soul, her son Abel's. Granted, she was damned for eating the forbidden fruit and convincing Adam to do the same, but how she viewed death disturbed him. So Death explained that he was inevitable. That day, knowing she would join me in hell, Eve set her long game to play eternity with Death."

The scene played out, Lucifer narrating the language spoken between Death and Eve. Until Death turned, thumping his scythe, exiting in a portal. Then it was all there on Eve's face if only he looked back. In that instant, she set her forever on him. Stalked him ever since!

A low growl rumbled in my throat, so pissed off right now that I could kill someone! In fact, I blasted the devil with death magic.

Sky blue eyes rolled. "You're not having sex with Death. He would fall. I would know. You are not bonded to him. You are not soul-chained to him. Yet you are ever close to his side. You don't so much as smell like him. No claim."

He waved a hand up and down at me. "All of this because you wield a gift of his power?"

His grin curled wickedly on his too-perfect-to-be-human face.

"Perhaps he keeps you close since a destroying angel will be powerful in the chaos war."

His hand swiveled like he swiped a new scene around us; now, we stood outside small rock-cut buildings, clay-colored like the distant fairy chimneys. Townspeople holding large stones surrounded a woman standing by the well. "Or could Death be keeping you near because you look like the wife of Thanatos?"

So that was why the dark-haired, olive-skinned woman with slightly angled green eyes seemed familiar. Zehra. Thirtyish. Minus my curly hair and over a decade in age? I saw a resemblance to her if I looked in a mirror. My heart plummeted. How could he see me when I looked like her?

"Familiar, no?" Morningstar chuckled. "Not twins but definitely sisters. You see, I full well know how valuable you are."

The gray stone groaned and rumbled, the scene swapping to action. The people hefted rocks, surrounding Zehra, whose baby bump was barely showing, ready to stone her. Then, a man said something I didn't understand; from the storybook, I knew he asked if any man would claim her. The crowd parted as Death approached, answering. The only part I understood was "Thanatos." That was all he had to do, claim her as his wife.

The rocks grumbled, then growled, the scene freezing again as Death stood outside Zehra's tiny home. Her belly was swollen with a child as she accepted the rabbit he handed her. Thanks to the book, I'd been receptive to Death as a hero even before he rebranded to Thanatos. The way we came together for our quest was like it was written in the stars...or the book. And it started here, speaking with her, his conceited resting bitch face perfectly intact.

Emotionless, except for his default look of arrogance, one ebony eyebrow cocked, like after he'd been shifted too long. Unnaturally still, he didn't know how to mimic emotions then.

A sharp pang tugged in my chest. And Lilith took Zehra's body for a millennium! "Why are you showing me this?"

"Finally!"

I snorted. Now the devil sounded like an angel.

"We can be allies. Or we can be enemies. Considering you are in hell, you can't stay shifted forever, and you'll fry when the dome goes down? Allies should sound appealing. Especially with Lilith on the way."

Smoke monster me tossed my arms then rammed the shield again, unable to phase through. If Lucifer didn't list off Team Horseman, then he didn't know about it. "What could you possibly want with me? As you pointed out, Death and I are not mated, chained, or trapped."

"Nearly six thousand demons, slayer." Flames flashed within his pupils for the briefest glance before disappearing. Lucifer poked Zehra's frozen image, standing beside Death. "He keeps you close. Why hasn't he marked you with his scent at the very least?"

"Cause he's not a dog, and I'm not a tree." Yep, the devil did not know about horseman teammates.

"Because—"

I whirled around to see Lilith. Red dress. Red nails. Red heels.

"—she does not know what to do with what she has." One brightly painted fingernail jabbed at Zehra's image. "Everything about you is more refined, except that unruly wild hair."

Lucifer sighed. "You must wait until he marks her. That is how it is. Then you can have her, so long as you guarantee he will fall."

The King of the Fallen raked one hand through cropped blond hair; his other hand, pointing at me, ended in claws. He clicked his ebony talons. "You will agree, a willing possession."

I scoffed, not terrified. They couldn't touch this smoke monster! "And why would I do that?"

Although black hair and green eyes, Lilith's attempt to have Zehra's body was a big Fail.

If you are named Grace....

The words from the book pulled at me. Serenity's handprint of worthiness glowed violet on my shoulder for an instant.

I pray the last Grace will know how to stop Lilith.

And I did. A demon blade. But suppose I willingly agreed to Lilith's possession? There was no way she would fail to tap into my shadowy smoke monster power, thereby avoiding being stabbed and trapped in the first place! No, consuming my magic would add to her power.

My pseudo wings billowed as I lifted one hand. Memitim power wasn't divine, so death magic passed my domed enclosure, hitting Lilith in the throat. Oh, she'd be back. But it felt good. I'd see how many hosts she brought for me to slaughter, those abandoned by their guardian angels.

"She'll be pissed," Lucifer promised. "You'll drain your shift if you keep doing that. See? We can help each other."

Everyone knew, of course, that making a deal with the actual devil never worked out in the end, except for maybe some guy who won a fiddle. I needed a way out on my own. And I prayed that Death didn't come for me. I was utterly invulnerable; he knew that! If he kept shifting, he said he might lose those gorgeous wings. I'd call for him the instant I escaped to a demon lair for a ride home. If Thanatos believed in me at all, he knew that. "No to a willing possession."

"You will. Or the Fallen's prophecy cloak will latch onto Kobayashi Maru. Hearing it means you're magically gagged on every subject you've heard."

Then Morningstar showed me the end: the cloak wrapping around Ashi, smoky black wings escaping an exploding mountain, dark angels blotting out the sun.

The terrifying vision stopped when Lilith reappeared, triggering a blast of my destroying angel death magic. The female, abandoned by her angel counterpart, dropped dead.

Chapter Twenty-Seven

Death

*Z*adie, come to me!

Insects chittered, actual crickets chirping…my surrounding noises gave the only reply when I tapped into Team Horseman. I did not panic. She would shift and stay that way. I couldn't communicate with my brothers once I stepped into the devil's domain. The dimensional difference cutting off our telepathy only confirmed Morningstar spirited her away to hell.

Of course, it was natural to think about her constantly. The emptiness of no reply felt like our connection was cut, stretching like a yawning black hole threatening to pull in all hope. Natural, for the now-awake territorial male to scratch toward the surface. If that part took control, I would mark her as soon as I had her back. And that mark, scent, or magical tattoo, would all but paint a bullseye on her back as my vulnerability.

As for my brothers, none of them said you should have made her immortal. Instead, each side-eyed me after I did not shift and go after her. Yet they didn't know her like I did. This was Zadie! She had her shifting power down to a fine art. And transformed, she was invulnerable.

Though confident she would find a way out without me walking into Morningstar's trap, it didn't explain my skipped heartbeats. Soon, she'd restore our telepathy and holler for me to come for her at the first lair leading out of hell.

My memory looped, remembering before we left a lair for hell. She rose to meet my kiss before I shifted but refused to kiss a villain after transforming.

The memory no sooner ended than I retrieved her family legend book. Sitting on her little bed, I flipped to a blank page at the very end. Then, using henna and my silver feather, I left her a message she would find at some point.

As recorded by Thanatos, the Angel of Death, mate to Zadie Grace: I love you.

As the wait stretched close to the twenty-hour mark, I knew she'd be riled if her yak wasn't milked. So milking Chuckles was the least I could do.

One after another, my brothers shot me with dumbfounded aqua, teal, and gray gazes.

It wasn't until I figured it out and milked her pet that Horse joined me on the beach. He stomped, spraying white sand, annoyed that I didn't flit after our teammate. In essence, he threatened to go after her if I wouldn't. Impossible, really, but a nice touch as each of his nudges into my shoulder pushed harder.

Yes. We were approaching the twenty-four-hour mark. She went longer than that in Tartarus, but eventually, she needed to shift. Fine, I'd shift and follow after her—an utterly invulnerable female—like some love-sick, tongue-lolling yak. Going meant I'd walk into Lucifer's trap wherever he held her in the vastness of hell. No other reason for him to grab her. Once in the same dimension, our team telepathy would reopen.

No sooner did I decide it than a dark purple vertical line appeared over the water. The rift split open like sliding doors. Smoke and shadows Zadie blasted out of the gateway as if shot from a cannon. She landed to float over the waves right where Morningstar nabbed her. A shark jumped in an arc to pass through her shadowy body.

In that instant, God declared, *She is yours.*

Zadie floated toward me, but I took flight, scooping her into my arms. I didn't release her after touching down on blessed land.

"I knew you could do it," I whispered. "I believe in you. After all, you're the hero."

Cradling her against me, I deeply inhaled her sweat pea and honey scent. She needed to shift, so I held her tight, thumb brushing her lower lip, nuzzling her neck, and helping return her physical feeling. "You're safe now."

Ashi, prophecy cape stalking her, stepped closer. "Are you okay?"

"Not so much." Zadie pointed at the cloak. Yet she choked hard when she tried to talk. Grabbing her throat, face turning crimson, she growled. That didn't stop her from pointing at the Fallen's cape again, choking harder, hand pumping with stabbing motions.

Flinging one hand at the cloak, Ashi detonated it with a fireball. It would reform and return.

Zadie inhaled a deep gasping breath. "Whew!"

With aqua eyes glowing silver, Pestilence cocked his head. "Magical gag?"

Long corkscrew curls bobbed as she nodded, finally shifting solid, still cradled against me. I couldn't seem to set her on her own just yet.

War grumbled, "Hrmm. So you can't say anything?"

Her hand rested over her throat as she shrugged. "Nothing I heard. I'm sorry. I have a plan if you can trust me, though I can't explain it." She rubbed her throat again. "But, since I was forcefully ejected from hell, still alive, I totally understand if you think anything I say or do is to benefit the devil."

"No one thinks that," I murmured, stroking one hand down her curls. Then I swept my gaze over my family. "Give her a minute. She was snatched and returned. We'll talk later about what happened between those actions."

Stalking away with her tightly smooshed to my chest, I heard her thought bubble. *I'm not her.*

No reason to play games. Zadie meant Zehra. "How many times do we have to go over that?"

"How can you see me? I look like Zehra!"

"From a distance through a sinkhole dust cloud—after a beam busted my skull." I threaded my fingers through her springy curls. "Your curls are only one way you look different. I see *you.* Bleeding as a glamoured blue-eyed blond, I could see *you.* But I returned for your name. And ruined your life when Lilith saw you because I was there."

Holding her eyes, I whispered, "Did he hurt you?"

"Some of his zones did."

"Should I have come after you? Instead of believing you would contact me the second you could from a lair?"

"No! Then you would...." She choked, face turning red, both hands over her throat. The magical gag.

"Easy." I headed toward the beach with her yak.

"Wait." She pointed in the other direction. "I need the vial in my backpack. Then I need to talk to your horse about my first potion."

My territorial male instinctively didn't want to release her. Still, she stared at me expectantly when we reached the massive forge and backpack.

After she retrieved the potion she'd concocted in the demon's alchemy lab, she approached my horse on the beach.

When Horse nudged her shoulder, she held up the neon green vial. "It's like this...you're immortal, so worst case, you die and come back."

Serenity joined us as Zadie continued. "Best case, you choose how you want to look, an illusion master like your dad. If you are happy as the palest stallion ever, then cool cause you glow! If you opt to take the potion, you could choose facades to help convey what you want to be named. Deal?"

"He's my horse."

After Horse nodded, Zadie popped the cork and tipped the tiny vial with the neon liquid. She was still ridiculous, chanting, "Chug! Chug! Chug!"

Horse sucked the contents before her first chug!

Serenity misted us with magical soothe. A backup plan, perhaps, in case Zadie killed him?

Horse bucked, belching emerald fire, then galloped off over the top of the waves. After he lapped near us, I started another entry for Are. You. Kidding. Me?

I'd seen that illusion for years; since knowing Ashi! The potion worked…if Horse meant to look like a puffy white unicorn with a rainbow tail.

I gaped before admitting, "I won't ride a white rainbow-farting unicorn."

"He's a comedian," Zadie laughed.

Horse morphed into a massive dark gray beast, draped in long shadows like she had when shifted, his eyes neon green like the potion.

"Whereas," she added, "that one is a bit intense, sort of scary, like he's the Grim Reaper's horse."

Then she pivoted to stare up into my eyes. "You have all the supplies I needed by now, yes?"

"No!" I exclaimed. "The roundup of cheese-making components and an alchemy lab stopped when my m—*you* were grabbed."

Both her hands lifted. "I know we need to talk, but I need those things sooner rather than later. We'll talk after. I have a plan."

Serenity waved her hand like shooing a pesky fly. "I'm with her."

Zadie hooked her arm through the Valkyrie's, tuning me out and walking off. "The blacksmith said he could make anything. First, I need to talk to Heph about a new order. Then Chuckles needs me."

She glanced at me. "Maybe you will be back by then?"

"Chuckles has been milked."

She stopped, pivoted, and grinned. "You milked Chuckles?"

I summoned my scythe, thumped it once, then nodded.

Zadie sauntered my way, a huge smile plastered on her face. She tipped onto her toes. "Thank you, Thanatos." Then she brushed soft lips over my cheek.

Just as quickly, she spun away to rejoin Serenity.

"Zadie—"

She glanced back at me. "Do you still not have the components?" Zadie dismissed me again, ignoring the thudding of my scythe as she had when she wanted me to fetch henna.

Instead, I followed them to the forge; I wasn't ready to lose sight of her again.

The blacksmith grinned at her, handing her a demon blade. "I made yours first, but I haven't seen you. Thin like a dagger, long like a short sword. Light."

Zadie accepted the overly long dagger, then a thigh holster. "Thank you!" As she tucked away the blade, the magical metal pulsed slightly with a glowing green light. Then she launched into details for her newest 'urgent' project, booting it before the mind-shielding helmet.

Leaning against a palm tree, I pondered why she wanted a crypt-sized stone vault covered in rune markings like the symbols outside Tartarus. Something that could be spelled shut, unbreakable, and exceedingly heavy so it would sink.

Yet when Hephaestus pressed her for the why of it, Zadie choked, her face turning bright red.

Until I stepped in. "Just make it as she described. Famine can pull up the rock."

Horse bizarrely charged toward us like he, too, would enforce her directions. But now, he was a midnight steed with glowing red eyes and smoke from his nostrils like a dragon.

My stallion used his magic to float her into the saddle while she squealed. Once I jumped on behind her, pulling her close, Horse trotted down the mountain, then over the top of the ocean. This, too, earned a squeal.

Horse, still black with red eyes and snorting dragon smoke, now had a black unicorn horn. I sighed. He was a comedian, making her laugh and me groan.

Still, this was nice; one arm looped around her waist as she relaxed against me, staring over the sea as we rode. *I want to mark you.*

She pulled to sit independently of me, trying to put space between our bodies in the saddle. "No."

"It has nothing to do with exchanging blood. Flesh to angels, carnal things? It is like white noise to humans. You simply don't notice it in the background."

"My body is like background noise?"

"Yours is like an orchestra masterpiece that demands attention. I guarantee it will pleasure you when I magically mark you."

She wheezed, one hand resting on her throat. "No."

"With my scent mark then."

"Nope!" Panic lit her from the inside, rolling over me through our link. The same way it had when she pointed at the cloak. Like that cloak, Lucifer must have mentioned marking. She suffocated when the gag kicked in.

When Morningstar nabbed her, the notion of marking her as mine morphed from a blooming idea to a desire. To a need. I nearly called her my mate earlier. The truth of who she was to *me* now honed to a fine point. And that was before God confirmed what I knew in my heart.

Yet I told her we wouldn't fall into that trap. The territorial male filling me with yearning didn't mean anything changed for her. Once upon a time, she considered me off-limits due to the family hero book. And if I lit up with desire, I might end up marking her accidentally—like War had stamped his magical mark on Serenity.

I stroked one hand down her glorious curls. "You make me. Then you break me apart to remake me. What do you need from me, Zadie?"

"The components for the alchemy lab and magical cheese."

I stifled a sigh, then opened a portal to Georgia, where my brothers and I left the gathered supplies. We'd stopped slaughtering risen crocodilian dinosaurs when Zadie used our team link to complain about Hades. It took me a minute to realize she was dealing with him at the time. It never occurred to me that Morningstar would glamour to trick her.

Summoning my scythe, I pointed it toward the pile previously collected. A large portal opened before I gave the mound a magical push, transferring it to the island.

Then I tightened my arm around her waist, pulling her closer. "Although the dimension of hell goes against everything I'm about to tell you, if ever you are separated from me again, tap into our link and summon me."

I touched her temple. "Call for me; I'll be there immediately. By the same token, if a magical gateway opens *and* you hear me telepathically calling you, I'm summoning you to my side. It's, unfortunately, voluntary. Unless it opens under you."

She glanced over her shoulder at me. "That's a pretty nifty trick."

Another might be our team. Since Morningstar doesn't know about Team Horseman, he doesn't know to block it with a magical gag. You're working out a plan you can't speak aloud, so you clearly recall what happened in hell. Concentrate on what you heard. I'm about to dig through your head.

As I opened a portal to the Seattle outskirts, riding into the misty rain obscuring Mount Rainier, I added the most important fact. Her willingness. "If you want me to?"

Chapter Twenty-Eight

"**F**ine, but first, let's talk tangletoes." Cause once he delved into my mind, he'd see it anyway. I exposed the truth before he saw it lurking.

One distant howl followed another, more Seattle dogs joining the chorus like the hellhounds had, announcing: *Death is in town!*

His green eyes narrowed. "Tangletoes? Is that your word for the day?" One ebony eyebrow cocked at my nod. "Meaning?"

"Nug-a-nug, fadoodling, joining giblets." When the oldest terms I knew still failed to fire recognition in his forest eyes, I added, "Horizontal refreshment." Finally, I sighed and looked away. "Coitus."

"Zadie—"

"Is it controllable…if you climax?" I gazed over my shoulder to gauge his face. *Marking? Is it automatic or controllable?*

Death blinked, then blinked again as his steed galloped around sinkholes. The only reply came from his horse, *clop, clop, clop,* as we rode past buildings coated in green ivy that began in Famine's reign, nature reclaiming on steroids.

Being ripped away from Death, the painful absence of our mental communication, left me aching for the teammate sense that made him closer to me than anyone. I'd decided that if I escaped hell, I desired to be closer to Death in every way, more intimate. Bluntly, I wanted to satiate my curiosity about sex with him.

Yet any magical mark was prohibited, or Morningstar's spell would nab me for Lilith. She and I were on a collision course. If she got hold of me, my power, she would be permanently invulnerable. Now, the Angel of Death was in my mind, searching for what happened, so I patted the demon blade sheathed on my thigh; *Lilith must die.*

Memories of shooting destroying angel death magic at her throat rose to the surface, startling me. One possessed female body after another fell, a memitim spell triggering each of the eight times Lilith appeared outside the dome in hell.

City dogs still howling, not a soul in sight; I sighed and shrugged. *She doesn't seem to prefer a dead host. She flees immediately.*

So that's why he ejected you from hell. Death sighed. *I guess I should be grateful you discarded your plan to let her possess you, so you could die together via a demon blade. Poor dull-witted human to have that idea as a solution in the first place.*

It didn't sting because I knew it to be accurate; it wasn't heroic. It was the stupidest consideration; Lilith would then be unstoppable. *In my defense, I didn't have your gifted power then. Can you renounce it?*

He steered his steed around a massive sinkhole that had consumed a city block. *No. I told you; it is a gift. But my power is your power. Death magic will be stripped from you when that power is cast into the lake of fire. You will lose it.*

I scoffed. *Who cares unless you think we need death superpowers in the afterlife?*

Still, as we left the city's outskirts, it was my turn to sigh. I wanted full disclosure before the horseman picked it up in my head. "I do need something from you. But not till the alchemy workstation is set up. And the first batch of cheese is aging. Because we're on a countdown clock! Then, Thanatos, I want to try out tangletoes and tea with you."

He emitted a slight choke, his surprise stuck in his throat.

I laid it out there for him. "As you said, you are not two separate people, nor are you split personalities. You are Thanatos, but also Death. If that part of you wants to take the memory when you do split, it doesn't change that I want to make love with you as you are. All of you."

Clothes and hair damp, I stared toward the obscured

mountain. Then I shared the hell-zone memory of Zehra in the doorway beside Death. "I look like her, but I'm not." *It will be me dabbling in earthly delights with you. And only if you can separate and control the angel horseman magic part. Definitely. No. Marking.*

His too-flawless-to-be-human face leaned near mine as his teakwood and leather scent intensified; forest green eyes grew smoldering hot. "Have I denied you anything since joining my team?"

"No. You're great about that."

"I will be in bed, too."

It was my turn to blink after the oh-so-vain Angel of Death boasted about excelling in something he'd never tried. Yet, I believed it was not all conceit. I hoped so; I'd warned about not really enjoying sex. Still, I wanted to find out if it could be pleasurable with *him.* Not magical pleasure, but the enjoyment of two bodies joining together.

"You will enjoy it," he replied as if I commented aloud. "They were not me." *People die in crazy positions all the time. I am Death. I've seen a lot. Horizontal refreshment is but one.*

You had to go and make it weird. And so will I.

Then I pictured the Fallen's prophecy cloak, replaying Satan's vision of it grabbing hold of Ashi. *Now we know it can do that. So for my plan to work, it has to be taken out of the equation.*

This time I pictured a stone chest, lid sealed with the cloak inside as it sank to the bottom of the sea. Angelic rune words glimmered, slightly pulsing with an orange-gold light on the black rocky surface. The same as the symbols had on the cliffs serving as prison walls around Tartarus. *How to bait the cloak inside, though?*

"Hmm," he uttered. Yet instead of discussing it, only one of his thoughts echoed through our team link. *She wants to have sex.*

His horse now morphed from black to his eerie, glowing pale form, carrying us through a heavy mist into the field near Keith's bunker.

Death gave my waist a quick squeeze. "Your chemist friend volunteered to gather the laboratory apparatuses. Stay here."

"In the rain?"

He grinned and vaulted off the back. "Yep." But he opened a magical gateway leading to Arcadia's sanctified ground. "Or we'll meet you on the island?"

His horse decided, stepping out of the rain onto the dryness of blessed land.

On the other side, in the misty gloom, Death strode toward the bunker door as the magical doorway spun closed. *I intend to privately chat with Keith to verify the tea works. I'm more than a man; impregnating you is out of the question. It would kill you to birth a Nephilim.*

Serenity and Eden escorted me to the island's backside, near the forge and blacksmith's hut, where the newly grown alchemy hut provided a roof and waist-high woven walls. Using her gift with languages, Eden translated my alchemy book into English.

A balmy breeze ruffled my wet hair, drying it, so frizz took over as Heph constructed a workstation. On one side, two burners acted as a kitchen stove. An empty section in the middle portion of the island worked as counter space to combine ingredients for either the kitchen or laboratory side.

After Keith joined us, we kicked into gear to mix magic and stamina potions with cheese to activate the magical components.

The Four Horsemen rode, never lacking targets between the unholy souls escaped from Hades or wild risen beasts spelled to attack mankind.

The ladies left to tend to their children before bed.

Cooled by a sea breeze, my golden orbs sticking to the leafy ceiling, I opened the alchemy book from the hell dimension library. Turning it toward the chemist, I pointed at a recipe meant to permanently bind a human's powers.

Keith frowned, folding his arms over his chest. "Latin. Why would you want to bind your magic?"

Then I flipped the pages to a detection bypass recipe. It was meant to bypass someone capable of detecting a demon's magic. Drink the potion to bind the power for an hour.

"I want to alter both recipes, make the demon one into a human one. An hour of binding is no good. More like twenty-four hours would work. See? A temporary nullifying concoction."

Keith raked both hands through his blond hair. "Damn, kid, you have a magical cookbook now! I wouldn't mind living on this island for a while. Give my chemist a chance to play mad scientist. Secure me an invite, and I'll help you convert the recipe."

Arcadia was a private family island and the horsemen's base. Thus far, Keith had spotted neither the dragons nor their den; we were on the mountain's backside. "How about...we open a portal so you can come daily to play with the book? I can offer you that for certain."

"That works for me; I'll swap my sleep schedule to match the time here." Keith grinned. "Your dad would have been proud of you, Zadie."

"Thank you for keeping Chuckles until you found me."

Then Keith's light blue eyes nailed me with a steady stare. "I'm not so sure of your dad's reaction to your choice of boyfriends. The Angel of Death and the last horseman of the apocalypse?"

I grinned at the boyfriend term. "My mom would approve."

With a slight *whoosh*, I felt Death when he walked out of a portal, immediately commenting on what he heard. "Approve of what?"

I choked back a laugh, deadpanning, "Your resting bitch face."

Keith dramatically slapped one hand over his chest. "Let's not upset the Angel of Death."

Death grinned at me. "You can't provoke me. I've dealt with Ashi for a *long* time."

Hitching my thumb toward Keith, I added, "He needs a daily portal to and from here. I agreed. Are you cool with that since you'll actually be the one to open and close it twice a day?"

"Not a problem; consider it done." With that, Death opened a portal leading right to the chemist's bunker door, returning Keith home.

After it spun closed, he pivoted to me. "Congratulations on creating magical cheese."

Yet he pointed to my open book's recipe: the demon anti-detection one. "What are you cooking up now?"

"Nothing yet. I need sleep."

His scent of teakwood and leather intensified as he stepped in close, running a finger down my cheek. "I know that you need sleep before tangletoes. There, I used your word for the day." His arms wrapped around me. "Time for you to—"

Sleep!

The musical-sounding command washed over me, closing my eyes as my world turned into dreams.

Until, all at once, the dynamic duo of bacon and coffee penetrated my sleep. I blinked to see Ashi, her eyes glowing like superheroes in old movies, wearing her hated chaos-battery tiara. Delicious nom-nom scents wafted from the food and drink she held my way.

"You can't speak, mime, or write it," she stated as I accepted breakfast.

Coffee!

As I sipped, she tapped into her private team-speaking ability. *Is the stone vault for me? Heads-up, I'm immune to runes. I can't read the markings, but I fully feel their intent. I'm immortal, so kill me first, then lock me inside. Hopefully, it removes me from the equation if I flip wicked while fighting my asshat father. Thank you.*

This time I gulped a drink. *Not for you. Not you as bait.*

Yet I seized up, needing to sit the plate and cup down until I could breathe without wheezing.

Ashi patted my back. "We need a code word."

Hand resting on my throat, I nodded vigorously toward my cottage doorway, where the prophecy cloak lurked outside. I knew Ashi's favorite superhero was Commander Integrity, like the poster in her old room, a teenager's bedroom, frozen in time. Before the apocalypse started, back when electricity and connectivity existed, the superhero franchise ruled in movie theaters. I was too young to recall it, but she told me the story, including the name of her superhero's nemesis. The supervillain. I glanced from the cloak to her. "Annihilator Anubis."

This time, the brush against the truth was not detected, not choking me, but Ashi heard me loud and clear. *Let's brainstorm!*

I nodded with relief. "Yes, please!"

We formulated a plan, not only for the cloak's demise but also for Lilith's. I delightedly volunteered for both missions. No moral quandary for me. I was only too happy to offer to stab a demon blade into whichever woman Lilith possessed, ensuring she died while knifed.

After caring for Chuckles and Yippee, I joined Keith at the alchemy workstation.

I pondered what Death's word for the day might be, further ruminating over a combined human and demon alchemy recipe. Yet I didn't get the answer to the first until I succeeded at the second. Well, in theory, it wasn't like I tested it yet. The potion, hopefully, could bind my power for a day, so if anything went wrong, Lilith couldn't steal it while I killed her.

Keith and I tapped coconuts, having a drink to celebrate, which was how Death found us.

Ignoring his sonar-like probe across my thought bubbles, I smiled and lifted my drink. "What is your word for today, Thanatos?"

"Mate."

Chapter Twenty-Nine

Death

"*B*oring, first off." Zadie's green eyes rolled. "Secondly, you said we would not get caught in the mate trap. There, used your dull word."

Keith stood. "That's my cue to split. Portal, please? But the kid's right; mate is a boring word for the day. So substandard. This daily ritual comforts her. She reads everything she gets her hands on. Don't you know her at all?"

Apparently, she had yet to find my entry in her family book. A rumble, not unlike a soft growl, accompanied the *whooshing* swirl of my portal opening. Keith escaped quickly.

Focusing my full attention on Zadie as her thought bubbles popped, I learned her point of view, then clarified that I picked it up correctly. "You will have sex with me but not be my mate?"

My stallion trotted toward the alchemy workshop, transforming into a kicking jackass. Then he morphed into a white unicorn with a rainbow tail. I enjoyed my comedian horse's illusions.

Yet not enough for her to ignore my question. "I tweaked my realm, created a massive bed, and considered keeping you captive. But never. That is how often I'd wear something stinking of urine—I wouldn't so much as change Bram's diapers. Never is also how often I vowed to milk a yak. And never is when I thought I would want to share blood. But you are my mate. I want to bond with you. I can give you immortality, but it takes many, many, *many* blood exchanges."

Her head shook, long black springy curls swaying. Yet she looked directly into my eyes. *Fairytale. Forbidden.* Her thought bubbles collided.

I lifted my hand and twined my fingers in her hair, further

stupefying her. "I knew you could do it; survive and escape hell, reach a lair to call for me. But the waiting stretched all kinds of new emotional muscles. First, I must claim you as my mate. Then the missed heartbeats and ache of loss while you were cut off from me? It will all be worth it. You want sex. I want to bond you. We can have both at the same time."

"But—"

"Scent marking, sure. But in simplest terms, no. I do not believe magical marking can be separated from climaxing. My overwhelming desire is all it would take to mark you."

She growled, face reddening, one hand on her throat as she broached a subject tied to the magical gag. *No. Marking. None. Zero.*

Or? Although she'd permitted me to head dive, I hadn't found what spell Morningstar tied to her before booting her out of hell for killing off Lilith's body supply. Lucifer certainly didn't let Zadie go out of the goodness of his black heart. I'd watched the memories of Zadie's memitim power kicking in each time Lilith reappeared, eliminating eight possessed bodies. *What happens if I mark you?*

I searched for the answer in her mind, but even that caused her face to redden. Then she choked.

"You go about without so much as my scent mark staking a claim on you. Moving about unclaimed as if you are not the most important person to me."

She blinked, then again. "That's Bram."

"He's safe."

Unclaimed…I am, too.

"What I feel for you is head-spinning, heart-thumping different than what I feel for Bram and the rest of my family. It's all-encompassing. You are my true mate. The need to mark you as such, to bond you—"

Stop! The prophecy cloak is not entombed. She tapped her temple. *But Ashi and I have a solution. We will revisit the marked mate situation after that.*

Zadie turned on her toes, dismissing me after I all but said I loved her, to greet Ashi.

I summoned and thumped my scythe.

"I'm ready," Ashi announced, nodding once toward the empty spot where the stone vault had been.

The beautiful cloak slinked behind the Nephilim. Each flutter forward showcased detailed black wings embroidered on the inner crimson lining.

Behind the self-aware evil cape, Pestilence the Conqueror stalked forward, shaking long golden hair. "Kobayashi Maru, no."

His aquamarine eyes glowed the same silver as my wings, his magic fully engaged, swinging to lock onto me. *Tell her that we won't seal her inside the stone vault. Not rely on the fact that she is immune to runes and could* maybe *teleport out? Before that cloak attaches to her inside there!*

I turned toward the redhead wearing a glittering jeweled tiara, a chaos battery, cobalt eyes burning bright. *That's unwise, Ashi.*

I'll be back before it sinks into the Marianas Trench.

My brother and I exchanged glances, pinging each other; we'd been riding all day to eliminate threats to humans. Neither of us knew where the stone vault was located now.

Zadie stepped in front of me, adding her voice to the group Team Horsemen link. *We trigger the spell to slide the lid shut as it sinks. Ashi can breathe underwater; she'll teleport out an instant before it fully closes and seals. I'll grab hold of the evil cloak before it claims her. Then my invulnerable smoke monster form will escape through the closed stone.*

I lifted one finger toward the stubborn glimmer in her green eyes. "Zadie Grace, no."

In return, she growled, "I'm not the pet; I'm the damn hero."

I crossed my arms over my chest, not about to give when Ashi clamped her hand on Zadie's wrist.

Zadie's scream pierced the air as they teleported, starting beside me, then sounding from over the water. Finally, she reappeared on a skeletal ship floating directly over the deepest part of the ocean.

An unkindness of ravens funneled to deposit Hades.

My brother and I summoned our wings, flying in starlight that danced and shimmered over the ocean. No more than two minutes had passed since the women appeared on the decrepit ship. Yet no vault, no women when we landed.

Hades lifted both hands. "Death, I warned her not to go to Lucifer when I saw past his glamour. I'm fond of your pet. I could hardly deny her when she asked for this little favor."

"Where is she?"

Hades pointed at the dark blue sea. "The Nephilim called it Davy Jones's Locker."

I roared, about to dive off the side, when Ashi reappeared on the deck.

Ashi wooted, hooking onto my arm. "Take that, Lilith!" Then she added, "Death, wait. She'll be here in a second. Invulnerable, remember? Zadie can't teleport, create portals, or fly; she has to *float*. Who decided that? Fail!"

I'd not gone after Zadie once; it was a mistake I would not repeat. So instead, I dove, wings pumping, propelling me underwater as quickly as in the air.

I knew the panic clawing at my chest was pointless—she was invulnerable. Yet, when we met underwater, I wrapped my arms and wings around her smoke and shadow form. I wanted her to wear my magical mark, to bond her. *And now, we'll go to my realm so I can claim you.*

Wings tightening around her, I permeated her with my scent.

"Mmm," she murmured, senses muted in this shadowy form.

With my mate now scent-marked, I opened my wings to breach the surface.

Poof! Zadie *disappeared!* Gone from my arms! Our team telepathy link vanished along with her.

I blasted out of the water, hovering over the moonlit ship and Hades.

Hades scowled, raking a hand through his short spiky hair. "She assured me that Morningstar's spell to yank her back to hell wouldn't trigger because it was controllable by *you.*"

I groaned. I marked Zadie. Only with my scent, but still.

Just that fast, I opened a magical door into Gogmagog's lair. The in-between. Shifting to incorporeal, I strode into the hell dimension portal. I tapped into our Team Horseman telepathy the instant I entered the same domain with her. *Where? Are. You?*

Stay. Away.

I sent out a blast of sonar. A satisfying *ping* followed, especially in light of Zadie's reply. But unfortunately, the next ping did not return results; the link between us slackened again. Zadie and I were no longer in the same dimension.

Pivoting, I exited hell. Standing in the lair, the in-between, not shifting, I reached out again. *Where? Are? You?*

Shift, Death. Before you lose your wings.

Flying north toward the team link's pull, I demanded, *Summon me!*

Reaching the Alaskan coast, I growled at Ashi and her teleporting! I landed; twenty rock golems served as sentinels around the women. I'd not seen Eden's druidess magic in action, but I knew the red mist emitting from the Valkyrie was not a good thing at all. Small lightning bolts and flames raced up and down Ashi's form.

The women *summoned* Lilith from the pit and temporarily bound her in the circle. With the spell triggered, Lilith brought Zadie along with her. The ladies retrieved her from hell and topside!

Immediately, Zadie zapped a blast of destroying angel death magic into the possessed woman's throat. "Oh, crap!"

The host still lived; no one could die while I stayed shifted. Afterward, Lilith's essence wouldn't stay contained in the circle long.

Standing directly outside the circle, Zadie pivoted my way. "Shift, Thanatos."

One small hand brushed the hair away from my face before cupping my cheek. Her other hand slid from my shoulder, down my arm, then up again and over my back. She was helping me shift. The thing was, I didn't want to. She, too, flickered away from smoke and shadows.

Her strokes returned sensations, feeling her touch more than the gentle wind. Emotions surfaced, pulling me from where none could touch me to where they all centered around her.

"Shift," she urged, tipping onto her toes. Her lips slanted over mine, kissing the villain.

I growled and wrapped my arms around her. Her mouth opened, our tongues touching. Wanting more, I shifted.

Ignoring our audience and Lilith's possessed body dropping dead, my wings came around Zadie as I lifted her to devour her mouth. Liquid fire flared through my veins.

When we parted to gasp for breath, she whispered. "I love you. I'm sorry."

"Sorry for loving me?"

"No." A mere whisper.

When a shard of pain shot through my chest, my glance dropped to blood puddling from a knife handle. Zadie stabbed me in the heart with her demon blade!

"Sorry for that. You'll resurrect. You told me that a horseman's death is to sleep and awaken. No need to shift and risk your wings. The plan is already up in smoke."

She caught my slump, gentling my fall to the ground, then yanked out the blade.

I blinked in confusion, noticing my brothers had not yet arrived. The Conqueror was nowhere nearby to heal me.

"It had to be fast." Zadie pulled back, flipped the cork off a small bottle, tossed the blue contents into her mouth, then swallowed.

Panic nipped on the heels of rage. Though I could not renounce my gift of power, her alchemy experiment bound that magical gift. *Poof!* The scent of her destroying angel power was gone! Zadie was now utterly, terrifyingly...human. "What did you do?"

My eyes shut, but I heard her whisper. "I'm trying to ensure Eve's shade stays dead."

Then silence reigned as sleep overtook me.

I woke underwater as I had the first time; the blue ice dome was now a sinkhole. Zadie killed me!

Roaring, scythe in hand, I opened a portal to where she temporarily ended me. Not so much as an echo of her power trembled along the line of team communication. As for our link? Gone. No way to know if my gift of power was still bound, cutting off her invulnerability. She must be back in hell.

My brother War, teetering on the line of berserker mode, landed beside me. "Welcome back. It just happened." He tugged on his beaded beard, then nodded. "Let me take you to her."

If she was in this dimension and our link didn't work? We were no longer on the same team.

"The women teleported from place to place, activating previously created circles in places of power, each limited in how long it contained Lilith's essence."

War opened a portal to the Black Forest, where I stepped onto an unstable, crumbling edge along a colossal sinkhole. "It happened minutes ago during the fallout; the slowly widening sinkhole swallowing more of the world."

It wasn't what I feared. It was worse. So much worse. I knew the instant I spotted Zadie, my mate; Lilith was in the driver's seat.

I shifted immediately upon seeing her in the sinkhole debris. Body and dark soul trapped as one below, skewered. Completely impaled from her back, the long demon blade poking from her chest. Even with Lilith in control, she could not pry herself up and off the sword.

Serenity coated me with a thick layer of green mist, Valkyrie soothe.

Pestilence held Ashi close to his chest as she cried, "Holy healing magic won't work on the unholy."

My brother added, "Morningstar's blood magic spell will kill the host if I exorcise the demon."

Undoubtedly possessed, she was still *my* Zadie, the part who raged a roar that held more power than she looked like she had to waste. "Shift! Nearly done."

Contrarily, she then wagged her fingernails my way. "Finally!" Lilith in charge. "Lift me off, Death. My powers are out of whack, but the potion will wear off eventually."

The thing was, she looked like, sounded like, my mate. She carried my scent mark.

"Shift!" Zadie added in a whispery growl.

"I cannot," I whispered. I bent to cradle Zadie tightly against my chest. Shifting my grip on her, the contact chewed into my shifted incorporeal form. I slowly hoisted her from the damn blade.

"No." A long pained groan.

I paused.

"Eve will escape," she whispered. "Shift before you lose your wings from shifting back and forth."

"I would give up my wings for you. If I shift, you will die."

"If you don't and pull out the blade? It was all. For. Nothing."

I nearly howled at the morbidity of it, holding her without lifting her from the sword.

Both my love and my stalker were trapped inside the same body. Lilith was powerful enough to shield any thought bubbles and poke around in Zadie's memories. Yet it looked like my Zadie, who gasped. "Changed my mind. Exchange blood with me; heal me. It's the only way. You said we could have both sex and bonding at the same time. It's that time now. Get me off this blade!"

Sadly, wily, it was Lilith wriggling temptations my way. Zadie would know that was off the table if we were no longer on the same team. If I bonded her while she was possessed by a demon, one step down from Lucifer's power level…I would be joining her team. I'd fall.

Decision made, I swiftly lifted her, pulling the blade from her body. "Poor dull-witted human. You believe I want to end Eve more than I want to save you."

Famine caught my eye. *She is Lilith, baiting you with Zadie. Lilith did not leave her when you freed Zadie from the blade. Now,*

Lilith is about to get everything she's ever wanted with you. The second most powerful demon in the world will gain your gifted power of invulnerability when the potion wears off.

Yet I gazed at Zadie in my arms; the one person who could pull me out of my shift held against me and mortally wounded. The unhealed wound would steal her life when I shifted if I didn't bind her into my realm. "It's a good thing you know the Angel of Death. That you are wise enough to bargain with me. I'm taking you to my realm. Like you said, I don't care if another part of you takes that memory with her into the pit. You won't die, but you will never leave. Thanks to that gift of power, which you'll regain when the potion timeouts."

She grinned, red foamy bubbles at the corners of her full lips. "A private prison world. With you. Sounds delicious!"

"Not with me. You won't torture me with Zadie, the woman I love. You'll stay confined. As you said, a private prison world. Not even you, Eve, can open a portal out."

"You won't stay away from your mate. I carry your scent. You want me to carry your magical mark. Do. It."

Her green eyes cleared; one hand folded over the hole in her ribs, Zadie wrestling for control. "Shift."

"You will *die*. Lilith will not leave you whether you're alive or dead. I warned you'd never be safe from her. You pull me toward corporeal now!"

Without glancing at my brothers, I carried one mortally wounded body—trapping both Zadie and Lilith—through a portal into my realm. Now neither could leave. Neither could die.

Sighing, I deposited her on the throne. Once upon a time, she claimed to need an elevator to reach the top of the rock. And when I tweaked my realm, I'd made a throne for two. But she'd let Lilith possess her. "I love you. I'm sorry."

Throwing those words back at her, I shifted to corporeal and left my whisper reverberating. "For this. Goodbye, Zadie."

I spun out of the realm, the most anguishing action required of me since Day One. She would not die, but I could never see her again. I loved her. And now Lilith inhabited my love.

Yet my foot stuck as if I stood in amber on my first step out of my realm. Emotionally devastated, I'd opted for the privacy of a mountaintop yet landed in a privacy bubble—stuck in the haze of another angel's magic.

"Pity that," rang in a deep voice. Raphael appeared, spreading his black wings wide. Not smoke like Lucifer's but summoned holy feathers the color of midnight.

The lightest green tinted the privacy shield, the archangel Raphael's magical color. The same as the runes arched across his chest. "The sinkhole expanded; Zadie lost hold of the demon dagger as she fell. Circle broken, the possession spell triggered again as she was impaled in a way she could not escape. You might suspect someone was guiding that, brother. Aphrodite, wife of Hephaestus, meddling. Supposedly to make you realize you love Zadie. But it could also be her anger; Aphrodite wasn't happy to regain her husband."

I raked a hand down my face to find his emerald regard locked onto me. "We are aware of the coming chaos war; we've seen your images, the state of the chains binding Sheol."

"Are you joining us in the war?"

"When God sends us, we will come."

With a swipe of his hand, an image of Morningstar wearing an ostentatiously jeweled crown materialized. "The King of Hell, once your close friend, was always of the opinion that you would join him and at least deserve an ending in the lake of fire. But you also earned a reward for never wavering faith in God. Until the last day, it only takes one to speak up. One angel. On behalf of her soul."

Raphael lifted his fingers to his forehead like horns. "I'm too dignified for lolling, but I know an angel who isn't. You spoke up for her. As will I."

So much for my plan to ignore doing that. I almost wanted to summon and thump my scythe.

But Raphael laughed. "Return her from your realm. She has the heart of a warrior and a hero, keeping me busy in my guardian stead. What else could she be, though? Raised on a hero family legend. 'Twas a spell, not willingness, that allowed her to be possessed. Though she won't thank me for the suffering, I did not allow her to die after Aphrodite's spell caused the wound."

He sighed, thumping me on the back. "After all, the entire concept of bonded mates came from you. Return her; I will smite Lilith from her, sever Morningstar's spell in a way that does not instantly kill your mortally wounded mate. You will not shift to save Zadie."

The privacy shield expanded, awaiting me to open the door. I'd sworn moments ago my realm would remain sealed despite the taunt from Lilith about not staying away from my mate.

"Trust me," Raphael declared in a low tone. "Did God not confirm she is yours?"

I opened a magical exit out of my realm as Raphael added, "Bond her to heal her the instant the unholy soul leaves. How obtuse of you not to recognize your mate within moments of awakening. You opened a portal right to her!"

Lilith, in the driver's seat, ran out of my realm.

Raphael's black wings brushed forward. Black and gold lightning struck the ground on either side of Zadie. "I *smite* you, the shade of Eve. Begone!"

Zadie fell sideways on the grass. With her mortal wound, I needed to act quickly.

As the dark essence of Lilith blew away like greasy smoke, Zadie's weak raspy words confounded me. "Wearing. Black. And red. Lace. Panties."

My angel brain fizzled out of service as I lost my chain of thought, remembering her wearing those as I applied henna tattoos. More of her backside was exposed than the sexy scrap of lace covered.

Just that fast, Zadie grabbed my hand. Her blood-smeared hand reached into her shorts, activating the protective rune symbol embroidered on the elastic.

A cottage-sized dome of golden light bubbled over us. Healing magic on steroids, thanks to Ashi's rune.

"I'm healing," Zadie announced as the stab wound pulled

together. "You don't have to bond me to heal me. Just because an angel more stuck up than you said so."

Although only she and I were within her protection dome, her voice dropped to a whisper. "I've seen him before. Many times. I thought I followed him into the crack to hide from the trafficker."

"That's Raphael." I threaded my fingers into her curls. "He's been guarding you all your life. He has to smite and run." Brushing my lips over her neck, I murmured, "Now that all's right with the world."

Horse charged our way, bucking up near Raphael outside the healing dome. Sadly, timing it with his rainbow-farting unicorn illusion.

"And on that note," Raphael laughed, "tell your brothers hello for us. We'll see you before the very end."

Chapter Thirty

Zadie

"You," Death declared from the grassy mountainside, "have much to explain." Then, from within my magical dome, he opened a doorway to his realm.

"Wait until I'm fully healed before sweeping me through. The need for medical attention is not a reason to marry." I indicated the golden dome of feel-good protection, closing my wounds. "It's a trap we will not fall into. You made sure of that. And I thank you for the choice of it."

"You wanted to end Lilith."

"Obviously, yet I still flipping failed to end the Eve threat. The spell triggered when you marked me like a dog peeing on a tree! I'm unsure how much clearer I could have been than…No. Marking."

I lifted one hand when he opened his mouth, cutting him off. "Thankfully, the ladies enacted their plan, summoning Lilith to retrieve me. Followed by my sneaky-stabby, so you couldn't shift to stop me from ending her, then my potion. It wasn't supposed to be me. That was just in case something went wrong. And it did. I killed Lilith's possessed body automatically with your gifted power. I was meant to stab her inside the circle and guarantee she died while the demon blade was in that possessed woman."

I sighed. "Then there was no living body. Lilith could only retrieve one if the ladies let her out of the circle. Lucifer's spell for her to possess me would yank me to hell when her evil essence returned; I would be the body. The women stopped that with the summoning, which pulled me outside the circle."

Death shook his head, long black hair swinging. "The

territorial male beast broke out when I scent-marked you."

"Although we removed the Fallen's prophecy cloak threat, I didn't have a lot of moves after Satan's spell fired. I didn't agree to the possession, so it was like we fought over control of my body. In the end, it's not like I dived onto the blade. It's just how it played out. The sinkhole expanded to break the circle, which superimposed her over me, then falling to be impaled upon the enchanted metal."

"I believe Heph's wife may have played a hand in that, so I would know beyond doubt that I love you. Because you're not the pet. You, Zadie Grace, are the damn hero." He grinned, lifting his index fingers to his forehead like horns. "I'm clearly the pet. Don't you know the difference when you see it?"

"Your tongue is not lolling; you're not running in circles grunting, so it is unclear." Then, when one black eyebrow cocked, I added, "Won't you deny you'd ever do such silly things?"

"Angels cannot lie."

He slid two fingers over my temple. "Our team link is repaired. Join me in my realm. You are healed. Now bonding—marrying me—is a choice. Say yes to your mate. I'd ask you to grow old with me, but I'm already ancient, and you will never age. Indeed, I'll start making you immortal immediately."

"I'm genuinely sorry I killed you; it was one of those cruel-to-be-kind situations. Save your wings from over-shifting in mini-god mode. How many black points did that earn me in the tally to enter heaven?"

"Luckily for you, I don't stay dead."

Like that, he pulled me to my feet and swept me into his portal, the realm house with a view of reapers glowing above like jeweled stars.

The disco ball spun light over the pool tub in the other room. A new addition on the other side contained a black counter with a magical burner heating a water kettle. "Tea?" He chuckled. "Before or after a bath?"

"That depends, Thanatos. Are we bathing together? Or is it

still too primitive for you?"

"Before, it is then," he rumbled. He pivoted back, holding out a cup of pregnancy prevention tea.

I sipped the hot tea, looking from him to the lightly steaming bath water. "I'll admit, the blood bond to marry sounded creepy as hell, but then I turned into a smoke monster, so...?"

"I suspect Lilith would have rebranded that name."

"I'm sorry I didn't end her." I tossed back the rest of the tea, setting aside the cup.

"I'm sorry you felt like you had to. I told you where Lilith, the shade of Eve, will end up. The same place where the Angel of Death has to sacrifice his shifter. On the day God puts an end to people dying, death and death magic will be bound there in the fire, too. I'm not yet only Thanatos as I claim you are mine."

A beautiful musical note later, a breath of power moved over my bloody clothing, removing it all!

"Eek!"

Silver feather-soft wings folded around me before I could gaze at his body. His teakwood and leather scent intensified. After he lifted me, I hooked my legs around his bare waist and locked onto his broad shoulders.

He carried me down into the pool as I flew higher than a flaming paper lantern over a poppy field, stoned on his angel scent. Furthermore, the disco ball spun light over the glass ceiling, showcasing a universe of star-like reapers who couldn't see us. This time, not a smoke monster with muted senses, the full force of his scent overwhelmed me. I sucked it in, intoxicated as it permeated me, writhing against him.

Holding me back against the pool wall, his wings vanished. When he opened his hand, it contained a needle. "Even a drop exchanges blood; it need not be gruesome to bond you. Will you marry me, Zadie Grace? Cause I'm marking you as mine either way before we leave this water. Go, team! Now join me as my mate."

He pricked his finger, one drop of blood welling. His green eyes smoldered as his hand waited for mine. Then, he poked my finger quickly.

When our fingertips touched, exchanging blood droplets, a liquid fire ignited from that point of contact, flooding me with high octane superpower. After the jolt of magic flashed into me, his finger touching mine, my mind conjured up Michelangelo's *The Creation of Adam.*

He lifted our joined hand to his lips, whisper-singing a musical word over my ring finger. A golden glowing tattoo encircled it. "Bonded," he translated with a smile.

I lifted his finger to my mouth, not attempting unpronounceable Angelic but vowing my whisper on his ring finger. "Bonded. My husband."

A golden glowing band appeared around his finger.

Silver wings suddenly folded around me. I still couldn't translate the red rune symbols lighting this magical bubble of just us. My hands slid over deliciously chiseled muscles as I kissed him deeply.

The line of fire from sharing a blood droplet spread down my body. Until it seemed like I fell deeper into this water, into a warm lake below filled with thick molasses. It coated me, suspending me in intense need. Never. That's how often I'd been this turned on.

That is likely why you didn't enjoy sex then. Death purred into my mind like I'd announced it.

In the next blink, he arched against me. "You are mine." That pound of his magical mark sent my mind spiraling out of my body, climaxing fireworks so hard that my muscles shook. I panted as his heart thundered under my ear, echoing mine since he felt exactly what I did.

Brain and body no sooner synced than he pulsed his magic over me again. I flew apart, his hands and mouth roaming, learning me. Then kissing me, he joined our bodies the third time I blasted off ecstasy's cliff.

Kissing a path up his neck to his ear, a trail of golden rune markings lit up where my mouth touched him. "Angelic?"

Instead of answering, he thrust again as he pounded his

magical mark over me. So while kissing him wantonly, he caught my next cry in his mouth before pulling back to roar my name.

Once I could finally breathe again, he shot a dazzlingly bright smile my way. "You enjoyed yourself, my love. I am Death. I had no doubt."

By the time we reached the bed, he was writhing as I kissed my way down his incredible eight-pack abs. I lifted my mouth, tracing the golden glowing rune. "What does it say?"

"Zadie."

Then kissing lower, I breathed, "And this one?"

"Wife."

Then he laughed. "My brothers are ringing. Unlike how I barge right in, they cannot interrupt us unless I open a portal. See how wise your mate is? We'll break in this bed, then see Chuckles and my comedian horse. We'll return to break it in again very soon."

"After my alchemy session and checking on the magical cheese."

He loomed over me on the bed, grinning while lowering his chiseled sinew over my body. "You were saying?"

"Was I?" I inhaled deeply. I had no idea what I was saying. Stoned on his scent.

"Please, Thanatos. That's what you're about to say."

***

"Please, Thanatos," I taunted in a whisper hours later; he'd liked it so much when I said it earlier. Except for this time, we were at my alchemy workstation, where I held out a slice of magic cheese. "One nibble. Then we'll make a run to eliminate threats to humans and slow the countdown on your fourth."

"We'll do that every day, but not today." He took a small bite of my magical cheese. Then he grinned. "You added bacon flavoring! You must love me."

With one arm around my waist, he hoisted me to his level before his wings launched. "Today, we'll find you and Chuckles a home. Our home. I'll sanctify the ground."

A portal spun open in the air in front of us. Death flew into a snowy night landscape with an aurora dancing in green and pink smears. It was where he brought me as the price for me to leave my underground home.

He landed on a mountain, on a cabin's deck. "I can't feel the cold, but if you like it here, I'll keep you warm." He slid open a glass door.

I grinned at him, tossing a light orb to stick to the wall. Gleaming wooden built-ins packed with books on each side, chaises to read, and an unlit fireplace. One wall consisted of a vaulted window. The scent of fresh herbs led to a large kitchen. "Oh wow, someone has been taking care of this. You didn't kill the owner, did you?"

"No." He brushed a kiss over my temple. "Rhea took him and told me about this place. Apparently, I did not consider soundproofing our lovenest in my realm. I fixed it, but…since you are a 'good sore,' it seemed like a good time to show you."

He pointed down the hall as I tossed more light orbs to stick to the high exposed wooden ceiling beams. "It has a room for Bram," he added. "Another if we watch the twins or triplets. The master bedroom has a big bed with a view."

"Plan to keep me warm then. Female yaks rule the herd. And if they aren't happy, no one is happy. But Chuckles will love it here; there's even a barn!"

"Zadie Grace, will you be happy living here?"

"Happier than in your realm, which is so perfect it's clearly make-believe. Living here," I swept one arm toward the wall of windows framing the stunning dancing aurora. "Reminds us what we're fighting for."

Death summoned his scythe, thumping it once. During the unnaturally loud reverberation, a perimeter shimmered to life. A glimmery light wall appeared around the grounds and premises. "I will bless every inch inside our warded fences and then return for my bride. And promptly fetch her pet Chuckles and her pet's pet Yippee. Afterward, we'll christen the bedroom —no, *every* room."

He stepped forward, reaching one finger to my forehead. White hot knowledge zapped my brain, then I grinned like an idiot. He'd taught me a new spell!

I held out my hand and tapped into the spell. A dancing flame shimmered into existence in my palm. Yet it didn't burn me. "Woot!" Mind confetti happily littered my curls; I could not wipe the stupid grin from my face.

He grunted. "You like that one. Now you can start the fire. Welcome home, Zadie Grace. Here, I will love you, wife. I will teach you magic and make you as immortal as I am."

Epilogue

Though the trumpet had not blown, the last dozen demon blades, magical metal infused with adamite, flashed from pale yellow to vibrant green fluorescence. The horsemen's pile of arms glowed as one in more pronounced and faster flashes. Humans had long been armed, thriving thanks to protection domes powered by Ashi.

Trapped in the Marianas Trench, the prophecy cloak could not hasten the chains breaking to free the Fallen. But I'd seen their failing condition five years back. Every year felt like a victory, continuing to ride and eliminate threats to humans. We kept the death rate as low as possible, nearly balanced with births, so as not to reap my fourth.

Before Zadie, I couldn't imagine this planet continuing for five years, couldn't imagine that we'd still be around to see Bram's eighteenth birthday. Or that we might yet live to see the double-fated soul chain role kick in on Bram.

Tall and brawny, curls past his shoulders, the mighty, magical young man picked up a demon blade. Bram shook his head. "I'm not waiting around. I heard you; you haven't claimed anywhere near your fourth. But the blades themselves announce the Grigori come."

Zadie handed Bram a bandolier, each slot filled with magical cheese. Ashi had added a protection and healing rune to the leather.

Bram grinned, now taller than Zadie and nearly caught up in age since I froze my wife as immortal at twenty. "Samson and I will fly over people who waited until the last minute to evacuate, give them cover to a magical protective shelter."

"Watch out for the twins," I muttered as the fifteen-year-olds launched ahead of Bram. Thankfully the triplets, now eight—the age Bram was when God put me to sleep—were on Arcadia.

As Zadie watched Zed and Zoe loop and arch over the land, I slid my arm around her waist, adding, "Relax; they're harnessed in. The kids don't need you to catch them at the last minute, so their fall turns into a float. Though we all know you can."

Zadie glanced at the demon blades, magical metal flashing faster and faster like in Tartarus. She sighed. "Sunshine and summer, an otherwise gorgeous day...even if it might be the last."

I pressed my forehead to hers as the instrument I'd been expecting to hear finally sounded. The entire sky seemed to blast with a trumpet note, acting like a speaker from another realm.

The sound reverberated against the earth, a blast of wind as the ground rumbled.

It's starting. Those who die will be added to my death toll, my fourth, as my reign is not ended.

Zadie threaded her fingers into my hair, kissing me. "I love you."

An unkindness of ravens funneled outside my protective warding. Hades pulled off his electric blue hat and tipped it. "Feel that? Tartarus cracked open."

A blast like an airwave preceded a red flash in the sky. A hot wind moving with supernatural speed accompanied darkness sweeping in. Thousands of dark angels swarmed into the atmosphere, giving the sky a nighttime look. The Fallen's smoky wings created black swirling clouds. The ebony mass of previously bound Grigori continued to expand and blot out the sun. Hundreds of thousands. While the swarm continued forming, power pulsed outward from ancient ritual sites, shooting red lasers into the ether.

The Fallen wasted no time in unlocking their elite leaders chained in space prisons. Those angels were so tarnished as to each be pegged individual satans; my brothers' wives were their children and grandchildren.

At least my Zadie was connected to none of them. She

strapped on cheese, a demon dagger, and the blacksmith-created headband—not a helmet—that would prevent the Fallen from messing with her mind. Then she shifted invulnerable, like a thousand candles puffed out at once; shadows wound around the smoke.

Thankfully, I could still feel her curvy body under there, tugging her close for a kiss. "I love you, Zadie. The Angel of Death and Thanatos, all of me. And I'll love you when I sacrifice my shifter and the power of death magic to the lake of fire, and it's just Thanatos."

I sat my wife upon my horse, now gleaming with a ghostly glow, opting to appear in his truthful yellowish-green form. Five years ago, my stallion chose his name, Houdini, celebrating his illusionist art.

We joined my brothers on the white sand of Arcadia. Four Horsemen. Four Horses. And the women belonging to them.

Stormbringer landed beside Ashi as the wind carried a dark whisper. "Kobayashi Maru."

The sky lit up with a colossal holographic projection of dark tousled hair, deep ocean blue eyes, and a sublime smile.

The Conqueror smothered a curse.

Ashi sighed. "Oh good, I take it that gorgeous asshat is my father?"

She hopped off Pegasus, still on blessed land, flames and lightning igniting over her arms and legs.

"Humans, I am Armaros. Be not afraid. We are the Watchers, the angel protectors of humans. Your true enemies are the Four Horsemen; they took everything from you."

Armaros lifted one hand, where a thin bracelet glowed neon yellow on his wrist. "This is the dawn of a new age. We will reboot this world and bring it all back using magical power. In addition, a new type of currency will be deposited in each individual's account. To use the credits, swipe your smart device over the interface. This wristband number is how you will be identified and paid for your allegiance. To this man."

Short-cropped blond hair, sky blue eyes, the image of Lucifer

Morningstar now flickered in the air.

"We need to stash our kids underground," Ashi whispered.

Morningstar nodded slightly to the planet's population, watching the magical broadcast. Humans would hear whichever language they spoke. "People of earth, I will usher in peace and prosperity. We start by handing out the wristbands to restore order."

Flames flickered for the merest of instances in Lucifer's pupils before a black ostentatiously jeweled crown appeared on his head. "Anyone refusing to comply, refusing wristbands, will be considered enemies of the Watchers. As the Four Horsemen and their families are. They are the enemies of us all."

But were we humans' enemies, though? Doubtful most humans regarded our divine reigns as fulfilling our God-given purposes. At the very least, Ashi was reasonably famous for helping humans survive for the last twenty years. So would people quickly dismiss her protection barriers, demon blades, and Mission Mankind dragon delivery drops? And instead, believe the King of Lies?

Then the wind carried a voice again, Armaros back in the shot. Ginormous hologram against the black mass background of dark angels. His dark blue regard swiveled as if, from this worldwide broadcast, Armaros could spot Ashi. *I'm coming for you, Kobayashi Maru.*

His gaze sharpened as if looking at each individual. "We will give you all of this, your world back only better as magic will run the realm. But, in exchange, you serve up the Four Horsemen and their families."

Zadie squared her shoulders, shadows lashing about her. "People will do anything to restart the world! And her asshat dad, along with Lucifer, made us the villains! That does not work for me. We. Are. The. Damn. Heroes!"

Ashi nodded. "We can take the Fallen, trap them one at a time. So let's do this; go, Team Horsemen!"